THE ENGLISH TEACHER

MICHAEL BRADY

The English Teacher

PART ONE

Love and Remembrance

Qui a inventé le cœur humain, je me le demande?
Dis-le-moi, et alors montre-moi l'endroit où on l'a pendu.
—Justine

PROLOGUE

1982

THIS IS NOT A LOVE STORY.

Yet it began in Paris, la ville capitale de l'amour, one smoky October night as I sat at the little upstairs bar in le Caveau de la Huchette. I had walked there after my lecture in the massive old Sorbonne building, making my way down the ancient rue Saint-Jacques through one of those sad autumn Parisian rains. What little light remained was retreating softly into the mauve evening shadows. As the old country song goes: it gets late early this time of year.

Inside the Caveau I was sitting by myself in the muted, mostly empty room—there was no music yet at that hour—thinking of the tried-and-true French adage: un homme seul est toujours en mauvaise compagnie . . . but I was not to be alone for long. I first saw her reflected in the mirror which hung behind the bar, coming directly toward me, her face calm, unsmiling, her deep-set Prussian blue eyes replete with indifference. She sat on the bar stool next to mine and turned sideways, confronting me with the pure look of youth, her flushed, unmarked face not yet frayed by life's vicissitudes.

"I liked," she began, "that you included Durrell with the other English poets. I was named by him: Melissa Artemis,

Notre-Dame des douleurs." She reached out and we shook hands. "And you speak very good French. You are a literary critic, no doubt."

"No doubt." I smiled.

"What do you do when you are not giving lectures on forgotten poets that nobody reads anymore?"

"I teach, or I write. Pas en même temps, vous savez."

"I will come to your class tomorrow. I am a student. What time does it start?"

"Tomorrow is Sunday. The school is closed."

"The university is never closed."

"Nevertheless, I have no class tomorrow. Are you enrolled at the American College? Because that's where I teach, not at the Sorbonne. Today was just a special lecture."

She shrugged. "I'm not enrolled full-time this term, but I am taking a couple of language courses, and I have friends who go there. I will audit your class."

"Melissa, you don't even know what I teach. You may have no interest in the course."

"Monsieur, you do not teach business law, marketing, statistics. You do not lecture about automation in the Paris Métro system. Or do you?"

"I don't."

Her velvet blue eyes looked unflinchingly into mine. "You talk about books and authors and poets."

"That's true."

"Then when is your next class?"

I told her and she proffered me a hint of a smile as she turned away and left the bar.

And that is how I came to meet Melissa Artemis, almost a year ago now. So much has happened in these last twelve months, yet I can look back on the events with absolute clarity, with the possible exception of a few days that are shrouded in dark sadness. I am writing these thoughts today in the little library of the International School of Florence. It is not Paris, but it is a refuge well designed for telling a story of Paris, the lost and found center of love and betrayals.

Why am I writing this histoire de tristesse now, in this beautiful Tuscan city far from the Gallic setting where all our sufferings and joys were acted out? Hopefully, the reasons will become clear at some point, if I can ever describe or even comprehend myself the difference between love and the remembrance of love. My luck hasn't been good enough to reach that level of understanding yet, but there is a first time for everything, they say. I don't know if I believe that, either.

Reflecting back on that rainy Saturday night when I first met Melissa, first talked to her, first listened to her bantering, teasing voice, I can't help but think of the lines Browning wrote a century ago: She should never have looked at me, if she meant I should not love her.

CHAPTER 1

THE AMERICAN COLLEGE IN PARIS, OR ACP AS THE students call it, is where I have taught for several years. Like the Sorbonne it is located on la Rive gauche, but unlike the Sorbonne, which dates from the 12th century, the ACP was not founded until eight hundred years later. It is not a prestigious university; technically it's not even a university. No one teaches there for the honor and glory or even the money. They teach there because it is situated in Paris, la capitale de la France, crossroads of the world, bustling, noisy, crowded; with dank, gloomy weather all fall, all winter, and most of the spring; full of aggravating photo-snapping tourists all summer, who leave you no space to pass on sidewalks which are themselves spattered by crottes de chiens; a city where Parisians say it rains thirty-two days in October, gray water streaking down dirty soot-covered buildings, grimed by generations of smoke and dust. Then why do we stay?

We stay because of the timeless, ineffable esprit of this city, distilled in her ancient centre, her picturesque streets and boulevards overflowing with ideas, le quartier latin, where, as the saying goes, Paris learned to think; emotions and sensual pleasures, where revolutions were dreamed up, given birth, and fought in the narrow, twisted rues: every block has a tale to tell. Paris embodies the voice of history, sometimes screaming

"L'audace!"—sometimes whispering in soft tutoyer—home to the Lost Generation and post-war new-found eccentrics, alienated existentialists and gifted writers, eating, drinking, smoking, and arguing in all-night cafés, with the uncaring Seine flowing heartlessly by as she has for millennia.

At night the river's placid surface mirrors the refracted light cast from old wrought-iron lamp posts and café lanterns, lumières de nuit watching over the water which glimmers faintly like candle-lit mica. Paris flaunts her moody beauty, her history, and her truth as she carries these gifts through endless time, inspiriting her poets and artists, while her great divided river pushes past both sides of the hulking Cathédrale Notre-Dame, the name of her architect long forgotten, if ever recorded, her treasury guarding the cold relics of love.

You can stand on the bridges or quais and watch the quiet current being sucked steadily into the dark western blue of a late afternoon, this river that remembers everything since the dawn of history, including all the sacred promises and lies told to lovers on her bridges. Like Vadim's stone-hearted, fire-scarred Jeanne Moreau, gazing out from a film made in another time, la Seine porte son âme sur son visage. And beneath the cover of the relentless daily pandemonium, under the noisy cobbled streets and the nonstop pounding of their autos and motos, lies the soft soul of the city of Paris.

This must sound to you like the sentimentality of lost youth, flickering memories enhanced or filtered by time; but nothing has been lost for me and the memories have not faded at all. Life in Paris for young university students, laughter, torments, dreams, the kiss on both cheeks, joys and sorrows all will leave their indelible marks and sometimes a few cuts, painful lessons imprinted in the hearts and minds of those young souls. They will soon leave Paris, it is true, but will take with them forever, if they have been lucky, unforgettably sweet memories of love, of times of intense happiness, and if they have not been lucky après tout, haunting recollections of bitter disappointments and unendurable heartaches.

And grief in Paris is like a shining steel blade—its sharp edge might wear away someday, but it can take decades. Though their following lives may be full of notable, even important experiences, these will not stand out in their minds like their time in Paris. When you're young and a student, you're always thinking of the months and years ahead, always waiting, planning, dreaming, and gazing impatiently into the future, never really catching sight of today. But as I was soon to discover, Melissa Artemis was not like that. She lived every day in the fearless now.

That did not, however, include my next class, which she did not show up for, despite her promise.

DIARY OF MELISSA ARTEMIS

October 9, 1982

I read somewhere that people write in diaries when they're alone and bored, or depressed, choked by grief, heart-broken even. The pages are blank when we're happy, active, at ease, quand tout va bien. I suppose no one would remember Romeo and Juliet if they had simply married and lived stress-free happily ever after. Some French critic got to the heart of the matter when he wrote it's only because they died that we know their names. Or was it Ned Rorem? I'm reading his *Paris Diary*, the main reason I've started my own. I did keep a dreadful daily journal for a French class when I was twelve—left behind somewhere and probably lost forever, grâce à dieu.

I should mention the lecturer we heard this afternoon in the Amphithéâtre Richelieu. I liked him, not just for what he was saying, but for how every now and then he looked out somewhere, waited a few seconds, and only then continued to speak.

One thing he said was that Lawrence Durrell left us more sensual poetry in the prose of his Alexandria novels than any English poet since the Romantics, with the possible exception of Yeats who, he added, "not to put too fine a point on it, wasn't really an English poet." He also warned us that there is something dangerous about reading *Justine* as a student, Durrell's not de Sade's, he smiled thoughtfully. Because afterwards, he warned, when you finish it, you're so immersed in his style, dazzled, overcome by it—a Byzantine mosaic was how he described it, one perfect gem-like phrase set against another—that you're tempted to give up completely and vow you'll never write another sentence or line of poetry yourself. It's like if you were a piano student watching and listening to Oscar Peterson play in some little jazz club, ripping through fast scalar runs and graceful arpeggios with nonchalant ease, and you decide never to touch your instrument again.

Darneau was the name of the lecturer, not an American sounding name. On impulse I followed him down to the Caveau, went up to him, talked about school, that was about it. He was sympa. I think I'll audit a course he's teaching at ACP, though I hate that place.

He lectured in slightly too perfect French, with just a trace of an accent—maybe he's French-Canadian. He has long Canadian hair. Could use a coupe.

I'll have to keep these entries shorter, because diaries tend to be mostly high-blown philosophical crap, tedious, utterly egotistical. En tout cas, ce n'est pas facile d'être moi.

Je suis trop sérieuse enfin.

CHAPTER 2

THE SECOND TIME I SAW MELISSA WAS A WEEK OR SO later, sitting in the back row of my European literature class. At the end, as I gathered up my notes and books, she came walking toward the podium like some Phoebe Caulfield marching her innocence down the school steps into her brother Holden's sad life.

"Salut, monsieur le professeur!"

"Bonjour, Melissa, comment ça va aujourd'hui?"

Like le petit prince she rarely answered my questions, except to pose her own.

"Monsieur Darneau, do you think that Professeur Adam was being disrespectful of young writers when he wrote that at age twenty all poets imitate?"

I looked at her. "Antoine Adam was too sensitive and perceptive to be disrespectful of young poets. What did he write after that?"

She shrugged. "I don't remember."

"I knew Professeur Adam, not well, but I took his nineteenth century French literature class years ago at the Sorbonne. What he said was, 'À vingt ans tous les poètes imitent, à trente ans quelques poètes imitent moins, et à quarante ans quelques-uns n'imitent plus.'"

"Yet Keats died at age twenty-five," she countered.

"He was not a French poet. They ripen more slowly."

The slightest trace of a smile wrinkled the edges of her lips. She turned away and left the classroom—that was the first, but not the last time I felt that I had seen her somewhere before, in another life, another age.

⚜

Melissa began showing up regularly for that class, always sitting in the back, sometimes with a friend, sometimes saying a word or two to me before leaving, sometimes running off without so much as a backward glance. It was only later that I came to realize what a compulsive reader she was. Melissa opened books like most people open bottles of wine. She worshipped words. I have to confess that I went into the admissions office and asked to see her application and résumé. She was born in California in late August of 1963, making her nineteen now. Only one parent was listed, a Nico Artemis, with a Zurich address. Her last secondary school of record was the American School of Paris in Saint-Cloud, and she had successfully passed the bac two years ago. I didn't feel right reading the rest of her application, so I didn't.

As it turned out, I probably should have.

CHAPTER 3

One Sunday morning, a couple of weeks later, I was leaving l'Église Saint-Sulpice after the organ recital, intending to stroll somewhere, I don't recall if I even had a destination in mind. In spite of the late fall season, that morning the city was washed in sunlight. I do remember thinking about the old, mostly-empty church I had just walked out of, the thousands of pipes in her great organ, her somber façade overlooking la Place with its monumental fountain and chestnut trees, wondering to myself why Paris never seems to change. And answering my own question: it does change, but not much. Her fashions change, hemlines and necklines rise and fall, the age-blackened walls of the historic buildings are cleaned maybe once a generation or less, the museums close for simple renovations and reopen six years later—but the vital fabric of this city, the ancient winding streets with their shaded culs-de-sac, the grands boulevards, the parks and quais and bouquinistes along the Seine remain reassuringly the same—though every year they are watched through new eyes by new lovers.

⚜

Musing half-consciously, I was aware of someone following me down the church steps into the great square. I would like to say that I knew her immediately, but I did not—although there was something about her, something that was ringing one of my rusty bells, faintly, but ringing nonetheless. It was not a Proustian madeleine scene. My memory could be ignited by the hurt of un amour manqué, but never by the taste or aroma of a pastry.

Then she called out, "Darneau?" and I stopped. Because her voice had not changed at all—after nearly two decades—even if everything else had.

"Yes," I said. "And you are . . . ?" But she laughed a little, because she knew I had recognized her before I could complete the question.

"Tu te moques de moi, et pourquoi?" in her flat American accent.

"Tu n'as pas oublié le français, Julie."

"But I have, really. I just rehearsed a few lines for you." After a short silence, "Can I buy you a coffee?"

When you're too bewildered to think clearly, or to think at all, you tend simply to go along with whatever you're asked to do. So we walked down to one of the innumerable cafés on the Boulevard Saint-Germain, the aromatic Paris morning air smelling of strong coffee, fresh croissants, and brioches, hot omelettes jambon-fromage with soft Camembert cheese, and we somehow resumed a conversation that had ended in pain (for me) a lifetime ago.

Actually, the conversation also began in pain, or at least in fumbling, uneasy hesitancies on my part. Julie, on the other hand, fell back naturally into her old expressions and glib demeanor, enhanced for me by her familiar mannerisms, remarkably unchanged—she was still a lustrous free spirit.

I studied the look on her face. She was older, naturally, but the Frenchmen in the café had glanced up and were watching her as she walked in. She was proof of the old axiom: nobody really changes as you get older, you just become more of yourself, and Julie was still beautiful, yielding nothing to time. We found a table in a quiet corner, and I let her begin.

"Aren't you going to ask me how I found you, Darneau?"

"I haven't been hiding from you . . . or anyone."

"Still, it took me forever."

"I wrote to you in California, quite a few times, at your parents' address. You never answered. In fact, as I recall, most of my letters were returned unopened."

Julie looked around the room, just briefly, then her eyes came back to me. "Darneau, if you wrote, my parents would have sent them back or thrown them away. They did not want a young, reckless, free-loving New Yorker in my life. I did receive one Christmas card that must have slipped through, postmarked London. That's where I first looked for you, years ago."

"I was in graduate school there for a while, but mostly I stayed in France."

"Doing what?"

"Teaching or tutoring English—faking the obligatory British accent to get jobs. And I was taking courses at the American College and then at the University of Paris, writing home for money, scraping by, dodging the draft, steering clear of Vietnam. Now, all these years later, living the expat life, still teaching English, still working on a French doctorate. There are nineteen years of my life . . . in three sentences."

"You were always pretty good at compressing the truth, Darneau. I pictured you married years ago—you were forever talking about it, about running away like teenage lovers. Alors, dis-le-moi."

"Married? Non, as the old song goes: Jamais de la vie. And you?"

"Yes, and no. A Los Angeles wedding one year, a Reno divorce the next. A catastrophic marriage—less a marriage, more a catastrophe. When we split up, my husband kept the money, the furniture, and all the good memories. I got the rest."

"No children?"

Julie picked up her Americano, took a sip, and hesitated before answering. Like Melissa Artemis, she rarely replied matter-of-factly to what I was asking; and now she answered my question with a question of her own.

"Darneau, do you remember when I left Paris right in the middle of the winter term?"

"Do I remember? Let me put it this way. It's not simply a memory really when it's something you've tried—and failed—to forget every day since then, month after month, year after year. Unfortunately, memories can't be sorted through like vacation souvenirs, some to be saved, some to be thrown away. I knew you, Julie, for what, about two months? As Cavafy might have said, I would never have believed the memory of those eight weeks could last forever."

"You exaggerate, Darneau. I have forgotten your talent for turning choses tristes into beautiful sad words. Your rhetoric is still pitch-perfect."

"It was not all tristesse. It's just that when you are young and in love, in Paris for God's sake, and then you are suddenly abandoned with absolutely no warning, no explanation, and here truly I don't exaggerate at all, I was crushed, stumbling my way through long empty days and longer, miserable lonely nights—my life was completely hollowed out. It was like an ice pick in the heart.

"And you, Julie, must have been considering it all rationally, living your peaceful life in Southern California, thinking yes, it was a sweet but brief affair, a summer romance in a Parisian winter. But over here I was dying. I know cœur brisé is just a figure of speech, but some heartbreaks go on and on in their own merciless way—et l'avenir dure longtemps as DeGaulle once said. Tristesse perpétuelle."

As we sat together again on that eventful morning in that nondescript café, my mind was wandering, as it often did, off into the hazy, unfathomable, inexplicable unknown, where it could do me or anyone else no good. Although my mind wandered, my eyes were fixed on Julie, reminiscing and remembering . . . and I couldn't help but think that if true happiness isn't always short-lived, nonetheless it's almost always transient, and trying to outwait the sadness that inevitably follows it is insanity . . . you'd have to live forever.

Julie looked at me, sighed, and continued her story. "In the fall I went back up to Berkeley to try and finish my degree. The sixties student life at Cal: we protested everything, the war, the draft, civil rights, college admissions policy, freedom of this, freedom of that. We marched for any cause, anywhere, everywhere, all the time, sucked in tear gas, that wasn't fun. We burnt our candles at both ends and in the middle. Sometimes we even went to class. Months went by, then years. I almost forgot you. And now, thirty-eight years old, we are sitting in a little Parisian café on a quiet Sunday morning. And you are looking at me as if I were a stranger, une ombre de la rue . . . which I am."

I sat there, mostly silent, taking it all in, listening to her rapid-fire stories as she went on: school, jobs, failed marriage, more jobs, some of them even good ones—life in the California maelstrom. When she finally asked about me, I filled in the blanks. It didn't take long. Our conversation was not painfully insensitive and not stalled or weighed down by extended, excruciating pauses. Yet it seemed that we were, in some way, not getting below the surface, not reaching the feelings between the words. I suppose that was not surprising after the long bleak years of complete separation. Long dark years, when a love can burn itself out, but not all loves; and not for all lovers.

Julie still radiated her own self-assured charisma. I could not help but continue to study her features as we talked: she had somehow safeguarded the luminous young look I recalled, though perhaps just beginning to show the gentle but irrepressible jabs of life's natural forces . . . le Temps, c'est l'Ennemi. Doubtless she was thinking the same of me. In the subjective mirrors of our own minds, of course, we appeared perfectly unchanged—the aftereffect of selected treasured memories overcoming matter-of-fact visual truth.

She was to be in Paris for a few more days—could we have dinner or perhaps just walk in the Luxembourg gardens or by the Seine? I said why not; we exchanged numbers and left, Julie to her hotel on the boulevard, while I walked down to the Pont Neuf and crossed over to the Vert Galant. There I leaned against the cold stone balustrade of the ancient bridge and looked down at the dark taupe river pressing by me on both sides of the île. And I remembered the last time Julie and I had walked to this exact same place and watched the lucent crimson fragments of a late winter sunset falling through broken clouds and down onto the Paris cityscape. We were just kids, really, in love forever. I thought we'd have a thousand more nights to watch the sun set into that perfect river vista.

We never had a single one.

⚜

I wandered back to la rue de Vaugirard and crossed into the Jardin du Luxembourg where I sat on one of those heavy old metal chairs that have been there forever. How many times had Julie and I hurried across those gravel garden paths, running late for class? Once in a while on rare sunny days, especially on weekends, we took time to sit and talk, watching les gosses sail their tiny boats around the Grand Bassin, racing around to guide and trap them with their long sticks before they crashed into the far side. Even then, mostly she talked and I listened, like to her fierce arguments against the death penalty and the impassioned, unwavering fervor of her young beliefs. Just to be annoying, I would sometimes chip away at her position, citing Adolph Eichmann who had been executed a few months before: would you have let him live? And she would immediately and cheerfully seize on my exception that was so hideous, she claimed, it somehow proved her rule.

Julie's family were half-hearted Catholics, but she was a whole-hearted atheist, so she fit in well with the European students of the 1960s. In one class they made an audible mockery of the poet Paul Claudel's mystical Notre Dame conversion, when it was recounted by our French humanities professor. And Julie made her point: what value has a religion if only little children can believe in its horned devils, its three gods, winged angels and miracle-performing saints? Once, I resorted to quoting the beautiful Chateaubriand response: le Christianism est vrai parce que c'est très agréable d'écouter une cloche sonner la nuit dans la campagne. (It sounds better in French, doesn't it?)

But Julie answered, "Wasn't it his father who said the only thing worse than a bad priest is a good priest? And I'd rather listen to Boris Vian sing L*e Deserteur* than to hear evening church bells in the countryside."

Along with thousands of other students we had arrived in Paris as the bitter, bloody Algerian war was finally ending. Emotions still ran hot in 1962 and unyielding French nationalists would drive around the Place de l'Étoile honking their horns with three short blasts and two long—the banned five beat signal sounding out "Algérie Française." Now, two decades later, from my seat in the great, sprawling park, I looked up at the Florentine Medici palace, wondering if Julie's heart and mind and soul ever wandered back, as mine did, to the same fugitive memories, or if her time in Paris was too ephemeral, cut off so soon by her sudden flight. For Julie, the images of our time together had doubtless blurred ages ago. For me they had not; they were still distinct . . . razor-sharp.

Le grand jardin was slowly giving up its walkers and joggers as a chill wind blew in from under the pale sun sinking obliquely behind the rue d'Assas. I thought back to my first freezing winter here, 1962-63: a bitter shock to Parisians though it seemed perfectly normal to me coming from the Finger Lakes region of upstate New York. It did seem to snow almost every day in Paris after Julie left, and the long nights were, as the French say, colder than a bishop's heart . . . as I checked my pitiless mailbox for letters that never came.

How long did I go on haplessly loving her after that last desolate day she slipped away? For months, if not years, I would walk around the Latin Quarter and see shadows of our past, in the Place de la Sorbonne, down la rue des Écoles, past the Cluny métro, language classes on rue Auguste Comte, ducking out of the rain into a little bar or café. For me it had been a true first love in all its poignant simplicity. For Julie, who can say? Even now did she still care for me in some senseless way? If not, why was she back in Paris, tracking me, following me down church steps?

I suppose the emotional fires in two lovers' hearts never

reach the same intensity at the same time. They burn at different rhythms in different ways, and even the strongest of them will invariably begin to flicker and finally die: smoldering, lingering orange embers for some loves; for others, gray-white powdery ashes quickly turning ice cold. Yet even the faintest embers can sometimes come back to life, reignited by the residual heat of love: new flames to gently warm, or burn and destroy. I wrote a long letter about this wretched nonsense to Julie in the summer of 1963. I don't know if it got through to her, though it was never returned to me. Maybe I never mailed it. It was drenched in self-pity and anguished self-righteousness; I hope now that I never sent it. Since then I have come to understand that only the young are truly shattered by broken love affairs, or by being suddenly abandoned. Older lovers can be hurt, but they grieve briefly and then go out looking for replacements, sweet substitutes; though this might not be true for everyone . . . some may still hurt after twenty years. They are the unlucky ones, cursed with long memories.

Dusk was slowly falling as I headed back through the misted city toward rue de Sèvres and my lonely apartment. Images of Julie, then and now, not so different really, rolled through my mind. Was I still in love with her? I had no clear idea, or at least not an idea I could explain. Can deep affection, if not love, linger on after more than nineteen years of complete disconnect? Or do those long stark years crush the feelings bit by bit, until all the little broken pieces are trashed away for good? And after such a slow, painstaking death knell can the love ever be brought back to life, back from near extinction? It seemed sadly unlikely—yet in the human heart anything is possible.

If I were being honest with myself, which I never am, I would have to confess that the memories of Julie were the only stars that sparsely lit those dark years for me, but those years and those stars had inexorably faded into the distance. Ours had been a brief, profound, even beautiful affair, but destroyed by none of my doing or wanting, and maybe none of Julie's. The intensity of it was only heightened because there had been no time or space in Paris to erode our passion or to be drawn away to someone else. There was no one else, not in that perfect interval of love.

It was dark by the time I got close to my apartment, where I ducked into the little rue de Sèvres market to pick up something for dinner. I passed a couple of students moving in the other direction, arms locked together, eyes full of love.

CHAPTER 4

THE NEXT DAY JULIE DID CALL ME, AND WE DECIDED to meet for dinner at a little left bank restaurant we had been to in the '60s: Aux Assassins on rue Jacob. Some Paris restaurants last for generations, a handful even for centuries; but many, probably most, come and go in a decade or two, often to be resurrected later with new names, new owners, new chefs. Aux Assassins was one of the survivors, and it was crowded the night Julie and I returned there, noisier than she recalled, with its long shared tables, beaucoup de monde. But we stayed anyway, for old time's sake, ordering steak frites and drinking a pichet of red house wine, pinard really, (not quite a three-man wine as the French vignerons call it: so bad it takes two men to hold the third one down to make him drink it).

I let her begin, as I knew she would. She surprised me by pulling out an old Polaroid shot of the two of us, taken by some nameless street photographer on the steps of Sacré Cœur whose great white dome reproved and looked down on us from under a pewter sky. I studied the snapshot for a moment, trying to reconstruct the possible events that might have followed. It was not the sort of photo that would win an award or be included in a coffee table book on Paris. But for the two young lovers portrayed, it was one to keep forever as it captured and froze the spirit of that forgotten afternoon.

I said quietly, "For me, Julie, you were Paris—our love and our memories were the essence of the city."

She looked intently at me. "How do you remember being so young?"

I shrugged. "I never think of it that way, not in the sense of being a certain age. But I can recall our time together almost hour by hour, sitting next to each other every morning in the Cours de Civilisation Française lectures, then walking down Boul'Mich' to the student cafeteria at le Foyer International, holding our breath as we passed the stinky pissotière, back to afternoon language classes, maybe a film at night in one of the little cinémas in le quartier latin, sometimes they'd seat less than fifty people. We walked everywhere, except when we took the métro to the American Express to check for mail or exchange dollars for francs. Then the resolute day you moved from your French host family to stay with me at l'Hôtel St-André des Arts, never letting your parents know. On s'amusait bien, non? I didn't choose to fall in love with you, Julie. There was no plan. It was the simplest happenstance."

"So what was I like? Have I changed so drastically?"

I'd forgotten how much Julie had focused on her looks back then, like most teenagers, I suppose. I answered her, "Maybe you've changed some, but not your voice or your laugh. It still sounds like arpeggios in some melodious key that you used to practice on your French family's grand piano."

She smiled. "I hear it more like a lament in some minor key no composer would ever want to write in. God, Darneau, look around us. You used to be able to pick out the Americans because they were wearing jeans. Now everybody's wearing them.

But I do remember getting letters at the American Express and, of course, moving into St-André des Arts with you. But do I look so different? You didn't recognize me at St-Sulpice. I was sitting across the aisle from you the whole time."

"Maybe my eyes were closed, listening to Bach."

"Maybe your heart was closed, too."

I stared at her, then shook my head sadly. "Pardon me for asking, but what is that supposed to mean? You were the one who deserted me without even the simplest goodbye."

Then out of nowhere came her calm pronouncement, like an unforeseeable bomb falling from a night-black sky.

"Darneau, I was pregnant when I left you in Paris. I didn't tell you because I couldn't trust what you would do in your crazy, romantic, immature idealism. Having a Parisian love-child, living in poverty à la Bohème, tout ça. So I went home to California to have an abortion—it seemed the only way out."

I sat there breathless, stunned into silence. When the words finally came, I said, "Julie, stop. . . . I can't believe what you are saying, what I'm hearing, what you did, how you left me. This is not true, is it?"

"I wrote you a letter."

"It did not happen to include any mention of being pregnant."

"No . . . for one thing, I wasn't one hundred percent sure."

"And the abortion?" I tried to maintain my composure, or at least keep my voice down. "I didn't deserve to know about that?"

"Would you have agreed to it, had you known?"

"Yes, if I had no heart and no conscience."

She looked away. "It wasn't your child."

We sat there without speaking. There are awkward pauses, and there are agonizing, earsplitting silences.

"Julie, listen to me. I have two simple questions: did you have an abortion, and are you certain it was not my child?"

"I have two simple answers: No, and yes. I couldn't go through with the abortion, and I'm ashamed to say I was pregnant when I met you."

I put some franc notes on the table and we left the restaurant without finishing our dinners. As we walked back toward the boulevard, the night wind was rising, cold and dry. We were both silent again, even Julie, who was never at a loss for words, thinking about everything, the two of us, I'm sure, running through completely different trains of thought.

Finally I said, "Julie, I can't believe you would let all these years go by with no contact, no letters even, and now you show up in Paris . . ." But I didn't know what more to say, whether to laugh or cry.

"For a long time I was ashamed to reach back to you, Darneau, just as I was too ashamed to say goodbye to you, face to face. There are two things I'm good at: shame and guilt. But look, we knew each other for how many weeks? Or should I say, we never knew each other at all. You were smarter than everyone, sensitive when it came to poetry, art, music, but you were not sensitive about people. You were spiritually and emotionally color-blind. Yes, you had a few friends, but you confided in no one, not even me, though I was living with you."

"I loved you," I said softly, without emotion.

"No, Darneau, you loved what you brought out in me, what I gave back to you. It was not real love of me, was it? I was an idealized figure created in your imagination, blended in with your obsessive love of Paris. Remember how you used to tell me that your only true virtue was your immaturity, and you were afraid you were losing it? That we had probably already reached our peak as individuals, then would gradually decline, year by year? I think that's how you put it. Now it seems to me that you may have been right."

"Julie, we were kids, I was talking drivel about youth, not love, or even infatuation." I tried to keep the bitterness out of my voice. "What I understand better now is an even more painful truth: that our innocence does slowly die . . . every day, one experience at a time. You can never get it back."

We sat on an old green bench near the ancient Saint-Germain-des-Prés church, beneath tall, almost leafless plane trees, as night shadows fell darkly between the deep pitched rooftops. Yet the boulevard was still alive with the sounds of the sleepless city.

"Julie, how can you be certain who your child's father was . . ." But I stopped here.

"I'm certain. There was only one other—you never met him. I knew him for just a little while before you . . . he was young and good-looking, I was young and foolish. I don't want to talk about it."

She still had a knack for inflicting pain. "What happened next?"

"I paid in shame for my stupidity. Then I got married."

"And the child?"

"It was a girl. She stayed with my mother when I went back up to Berkeley; sometimes she was with my husband after we separated. It was the sixties, remember. I was twenty years old, a pleasure-seeker, occasionally slightly ambitious, always utterly selfish, solipsistic, like Anne Boleyn without a king. There was no greater egoist in the world."

"What happened to the child? What was her name?"

"Audrey, and she left when my husband left—I lost touch completely for a while. I was living in a bay area commune with other losers, my life hauled around like a garbage truck. It was a squalid time, yet we thought we were on a great adventure. We believed in free love. 'It works perfectly in practice,' as the French engineer said of his great invention, 'but I fear it doesn't work in theory.' Anyway, I didn't see my parents really for three, four, five years. Don't ask me why. We just left each other's lives. Actually, I have seen them in recent years—they're getting old, but they're so valiant about it."

"And that's the end of the story? Now it's back to California and I'll never hear from you?"

"No, not like that. You and I will be close again, we will write letters."

"The written word doesn't quite make you friends, does it?"

"Darneau, you were drinking wine one night and I remember your joking: life is incomprehensible—once you understand that, you're in. Do you still believe that?"

"I never said that. If I did, I was just quoting some idiot."

"You also told me, maybe you were quoting again? Set the bar low; it's the secret to a happy life."

"Where do you find these jejune platitudes? Maybe they would sound better in French."

"You said them, Darneau. I wrote them down."

"I remember now: you kept a journal. You wrote it in pencil on the squared graph paper of a French student's exercise book."

"That's true. I brought it with me to Paris and in fact I was going through it last night. The writing level is middle school Californian, the thinking and posing even worse. But I like it because it brings back those times, the Latin Quarter, the smells of Arab and Greek restos, the different languages and accents, the little bars and storefront movie houses, sneaking into the Mabillon student restaurant. Remember the old style of bus with the rear platform half open to the air? We would run and try to mount the platform en marche as the bus pulled slowly away from the stop. And les grèves, picket lines, les flics and their ear-splitting sirens: loud honking rhythms of sound breaking up demonstrations, DeGaulle droning on the radio about la liberté et la gloire de la patrie, students laughing at him, mocking, digging up cobblestones from the sandy streets to throw at the police while shouting, 'Sous les pavés, la plage!' You always found a way to slip through the student picket lines to go to class, Darneau."

"Yes. There are many doors into the Sorbonne. It was either that or waste time and money in a café with other lazy students."

"Like me?"

"No, you were not lazy—absent-minded sometimes, but sincere . . . I thought innocent. I was wrong."

"Yes. As I got older I began to replace innocence with common sense. It was pathetic. Still, I was not good at the business of life, which meant I was not good at the business of love." She spoke with faultless equivocation.

"And then?"

"And then I found Jesus, like Claudel standing by the pillar in Notre Dame."

"You found Jesus in California!"

"No, just kidding. I'm still an atheist."

"Thank God."

"Darneau, remember that story you told me about the young African student sitting on the métro, and a woman got on, went over to him and said, 'Jeune homme, in our country we give up our seats to older ladies.' And as the student got up he told her, 'In our country, we eat them.' You made up that story, didn't you, Darneau. What did the boy really say?"

He said, "Chez nous, on les mange."

Then cooly, "Darneau, you have not asked me to stay in Paris."

"Haven't I? Or should I say, why would I?"

"We had something, Darneau. I just wasn't strong enough then to love you completely. Paris, as I look back, was wasted on me—I was nineteen, hopeless. But we had a beginning, didn't we?"

"Yes, perhaps. But it was also an ending. Great loves, Cavafy says somewhere, last no longer than a spring breeze."

Her eyes flashed. "When did you become such a relentless cynic, Darneau, hiding behind your old Greek poet? You were once a dreamer."

"Some days I still have dreams, and hopes, some days doubts and sorrows. I can live with all of them. But not self-deception and lies—they would kill me."

She gave me a long look. "Sometimes lies tell us more than the truth. Did you never want to have children?"

No one could accuse Julie of being tactful, or even polite. But I answered her question. "I have children. I look out at them tenderly every day in my classroom."

"Is it the same? Is that enough for you?"

"Perhaps not, but even in Paris it's difficult to have a child without a wife. You are thirty-eight now, Julie? How many children do you have?"

"None, really. I have none. The one I had I lost long ago. Forgive my self-pity—it comes with my selfishness. I can be overcome by both. And when it comes to potential fathers, I have a talent, perfected after I left you, for picking nice-looking neurotics. When my life becomes too tiresome, I leave it behind. That is my chanson d'amour."

I had no idea what this meant exactly, but I said nothing more. A fragile dark-violet stillness hung over us, as if it were descending to kill off the rest of the despondent evening. Whatever random lucky stars that might have been out there somewhere were sadly outshone by the unfeeling Paris street lights or blocked entirely by the massive old buildings of the district. Julie stood up to leave—I offered to walk her to her hotel—but she said it was just a minute away, across the boulevard. Then she looked up at the ancient Saint-Germain church walls and said, "Remember the five sorrowful mysteries of the rosary, Darneau? The last one is love."

And she left, not looking back, never saying goodbye, and I wondered if either of us believed we would ever see each other again. What did she mean to me now? We were escaped prisoners, wandering blindly back into our sad history, linked together by an old love affair and its shadow of remembrance—but those links can snap suddenly or, if they don't break, time will patiently rust them away. At this distant point what did Julie and I retain or what could we recover from those long ago days we spent with each other? What was left for us to share in the here and now—between un ange déchu et un homme blessé? Fascinating how it's only the failed, damaged loves that leave you with meaningful lessons . . . d'apprendre le cafard.

I turned away from the boulevard and walked up la rue Bonaparte to the Seine, heading into the cool remorseless flow of the night-river air, seeking isolation, trying to free myself from the ghostly prison of senseless memories. Was it Pursewarden who said the better your memory is, the shorter life seems? Probably not, but I know he said: il faut chercher une femme qui valait peut-être la peine d'être aimée. He was talking about Julie.

She complains that her Paris recollections have been dimmed by the passing years and long estrangement from the city, but I'm not sure I believe her. She remembers a lot, though perhaps not with the clarity and sharpness that accompany pain and loss. My own recollections come with that clear disadvantage. And she could not help but defeat me: her staunch insensitivity deafening my weak inner vision. I knew that at some point in those haunted years following Julie's escape I came to realize that I had always loved her more than she had loved me . . . For me, unlike for Julie, it was never just some romantic, fantastic illusion, some folie à deux.

It was getting late and the side streets were almost empty. I headed back through shafts of darkness down rue Bonaparte, walking slowly towards Julie's hotel on the boulevard. Some force I didn't understand was pushing me back to her, though I couldn't have told you what I was going to do when I got there, or what I was going to say. I went into the ornate lobby and decided to collect my thoughts in the hotel bar. I hesitated at the entrance and looked in.

Julie was sitting alone at the far end of the mahogany bar, her back to the door where I was standing. I wanted to go to her, but for some incomprehensible reason I could not. I turned slowly and walked out of the hotel. Julie never looked around, she never noticed me. She didn't see the defeated look on my face, caught desperately somewhere between love and fear.

DIARY OF MELISSA ARTEMIS

October 28, 1982

I sat in the back of Darneau's class today, listening to his discussion of Mallarmé's poetry. I took a few notes even. This was the line I liked best: 'La chair est triste hélas, et j'ai lu tous les livres.' When he recited it, there was a deep, timeless melancholy in his voice, deeper than before, sadder than ever.

I went up to him after class and asked, "Have you read all the books, monsieur?"

At first he didn't answer me, then shrugged and said, "Il y en a trop. I read more of them when I was your age."

I told him, "You were not yourself today, professeur. There was no bonheur in your voice."

He finally smiled, barely smiled I should say, and looked at me with a trace of pathos in his dark blue eyes (or do I imagine this) and said, "Can you detect happiness in voices? Then you have a gift."

I told him I had watched his mood change in an instant from expressing the precarious beauty of a poem into one of inconsolable sadness, as if they were the same thing. And he gave me his characteristic, inscrutable look and said, "How are they different?" As he walked away I felt the icy shiver of his sadness knife through me, like a parlous, shriveling, stabbing blast of wind. I promised myself not to use too many over-the-top metaphors in this journal, but it's a promise that I am constantly breaking. Clichés are my forte.

Mallarmé also wrote that we are not born to be happy—it is not our métier, not in our evolutionary design. We are lucky if we have quelques moments de joie parmi les heures d'ennui.

When did this blue mood find me? J'en ai marre.

Finis.

CHAPTER 5

After leaving the empty classroom and watching Melissa Artemis head down toward le Pont de l'Alma with one of her friends, I decided after all to phone Julie at her hotel. I was told she had checked out that morning.

I shouldn't have been surprised, I suppose, which I wasn't really, after thinking about it. Her leaving Paris was as sudden and unannounced as her return. And I shouldn't have been disappointed either, and mostly I wasn't. And yet . . . and yet . . . was it Shylock who said, "If you prick me, do I not bleed?" There was the inchoate, vaguely familiar sting of another joyless, if not as calamitous, separation, this time after just a brief rencontre, following so many years of total, uninterrupted silence.

I walked slowly back down the rue de Sèvres toward my little apartment, my mind and heart reprising the bittersweet memories of my time with Julie, now so long removed. Seeing her again, svelte in her stylish southern California outfits, reminiscent of her Sorbonne days, always looking good back then in her perfectly starched blouses with their Peter Pan collars, her fitted skirts, tight capris, her little pointed heels, handsome lambswool sweaters or French styled vestes, often wearing the bright colors she favored: bleu, blanc, rouge, like the tricolore revolutionary flag, I recalled how she stood out from the other foreign students who were more casual, informal, dégagé; they were not like Julie, who would forever be checking her eye makeup or her blond ponytail, her Heidi braids or French twist in the compact mirror she was never without. Not that the others were all more serious students than Julie—she had a good ear for the language—but she also had a good eye for the pleasures of the Latin Quarter. She soaked up and sparkled with Parisian joie de vivre.

The very first night we met she was sipping wine in a café on rue de la Harpe with five or six American students loosely connected by our various inefficient efforts to kick off the new semester of the Cours de Civilisation Française de la Sorbonne. Those efforts consisted mainly of trying to locate, then waiting in, long, slow-moving lines to apply for cartes de séjour, student restaurant assignments, language class placements, library and museum permits, and so on, the torments of la bureaucratie française. That first night we all ended up wandering through le grand marché of les Halles, watching the French ouvriers noisily unload their trucks, gridlocked and parked at odd angles, of the crates of fruits, vegetables and other fresh foodstuffs—to stoke Zola's belly of Paris.

Sadly, the ancient market now has completely disappeared, trampled by modern civilization, removed from la centre ville to suburban Rungis. Julie and I did not realize then, of course, that we were standing in the dying twilight of the market's long history, or that the medieval center of the city was soon to give up forever the transported paradisiacal beauty of the countryside and its fresh products of nature. Its epitaph is written on the wall of the district's great church, Saint-Eustache, ending in these stark, poignant words: L'image des Halles Centrales dans le cœur de Paris est maintenant un Paradis Perdu.

Leaving the packed streets and alleys of the market, we had found the famed restaurant Au Pied de Cochon—it must have been one or two in the morning—but crowded even at that hour and famous, bien sûr, pour la soupe gratinée à l'oignon. Now, as I write this so many years later, I think back to February 25, 1963 (I still have the program notes) when Julie and I squeezed into the Palais de Chaillot for the historic first Paris reading by the young poet Yevgeny Yevtushenko, where he recited his poems in Russian following French translations read by Jean Vilar. In tongue-in-cheek homage to the Pied de Cochon signature dish, he had written: On goutte de cette soupe-là comme on va à la messe.

But not all his verse was light. The poem "Babi Yar" was his dangerous salvo against antisemitism. It was recited by the French actor in a voice trembling with emotion, finishing in a dramatic burst so intense that the young audience froze in one of those rare hushed moments that sometime take place in a concert hall after a sublime musical performance, a deep silence lingering after the last note is played or last word sung. Then came the long stirring ovation, even as the French reader, stunned and bewildered himself, turned and instead of leaving the stage, remained motionless, looking down at the poem which he still held in his hand. Yevtushenko went to the actor, smiled at him, then embraced him: I can still see the scene so clearly.

After the program, Julie and I had filed out quietly into the dark evening, though in reality this city is never truly dark. One can rarely see the moon let alone any stars in the Paris night sky. Out in the streets a thousand cafés and shops and carrefours are lit up: now by luminous electric powered lights, a century before by lambent pale-yellow oil and gas globes, and even before that by myriad glass lanterns with their tallow candles flickering like white gold behind the shadowy Parisian casement windows. It had been a cold and damp yet unforgettable winter night, a night of Russian poetry.

After I had gotten to know Melissa Artemis, I happened to mention to her about seeing Yevtushenko in 1963. She was always asking me for stories of my student days. But after this one she informed me that Yevtushenko was not a great poet like Mayakovsky. I told her that Mayakovsky did not come to Paris to read to us, and she said, "Darneau, he killed himself before you were born, but like Keats, he was a true poet who died young. There was another true Russian poet whose name I can never get right. Her first name was Anna."

"Akhmatova, but she didn't come to Paris then either."

"She was a woman and a genius. What chance did she have to travel under the Soviet boot?" And Melissa scorched me with her most ardent feminist stare.

For so short a love affair, Paris gave Julie and me many such nights to remember—this city of half-truth and half-fiction, emblazoned everywhere with immortal names from centuries past: mad artists and poets, novelists, literary swordsmen, musicians, composers, murderous rulers and generals, and quite a few patron saints and martyrs, their names carved onto the street corners of ancient stone buildings (sometimes with just the word "saint" scraped away from the original nom de la rue by anti-clerical revolutionaries). The streets, the squares, les belles places, métro stations, their names flashing onto the screens of our memories, fixed there indelibly as we moved around the city day by day—names like Jaurès, Balzac, Hugo, Foch, Gambetta, Danton, Ravel, Debussy, Django. We were young and naïve, Julie and I, tossed into a Paris rêverie where we hurried everywhere and didn't have time to fall out of love. We trusted and believed. Later, I learned to my chagrin, you should never trust any of your young beliefs, which can vanish overnight like a false satanic creed.

Yet on that first night when we met and fell in together, Julie and I were not thinking about the distant future and not worrying about anything at all. We made the long walk back from the Châtelet-Halles district—the last métro had left hours ago. We had talked in the restaurant about schools and studying French, learning about music, history, art, and wine, and traveling around Europe. It wasn't until later, as we got close to where she was staying, that we touched on more serious things: what we hoped really to achieve here in Paris, how we would refine our language skills and perfect our French accents, improve our own writing, explore every library and every museum, watch films like *Orfeu Negro*, *Jules et Jim*, and *Les Quatre Cents Coups*, how we would grow and change and deepen our shallow lives.

Of course, we never actually accomplished any of these goals. They were fantasies, pipe dreams, though we did watch a few movies.

When we arrived at Julie's host family's building off the rue du Quatre Septembre, she unlocked the massive old wooden doors and we sat inside on the stairway landing, talking quietly, listening, hanging together, fighting off sleep and falling in love—or so we believed. C'était le triomphe d'une jeune naïveté sur une vérité dure et implacable. But that is truth seen perfectly through the cold lens of hindsight. By the time I left Julie that first night the sun was already threatening to return, a faint promise of light climbing up the east edge of Paris: dawn besieging the dark city. The façades of Haussmann's great stone buildings were slowly emerging out of the murky morning like gun-metal gray battleships floating down the English Channel. The streets were as quiet as they ever get, all the city of Paris holding her breath.

I went up the steep stairs to my little hotel room on the quatrième étage and tumbled into bed, dreaming of a future that I hoped would change me forever, in a city that itself would never change.

CHAPTER 6

A FEW DAYS AFTER THE AUX ASSASSINS DINNER WITH Julie I received a letter from Los Angeles, neatly enclosed in a pale blue airmail envelope with red chevron trimmed edges.

1 November 1982

Mon cher Darneau,

I am not adept at farewell scenes and I would express regrets, if I knew how, for leaving you in Paris a second time, but I have never been a willing or successful apologist. Who was it said never compound a serious blunder with an apology? Perhaps I should reread Plato's Socratic dialogue on the subject—I can hear you muttering, don't bother, it wouldn't help. Yet it might lead to a little more reflection on my part, and a little less consternation.

Let me first say that I am not sorry I found you after all these years. For me it brought back the Paris of those old days, times I had not totally forgotten, to be sure, but that year after year had grown less distinct, like a fading watercolor left hanging too long on a dry, sunbaked wall. You once told me the French definition of memory: ce que nous pensions avoir oublié . . . memory is what we thought we'd forgotten. I wrote it in my journal. I realize now that my failure was I loved you honestly and passionately back then, yet I was also able to go on living without ever seeing you again . . . until I did see you again. And I felt those punishing memories return and begin to gnaw at me, reminding me how I utterly lacked the courage then to prevent our separation. I know what I did was inexcusable: I couldn't face you then and nothing is making it any easier now.

Yet being with you again, walking down the Boulevard Saint-Germain and rue Jacob, it seemed to me that the quintessence of Paris, the city as I remembered it, was surprisingly unchanged—despite the obvious superficial differences. Can that be true? Even the winding streets lit by the old streetlamps gave the same vintage-like quality to the city. You who have continued living there through the years must see it totally differently, the new horrendous Montparnasse skyscraper spearing the Parisian skyline, the ugly périphérique ring road, nobody under thirty-five wearing dresses or skirts anymore—I'm sure you gradually got used to all of it, and now don't even notice it. On dit que tout le monde adore Paris: expats, exiles, artists, writers, pickpockets, jazz musicians, and of course students from everywhere. Everybody loves Paris except the Parisians—didn't you tell me that? Les riches moving to Monaco or Switzerland, but not les petits bourgeois, they can't afford to leave. You were pretty cynical about them, Darneau, but of course, you were pretty cynical about everything.

I've thought a lot about what you said to me as we sat on that bench near the old church—and also what you didn't say. I used to believe that the romance of love is less important than most young people think. They put it up on a pedestal; I never did that. Yet I'm not so sure I got it right, though we were never truly in love, were we? I mean you never really loved me for myself—perhaps our time together was just too short. You couldn't have understood the person I was, let alone who I would turn out to be. Now, especially after seeing you again, I think it was the time itself you fell in love with—the time and the illusions and the city—not me. I was part of that, of course, but not the essential part. The romance was mostly in your mind, not between the two of us. Paris, and yes we were inseparable there, but Paris was your real love. Aren't you happy that I can explain your life to you after all these years? Well, these are the feelings I took away from our dinner and our slow sad walk back to that dark sad bench.

Darneau, I came back to Paris because some inexplicable, unstoppable force had gradually built up in my mind and enticed me to search for you. I found you years older but somehow looking the same despite your long hair, now speaking beautiful French and completely settled in your Parisian life. I didn't expect you to fall in love with me again—I'm not that delusional. Long lasting love, is there such a thing? Perhaps we're only entitled to one coup de foudre in life, and after all that happened or didn't happen, that's okay. Still, I sensed my own feelings for you had suddenly become stronger than yours for me, and I didn't like it. You were friendly, warm even, but vague at times, without conviction. How can it be that two people in love are seldom happy in the same way at the same time, or is it simply that two happy people are seldom in love at the same time? Maybe it's because they are constantly fearful of being rejected, of losing, of being left behind, or maybe worse, that they will fully and finally possess the elusive beloved and it's not what they expected it to be.

I was hurt when you didn't ask me to stay on a little longer. You didn't even seem curious about my life, my ideas, my plans. I know I wounded you once when we were young. I never thought I would be wounded by you all these years later. It's like the old song: you cried for me, now it's my turn to cry over you. You have played a trick on my heart, Darneau. I guess my time for you has burned down, like those little trembling white candles lit in the side altar of some dusky church to save a soul. Sorry, I don't mean to sound maudlin. I know love can fade, like any other flower—mais d'une façon, je t'aimerai . . . toujours.

Julie

Naturally I was touched by the rambling feelings she expressed, and the French phrases she tossed in. They stirred my own intense emotions and some I had almost forgotten. I had loved Julie too much, I realized, not enough to die from her disappearance—from my irretrievable loss—but enough to damage years of my life. I kept the letter for a couple of days, then wrote back. I asked about her daughter and where she lived, if Julie even knew. And I did finally ask about her own life in California, her work, what she did, what she read, what she thought.

She wrote again, but her next letter was different in tone, even more somber, almost desperate, or was I reading too much between the lines (where, according to Pursewarden, all the real writing is done) searching for the true meaning, comprehending what was not there?

Dear Darneau,

You asked about my child. She was born in the UCLA Medical Center in Santa Monica, not far from the little honey-colored stucco clinic where I had been scheduled for an abortion. The night before that appointment I had barely slept, and when I did I dreamt of tiny pink fingers and toes . . . I just couldn't go through with it. So the baby was born, I went back to Berkeley and left her with my mother. After I got married the following winter, my husband actually grew closer to the little girl than I ever did. I did see her at Christmas and holidays, vacations, and so forth, but she clung to my mother and cried when I picked her up, but not, oddly, when my husband held her. He told me I didn't hold her firmly enough, that she cried because she was afraid of slipping, or falling. So I would hand her off and she'd be fine—so much for the maternal instinct. In me it was replaced by infernal guilt. How can you love a child, if you don't even know how to hold her?

I had three more years to go at Cal and I saw her less and less. After our divorce my ex eventually moved to Pasadena and he stayed close to my parents. I think for years Audrey thought he was her real father. I rarely saw her—I know it sounds heartless, it's even worse when you really think about it. I didn't deserve to be in her life and she didn't deserve to have me poking back into it. Of course I rationalized that she was in better hands and didn't need a pot smoking counterculture Berkeley hippie ruining her life. Then 1967 came: the Summer of Love, they call it. It was more a summer of endings for me: leaving behind our college classes, our noble causes, our drugs and jug wine, my friends joining the Peace Corps and heading out to Ethiopia or Nigeria, some of the guys drafted and shoving off to burn the huts and jungles of Vietnam, the smart ones escaping to Canada or Sweden. I moved on as well. But it was too late, I told myself, to become anyone's mother or wife. I basically dropped out of Audrey's life and might not recognize her today if she walked through my door—though I have seen her occasionally.

My parents separated for a while and my dad's work took him to Europe a lot. He stayed friends with my ex, who was working for an American company in Zurich the last I heard. He eventually put his step-daughter in a private French school in Geneva. She understands now that he's not her biological father. This is about all I know. He may have remarried. I hear you thinking as you read this: what an unspeakably worthless human being she turned into. Tu as raison quand même, mon vieux. Does it sound less despicable in French?

I guess I don't really want to answer your other questions about my haphazard life in California; it's not worth the ink or the paper, but thanks for asking. High speed train wreck, the ship be sinkin'—pick your own metaphor for grim scenarios. I've had lovers, but I can never quite figure out how to return their love. Maybe that's your fault, Darneau. Am I wrong? It took me years, but I've come to believe that no one can stay happy in love for very long—it's not part of the human condition. Love is just a temporary disruption of our loneliness. My loves always have a beginning and an end. (I suppose by definition a love affair only becomes a love affair after it's over.) And mine usually end when I start to feel self-conscious—I do better when I don't dwell on them. Love withers when you think too much about it, and it dies when you try to explain it. Voilà.

Your last question about where my daughter is now? The answer is I don't know for sure, and I don't know if I would care to tell you if I did. She has nothing to do with you. I will close now, enough desolation for one letter. It's cold here today for L.A., and limpid soft rain is falling like tears, matching my mood.

Julie

P.S. You know, I almost considered pretending to you that my daughter might have been your child. In the end I couldn't bring myself to do it—there are some lines even I can't cross. Keeping the rest of the truth from you felt bad enough.

I read the letter a second time, sensing that it was in some sorry way sprinkled with fiction, not blatant lies exactly, but self-deceptions at least. Julie could be extremely hard on herself, but la vérité was more complex. I didn't know what to write back, so I didn't write anything. Was I tempted to ask her to return to Paris, to look again for what we had found before? Yes, but not so much as I might have imagined. To me, now, for the first time, after seeing her in person, it felt like my love for Julie was practically from another era, almost from a different century, and the relentless waves of existence had begun to wash away even those most profound passions and longings and memories that I thought would hold me forever. I reflected ruefully: was that terrible moment when Julie left me going to be the pinnacle of my emotional life?

Julie had asked me why I never left Paris. Of course, I had, briefly, but never for long. I was a captive in the midst of this restless city: clinging to, yet at the same time trying to excise, the beautiful ghost-memory of Julie herself—for years comparing everyone to her and every experience to what we had shared in our time together. I'm still here because this was the place where I felt the most young, the most alive, the most happy, and I'm still trying to learn a lesson from it. What is the point of a great love if it only leads to suffering?

To be sure, I have not been isolated like a monk through all these years. I have gone through short-lived periodic affairs ranging from minor failures to major disasters. There had been only two lasting serious liaisons in eighteen years, where we shared an apartment and a life, two people sipping vin rouge together in the evenings, talking, laughing, arguing, sleeping side by side comme vrais amants. These were my two successes—that is, we were happy . . . until we weren't. Until we began to inch away from each other, as if our allotted time had expired, like the short drinking life of a faithless Beaujolais Nouveau.

Thinking back now, I was struck by how even these two longer affairs had mostly slipped from my mind, to the point where I had difficulty recalling their features. They had not left permanent imprints, in contrast to some of the sharper recollections of my briefer, more transient failures, des affaires ratées, rejections, letdowns, disappointments, memories of which clutter up the attic of my mind. Song lyrics don't do justice to failures:

"Regrets . . . but then too few to remember" or Piaf: "Non, rien de rien, non, je ne regrette rien." But for me, beaucoup de regrets, and Julie, needing no more than two months, had struck home with the deadliest weapon, made the deepest slash, and left the gravest wound.

I always told myself it would heal in time . . . yet it's been half my life. Time is slow, uneven, obscure, undependable. If the remembrance of the days and nights of my short life with Julie has blurred some, the scar, though worn fainter, has not disappeared yet, and may never disappear. Yet love must be about the future, I realize that. Even though memories of the past are beautiful and true, we have to acknowledge that they are in the past, and the past disappears—we cannot change that. The future of love is truer because there is still hope and anticipation that it might be perfect, eternal, better than any memory, because it is still coming, it is unstoppable. Only the future matters, we know this—yet at the same time we suspect it may never be.

But I wrote none of this to Julie. I felt an irrational fear that we could be headed for unforeseen dangers, that everything would be wrecked again, that I was doomed to repeat my failures. I was aware of this without being able to explain it, or escape it.

DIARY OF MELISSA ARTEMIS

November 17, 1982

Darneau talked nonsense in class today—he claimed that poets don't compose great poetry out of spontaneous inspiration or from deep heartfelt emotions. Instead they must be—what did he call them—better craftsmen, thinking about themes, rhythms, symbols, and images, planning carefully, figuring things out—then they begin to write and write and blot and rewrite till they arrive at their final perfect version. Then maybe they revise it later. They might read it over twenty times and never change a comma. It might take years.

The trick, Darneau said, is to make the reader, not the poet, feel the fresh spontaneity of the lines while never revealing the immense effort it took to get there, to get below the ragged surface of reality. He quoted Goethe's remark about some play by Marlowe: "How great it is all planned!" Didn't some other critic respond, "How great it is, considering it isn't planned at all?" (I should take better notes.) Darneau also said (of Coleridge, I think) that great poems are not written under the influence of drugs, because when you come down from your high, it turns into garbage. I'm not sure I believe that, either.

I'm thinking of the last line of a poem I read somewhere, though I can't remember who wrote it. "A poem should not mean but be." I'll have to show that one to Darneau, see what he thinks about that.

I saw him talking to my German teacher, Annelise Petermann, after class. (I can't allow this diary to become a collection of common gossip, can I? Although I suppose that's what most diaries are for. Was it Pascal who said that it was vanity to write what no one would ever read?) Professor Petermann's all right, up to a point. In a word, coldly attractive. I guess that's two words. Like most Germans she sees the big picture but misses the sensitive details, which are usually more important, or at least more interesting. And like all German teachers she worships at Goethe's shrine. She quoted him on Byron today: "Sobald er reflektiert ist er ein Kind." That is both demeaning and untrue.

Byron is one of my favorite poets, maybe not one of Goethe's. What he should have said was that Byron's poetry burns with the spirit and light of youth, calling for freedom, rebelling, wringing out passion from the human soul, love, fear, revenge, whatever. Frankly, Annelise Petermann is too Teutonic to teach about Romantic poets. Maybe a French woman could, but they don't get hired at anglophone schools. Perhaps they're too impulsive, too emotional, too feminine. Or maybe they all move to the UK or universities in the States to teach the French way of contemplating poetry or how to read the subtleties of Nouvelle Vague films. I'll have to ask D. about that, too. He'll have an opinion, I'm sure. (I wonder if the ink of these words will fade completely away before anyone ever reads them?)

CHAPTER 7

Melissa Artemis cornered me after class a few days later. She immediately started blistering me about how callous and shallow I was to have said that great poets don't write beautiful poems inspired fresh from the hand of God (or their fallen angel?). To prove her point she quoted some obscure lines from Cavafy that she must have found in *The Alexandria Quartet,* beginning with "eyes greener than an emerald's mineral gaze." I couldn't fault her choice of imagery, then told her that Durrell didn't so much translate Cavafy as he took the Greek lines and completely reworked and reset them freely into his own poetic vision.

Melissa countered, as she always did. "How do you know that? Do you read Greek?"

"Pas du tout," I conceded. "But the best poems succeed because they are complex, even if they don't appear so. Writing poetry is an art that has to be learned, like painting a storm at sea or sculpting an old man's face. It is not easy. Robert Browning once said that his 'poetry was not meant to be a substitute for an after-dinner cigar.' And if poetry is the guide to the human soul, you don't write a guide without a plan."

"Darneau, we are talking about poets, not Michelin guide-makers. Do you know who wrote, 'If you rush into love you will often suffer remorse, but if you don't, you will always suffer regret?'"

"No, I have no idea who wrote that. Did you get it off a Hallmark greeting card?"

"That's cruel, Darneau."

"Yes, I know. I apologize. How can I make up for it?"

"You can't."

"As you know, it's not in my nature to be critically uncharitable."

"Assez, Darneau. Sometimes your irony simply descends into stultifying, banal lies."

By now Melissa and I were outside, walking through a sharp breeze rifling up the Seine, her wind-swept hair flying about her face, those cornflower blue eyes fixed on mine, shining with pleasure, questioning, challenging. I couldn't help but begin to fall back a little, at least rhetorically.

"Melissa, if there are instances of true poetic inspiration, I think perhaps they come from the hearts of writers when they are still young, fighting their way up through their angst-ridden, mutilated emotions. Sometimes they do give us terribly beautiful, moving poems. But as they grow older and live through more lies and more truths, some of these poets, though not all, will advance beyond their initial raw sensations, and then someday, whatever moments of inspiration they are blessed with, will come down to us poetically sifted through those life experiences, their own comedies and tragedies. Then, hopefully, if they have luck and skill and energy, their work will be honed by hours of reflection, contemplation, even devotion, and after endless meticulous revisions, it will be shaped, aged and perfected like a 1945 premier cru Mouton Rothschild."

She glared at me. "Darneau, you're starting to get on my nerves again. You know I will never believe all this rot."

I wondered if she was joking, yet there was no way to tell. She pushed on: "Your arguments are meticulously drawn up, but, and I don't want to hurt your feelings here, they are neither eloquent, succinct or persuasive."

"Then let me finish," and I tried to sum up my thoughts. "Melissa, the true poet looks at his blank page for a long time before he puts a word on it. It's like listening to Horowitz or Heifetz or Rubinstein play their instruments so beautifully you can't conceive that they were ever beginners who had never played even the simplest of tunes. Picture them as a little kid, just a toddler, going into a room with an old upright piano, and he reaches up and plinks his first note. He doesn't know it, but he's about to begin a long journey of hours and years of practice, work, and growth. But great artists leave little to chance or inspiration. Your spontaneous, suddenly inspired poet too often writes fast, sloppy, self-indulgent verse, like a young painter relying solely on his creativity, allowing his faltering technique to belittle his innate gift, and his work will fail."

Understandably, partway through this uninspired monologue she abruptly changed the thread of conversation, or should I say, severed it completely. No one is more skillful than Melissa at leaving behind any subject she does not wish to examine further.

"What do you think of my German language teacher, Annelise Petermann?"

At this point we were walking by a smoky little café on Quai Voltaire where students hung out to drink and complain about their easy lives, but we didn't go in.

"What makes you ask that?"

"Don't you find her a bit stuffy?"

"I find her le contraire of stuffy."

She frowned. "Go on!"

So I did. I explained that I would never tell my students what I thought of another teacher at ACP.

She looked at me and said, "I'm not one of your students."

But she was almost smiling in her wistful, oblivious way, with neither guile nor self-consciousness in that look—and immediately reversed the subject again, this time inflicting the coup de grâce to my lecture on young poets. She condemned it in her unequivocal French: "La jeunesse est spontanée; la vieillesse réfléchit trop."

I shrugged and said, "I don't want to preach to you."

"Yes, you do."

"Remind me again what that would accomplish, exactly?"

"Nothing, Darneau. Because you don't know how to preach. You don't believe in anything remotely spiritual. You have a good mind, you probably have a good heart, but you have no soul."

One of Melissa's most interesting and aggravating talents was her ability to hit back at me with my own beliefs, sometimes in my own words. I said nothing more then. She had a bemused expression on her face that I had never seen before. Sometimes I can't begin to penetrate her mood or understand her thought process. But someday I will.

And she herself did not return to the subject of her "stuffy" German teacher.

⚜

In fact, I had dinner with Annelise that night. Like all Germans, she favored Italian cuisine (now I'm painting with Melissa's ubiquitous broad brush), so we met at a tiny trattoria di famiglia on la rue du Cherche-Midi.

As Melissa had somehow intuited, Annelise and I were close. How should I put it? Lovers, but not in love? A specialty of Paris, one could say. I knew too many examples to count, and why would you care to count them? Three months later half of them would have moved on. I don't mean to sound cynical, because truthfully Annelise and I were fine together—we had gotten to the joy of love even if we had (thankfully?) missed the crush of youthful infatuation with its suspicions, distrust, and deep jealousies. We had skipped that grade up to a different level. We both understood that even without the pure bliss of falling desperately in love, you can still find happiness—or a true passion perhaps insignificant to everyone but us—even if (fortunately?) it doesn't promise to last forever.

Forgive me if all this sounds hopelessly pessimistic. Only the young are ever true optimists: they trust the future of their love because they don't yet have a past full of defeats and failures. But they will. They are waiting there, standing on the threshold of life's incalculable disappointments.

At some point in our dinner I asked Annelise about her

student, Melissa Artemis. She smiled. "She is young, I have seen her waiting for you. Does she bother you?"

"A little," I lied. "She finds a way to cut into almost every literary thought I throw out."

"Darneau, you are lucky to have a student who loves to read and who listens to you. She pushes back against your ideas because that is what the young do." She smiled again. "Perhaps she has a crush on you?"

"C'est absurde! Tu dis des bêtises! She did tell me how little she thought of Goethe's remark on Byron reflecting like a child."

"Did she? She never mentioned it to me. Darneau, you will have to take care with Melissa Artemis. I know something of her history. She lost her mother, had no real father, bounced around different schools in Switzerland and France, and she follows you like an abandoned puppy looking for a home. Just because she is smart doesn't mean she isn't fragile. She reminds me of a Lalique wine glass, precious, yes, but easily shattered. And you, beneath your sardonic veneer are a romantic push-over. Don't let your heart get in the way of your head, if you'll forgive me the cliché."

"Annelise, she's just a kid. You are a born worrier, forever uncovering perils that aren't there. She is not so fragile as you're making her seem."

We went on to speak of other things, and after finishing with un petit noir went our separate ways. I reflected on what she had said about Melissa, and I had to admit to myself that Annelise was always right—well, almost always. Perspicacity is her inborn strength. And she worries about things that I never even notice.

⚜

The next day Melissa was in the back of my class again, looking nothing like an abandoned puppy. But I haven't described her yet, have I? Despite being a devotee of romantic literature and teacher of lyrical poetry, I have no gift for depicting la femme. A beaux-arts professor would doubtless do much better. To me, Melissa looks like a young university student caught between two worlds, not too French, not too American, a mélange of styles. Outfits not consciously casual, more careless perhaps, or inattentive if that's a fashion term. She moves easily with the natural grace and confidence of youth, somehow looking good no matter that she doesn't much care, but never actually sloppy. Her hair, not exactly lustrous, streaked some nameless color, longer than most, shorter than some. I told you I was not good at this.

I suppose she could have worn makeup, had her hair done, but since she didn't need to, what would be the point? She was noticed, however. As with Julie, people's eyes would follow her when she came into a room. I think she knew this, but never showed it. Without question her most striking feature were her deep-set, unsullied sapphire eyes, of almost an unnatural blue color, eyes that held farness in them. These were her jewels. You know the old adage that the eyes are a window to the soul? Melissa's window was almost always impenetrably shuttered. A smile from her did not often reach those wary blue eyes. Her gaze could be more than sardonic. It was often preternaturally full of scorn. Yet somehow Melissa made me happy when she looked at me like I was a moron.

She listened to a song no one else could hear.

Today she stood irresistibly alone and motionless in the doorway as I went to exit the lecture hall. "Melissa, you are blockading me like the U.S. Navy did Cuba when I was your age."

"Désolée. I want to invite you to lunch." She disguised her serious intent, as she often did, behind her light, effortless demeanor, as if she knew I couldn't refuse her. And I didn't, overruling my first guarded instinct to say no. It was probably a mistake, not a major one, perhaps. Those would come later.

We walked together to a small bistrot on the Avenue Bosquet where we heard the recorded rhythm of gypsy guitars. Two hours later we were still there, Melissa doing most of the talking, moving aimlessly from one subject to another. If for me that afternoon was the beginning of a new, different feeling about Melissa, I suspect it was also a moment of change for her, though not something either of us could have recognized, let alone put into words.

No longer the glib coquette, she was now, for the first time, struggling just a bit to express herself. She told stories of her past, her schools, her stepfather Nico, who was never around . . . until she really needed him. Then he would come and save her, usually from herself, before withdrawing back into his own life. Melissa defended him quietly, dispassionately, insisting that in her stepfather's mind he never abandoned her, but pushed her out to face down her own reality, much like he handled his business affairs. It wasn't that he looked for her to flounder and fail on her own, he didn't necessarily believe she would. But he gave her that chance, always holding himself away until she was about to implode, then he would reappear, unsummoned, for the rescue. At least that's how Melissa put it. When young people talk about themselves, who can ever distinguish between what is entirely true, what is mostly true, what is somewhat fictitious, and what are perfect lies?

"Alors, Melissa, Nico more or less raised you with no help from your mother?"

"How could my mother help? She was never there. I raised myself. Nico indulged me, protected me, son enfant terrible. And he gave me my real name, Melissa. He told me it goes with his surname. Years later I understood why, when I read the *Quartet*: Durrell's lovely, sad Greek dancer, Melissa Artemis." Spoken for once without a trace of her normally unrelenting sarcasm. Then there was a short perfect silence, like all silences full of dangers to come. "So, my German teacher, Annelise, how long have you been seeing her?"

Another brief silence.

"I see," Melissa sighed. "Are you tupping her?"

I said, "If it makes you feel good, you may continue to insult me."

"No, you don't understand. I don't lie awake at night worrying about it. It was just a passing thought, insignificant. Et tant pis si vous ne me comprenez pas."

"I do understand, Melissa. Your questions always begin in your heart and are seldom filtered through your mind. That is a hazardous way to go through life. But perhaps you cannot help yourself." I smiled. "You wake up every morning crazy, non?"

"No, not crazy. Entranced, maybe. I've been feeling lucky

lately, even sitting back in your class with all those fake students, some listening to you from time to time."

We left the restaurant and walked over to the Quai d'Orsay, the afternoon cold but still bright, with copper-tinged sunlight sprayed everywhere. We headed east, wandering along the Seine as it flowed past us and on toward the farmland and orchards of Normandy, and then eternally into the sea, this shivering river that has seen so much life through her soft gray eyes.

We stopped at a bouquiniste's stall and I saw a second hand copy, un livre d'occasion, of *The Magus* by John Fowles. I picked it up and asked Melissa, "Have you read it?"

"I don't read best sellers."

I bought the book and handed it to her. "You will this one. Give it twenty pages and you'll be up all night reading it." She gave me one of her pouty looks, but she took the book and stuck it in her backpack.

J'ai regardé Melissa et sa jeunesse libre, à côté de moi, un homme un peu inquiet. (Sometimes it's easier to mask these incipient misgivings in French.) She shifted subjects again, out of nowhere, though I had learned she would often return to her favorite nineteenth century English poets, her literary stomping grounds, like a little child holding on to her favorite toy, her oldest, tattered stuffed animal.

"Darneau, who was it you said wrote that one is only capable of love when the loved object is unattainable?"

"I think you may have it wrong. She wrote that the loved object doesn't matter. It could be anything—a tree, a rock, a cloud."

"That wasn't a poem, it was a story. And I'm talking about

real people, real life. A cloud may be beautiful, but it doesn't love you back. Which poet was it, Darneau?"

"Lord Byron had a daughter with one of his lovers—he named her Allegra. She died in an Italian convent at age five, not long after writing her father a heartbreaking note in childish Italian, to come visit her, which he never did. Tormented by guilt, Byron had these words engraved on her tombstone: 'J'irai à elle, mais elle ne reviendra plus à moi.' That was unattainable love, and unbearable grief."

"You made that up, Darneau. Byron would have put it in English, not French."

"It's from the Bible. Perhaps it was carved in Hebrew, or Greek. I never saw it. But you know, Melissa, that God listens to no one's prayer unless it's in French. He understands le langage de l'amour. God is deaf when English is spoken to him."

"I think you make up a lot of things, Darneau. Your students cannot tell what day it is, let alone if anything you say is true. And I don't understand you when you are not telling the truth."

"I had a professor at the Sorbonne who once said there are only a few things that are true, and you have to keep changing them around so they don't become repetitious. Like poetry, teaching is a craft, not an art, just a lesser craft. But I'm rambling."

"Yes, it's not like you to talk about yourself."

"It won't happen again."

"You think?" Melissa was smiling. "I am going to write a novel someday, half in French, half in English, nothing translated."

"Perfect. Then ninety-nine per cent of your readers will only get half of it."

"Yes, thank you. By the way, Darneau, which do you think was the best book written by a French teenager, *Le Diable au Corps* or *Bonjour Tristesse?*"

"What would be your choice?"

"Françoise Sagan. The ending is beautiful: so much peine de cœur."

"Maybe you pick *Bonjour Tristesse* because you are hearing the echo of your own voice. For me, though, Radiguet was the better writer; it was a tragedy he died so young. Sagan's prose does not quite flow like his beautifully constructed sentences. And, not that it's relevant, but his novel's movie was much better. Gérard Philipe was unforgettable as Radiguet's young lover; Jean Seberg could barely read Sagan's lines, though she did look the part. And Radiguet was also a poet."

"I think I'm beginning to understand you, Darneau. Myself, I am impulsive—you are the opposite. You carefully examine everything, and then you hide your final answer like a dark secret—from me and from yourself. You cover your soul with the words and thoughts of your iconic poets and writers. They're not just your mentors and idols, though. They're more than that to you. Their poems and stories sink into your life and breathe their beauty into you, but I think their words in the end don't penetrate deeply enough. They get deflected by your defenses before they reach your heart."

I laughed then, but felt the truth of her thrust.

"You think I'm jokin', monsieur?"

I shrugged slightly. "Mais non. Brava, ma p'tite!"

Then out of the blue she asked me why I had left Paris years ago.

"I didn't."

"But you moved away for a while."

"Yes."

The sky had begun to darken, and before I could say anything more the rain began, sprinkling lightly, just a few drops. Clouds of sad mist hung low in the air, drifting off the Seine, forming tears on Melissa's cheeks. There is nowhere in the world as melancholy as Paris in November—there are never rainbows in her veiled, leaden skies. For the first time she slipped her hand through my arm as we walked. It was nothing to her, I'm sure, but it felt like the birth of something frightening to me. I gazed down at her raindrop-dampened hair, into her blue-marble cat's eyes shining lucidly up into mine, aimed firmly at me over her sublime, unwavering, untrusting smile.

DIARY OF MELISSA ARTEMIS

November 24, 1982

Walked home from le fleuve through a heavy misty rain settling down on me like a cold wet clinging shroud—I was soaked. And the day had started out si plein de soleil. I linked my arm through Darneau's, squeezed together, but still couldn't stay dry, or warm. Rain in Paris always makes me think about my wasted life, where I've been, where I'm going. Once, half-kidding, I asked D. how many times you can find eternal love. It depends, he said, on how good your memory is. I wonder if he nicked that line from Pursewarden.

It's blowing harder now, the rain rattling and pounding against my shutters like the hammering of my dark heart. Another one for you from the Queen of clichés. Hand me my crown, my rod and sceptre, and I will bury you in mindless, slipshod, purple imagery.

Why do I keep this diary? No one will ever read it unless I become famous or marry someone famous and some scandal blows up later. (Just thinking—if I die young, I'll never turn gray and I won't grow fat.)

But I have to write things down, the odd remarks Darneau makes. Some are pretty crazy, some are pretty mean. Like when he said his mother has a heart of gold, but her mind does not glitter at all. Or he wouldn't say she wasn't a good cook, but in their house they prayed *after* the meal. Where did he steal that one? Some are baffling (to me): "It wasn't love and it wasn't the opposite of love. It was something in between." Qu'est-ce que ça veut dire?

When I asked him today whether I will still love him when I grow up, I was just joking. But he said half-seriously, which is as serious as he ever gets with me, "I'm afraid I'm not the one who should be answering that question. But you know, Melissa, the deepest love happens before you grow up." I think he said that because he's afraid it's not true.

One day, I have to admit, I followed him and Annelise from the American Church building to a café nearby, just to see where they were going. Am I jealous? More curious, I would say—well, maybe un peu jalouse—she is definitely not his type. I hope. I loathe her.

Et maintenant, au lit . . .

Bonne nuit, tristesse.

CHAPTER 8

Melissa and I would sometimes leave school together, not really by chance. We would meander along the river, or cross over to the Tuileries on nice days, like the shiftless flâneurs we were. As Victor Hugo said, "Errer est humain, flâner est parisien." More often we sought refuge from the darkening winter afternoons à l'intérieur of some run-of-the-mill café-tabac, where Parisian workers stood at zinc counters smoking, killing time, drinking their espressos or petits verres de vin. Occasionally I would make a note of her wild, heartfelt critiques, right then or later, thinking back to my own student years when we trusted no one over thirty: we accused them all. Melissa, on the other hand, never wrote anything down (in front of me), and I knew nothing then of her diary.

One day she remarked, "I've been reading some of your book reviews."

"Good, aren't they?"

"Darneau, they are mean-spirited, often cruel; clever rather than sensitive."

"Thank you. Understand, I don't get to choose the authors I review. They give me losers. I write about them so students like you won't waste your time reading failures."

"But I have the time. You told me boredom is a luxury of the young."

"I never told you that. You must have read it in Sagan somewhere, or it's just a filament of your inondation, as Joyce would say."

An eyebrow raised and her mouth curved delicately in the slightest of smiles. But she was not done with my reviews. "Darneau, you insulted the poet laureate with a line you filched from Chaucer."

"And what was that?"

"'Thy drasty rhyming is nat worth a toord.'"

"I remember that review. I was just being facetious really. And Betjeman may have sneaked in to be dubbed the English laureate, but how can I put this more kindly: he is no William Wordsworth."

We talked about love and passion and style in the novels and poetry she was reading, and love's singular paradox: the constant, fearsome, aching threat of losing it versus the pure joy of reaching for it. She never tired of scrutinizing these emotions, while I mostly listened. One time she started in on me: "Darneau, why did you claim in class yesterday that all poets fixate on the passing of time, that it is a recurrent theme of great poetry? That may be partially correct, but it is not the truest and most meaningful theme. Do you know what is?"

"I know what you will say it is."

"Darneau, great poets write about the loss of love—that is the most beautiful, most poetic of themes, and the saddest.

Durrell said that the great tragedy of love is that we cannot compel it back from the one we love."

"Where did he say that?"

"Maybe he didn't, it doesn't matter. You want to know what I think? Someone who has lost a great love obsesses about it every hour, every day. Yet when she had that great love in her hands, she probably thought about it much, much less."

"You are talking about dreamers, Melissa, young idealists. The passions of French poetry, novels, drama, music are relived every day by your role-playing fellow students on the streets of the Latin Quarter. For them, falling in love is intoxicating—breaking hearts and having theirs broken—miraculous, un rêve. But let me put it this way: you won't find love by faithfully following the North Star—if you find it, it will be by sheer luck. Of course, staying in love can turn into a bit of a hangover. For some happy few it doesn't have to."

"Some happy few—now you're stealing from Shakespeare. He didn't even write all his plays."

"Perhaps not. But if William Shakespeare didn't write them, then someone else named William Shakespeare did."

"You are smiling, yet I find your remark rather sad—its truth demeans the man."

"The man is not important. We will always have his words."

"Then why dishonor him?"

It began to rain hard again, driven by a fierce rising wind, so we stayed inside. As the French say—il pleuvait comme vache qui pisse—one of those dark torrents where you can't see where the rain ends and Paris begins. That happens a lot here in the City of Light. What with the roiling winds and no sun all day long, how should I put it? This is not Paradise.

I didn't quite understand then that behind Melissa's wry questions were subtler, more piquant feelings. One time she stared right at me with those blue-starred penetrating eyes and whispered plaintively, "Why do you always have to be right?"

"I don't," I said softly with a quick smile. "I just want to have the last word. Melissa, when I was your age we didn't believe any adult could possibly understand us. Then fifteen minutes later we were in our thirties and counting."

"The sixties were different, though. You had honest causes. Now I'm leading a life with no meaning, and it's frightening. I want more, can you see it from my point of view? Do you understand me?"

"I'm sorry to say that I can barely understand anything even from my own point of view. But what bothers me most is when my world-weary students start complaining about their poor sad lives, basking in their depressing ennui, when at the very same time they are surrounded by this euphoric city overflowing with new ideas, dazzling art, music, dance, history, the ecstatic rhythm of her street life, cafés, cinémas, jazz clubs, boîtes de nuit. Of course Paris does not allow us to thrive here cost-free. You must be willing to give her something back, to tear into the fabric of her life with all your psychic energy. Don't fritter away your time here, Melissa, or you will never be able to win your heart's way into this city. She does not have to love you back . . . but forgive my exuberance, and feel free to ignore my worthless advice."

I thought that I was beginning to understand why Melissa tagged after me: I personified what she both liked and disliked about herself. She smiled the other day when I remarked that a French psychologist I admired once wrote that you can never truly, selflessly love another person. You love, he explained, the mirror image reflected in your own mind, and that becomes the portrait of your created ideal. This can bring you happiness, but it doesn't have to last forever. (It never does, Julie would have added.)

Melissa rolled her eyes and told me the only reason I admired that psychologist was because he put into words precisely what I already believed: nothing new there, she pointed out reprovingly.

Some days Melissa reminded me of Julie, though not so much in appearance, because usually Melissa's hair and clothes were disheveled tout en même temps et de la même façon, as the French would say. Melissa was the type of girl who sometimes forgot to brush her hair, or sometimes forgot her brush completely. Julie was the opposite in that respect, although on another level they did share similar doubts and skepticism about love and life. The night we were sitting on the bench by the old church, fumbling our memories away, Julie had warned me, "Love is like running down a steep hill. You can't stop even if you try; or you do try and then you crash and burn."

I asked her, "Why would you have to burn?"

She sighed. "It's just an expression, Darneau. Don't be so literal."

Melissa could be serious, too, though normally she didn't stray too far from her natural inborn sarcasm. She recently poked at me, "Darneau, you excel at disguising the truth. You know, I can pretend that you care about me."

"If you like."

"Have I told you lately that I hate you?"

"Some people hate what they want more than anything in the world."

"Do you think I'm trying to seduce you?"

"Aren't you?" I said with what I hoped was an enigmatic smile—it was a jest really.

But her winter-blue eyes burnt back fiercely into mine, erasing the jest.

⚜

Melissa and I had never, in our rambling conversations, talked much about religion, but one day she blurted out, "Do you believe in God, Darneau?"

I thought of Einstein's famous response: "I believe in Spinoza's God." Instead I said, "Religions are about absolutes. When I was your age I believed in them. I used to argue with a Swiss architecture student at Cornell named Klaus Herdeg. He said there are no absolutes either in art or life. He challenged me to name one absolute that helps us to understand the world. Years later he sent me a beautiful book of Persian poetry, translated into English, fortunately. He inscribed it: 'Always listen to your heart, Darneau. It's the only valid absolute.'"

"That's nice rhetoric, professeur, but you are not a Christian after all?"

"Do I believe in water miraculously converted into wine, a virgin birth, purgatory and the fires of hell? I did as a child."

"So you are not a man of faith, hope, and charity?"

"And how do you know that?"

"Because you understand exactly how to hurt someone."

"I do? And you at nineteen are already an expert on how it feels to be hurt?"

"Yes. Sagan said let someone get hurt once and she'll learn forever."

I looked away. "I did get hurt once, but I don't know if I learned anything."

"You didn't."

But I wasn't totally convinced. I shrugged and said, "Maybe I did learn something, maybe how to wait patiently." This was followed by one of Melissa's incredulous, scornful looks, and I said nothing more.

But she was relentless. "Darneau, do you think it's possible to love someone completely while wounding her?"

"Am I imagining this conversation?"

"Don't resort to ad hominem mockery, Darneau, it doesn't become you."

"It was self-mockery, really. But you are serious today, mademoiselle."

"Am I? Maybe it's because I'm thinking how life is short, but not sweet. And it isn't pretty, either."

"It is not short when you are waiting for someone to come back to you."

"Now you are brooding again, Darneau. So maybe you wait and wait and the person never comes back. So what? It's just a rare happenstance anyway if you love someone and somehow, by some bizarre coincidence, you end up happy together. It probably never happens. So she never came back to you, and you haven't forgotten."

"Melissa, someday even you will learn the art of forgetting. For myself, I try to conjure a huge dark shadow to block out certain memories, not that it works every time. Sometimes my mind just ignores the mental block and hoards the memories subconsciously . . . neatly stacked up and engraved: Never To Be Forgotten."

"Alors, c'est dommage, mon ami. Did I tell you I read somewhere that the need for love is more real than love itself?"

"What great philosopher wrote that? Casanova?"

"Maybe it was Monet. I think he said it is of the idea that we are enamored, not the reality."

"He was talking about painting."

"He could have been talking about love. He was a dreamer."

And so ended our religious philosophical discussion which, like many dialogues with Melissa, had trailed off into her thoughts on love and unhappiness.

⚜

One sullen cold day, when the low sun was struggling to throw shafts of light down the empty off-season streets, I received a short letter from Julie, after nothing for several weeks. She wrote that she might be returning to Paris, that she had been in touch with her ex-husband (whose name she seemed reluctant to mention), and that she had a "lead on her daughter's whereabouts," was how she phrased it.

Reading it, at the time, I felt a rush of mixed feelings—including, I admit, something of our distant love, that old candle still flickering bravely, still refusing to go out. If time heals all wounds, as the saying goes, nevertheless it doesn't efface the marks left by the very deepest of them. In the end those desolate, jagged souvenirs will outlast time's best efforts. What Julie now felt on her part, I had no idea. At Aux Assassins she had said to me, "You are a refugee from the Romantic Age, emotional, sentimental. But that does not mean I cannot love you . . . with passion."

I told myself that so many years have gone by, our feelings cannot help but have profoundly changed and will go on changing: diminishing probably, or perhaps even growing back stronger, in different ways, at different tempos. Yet the abandonment of her child remained for me the most inexplicable, unforgivable act. When I think of how casually she told me about it, I still can't believe it.

I didn't answer her note. Perhaps if I had, I could have forestalled the painful trauma of the eventual encounter, inevitable though it was. Later I wondered if Julie had planned the two unfolding events to coincide—her search for her daughter and her reaching back to me. Still, there was no way she could have foreseen everything that was to happen.

CHAPTER 9

Melissa and I had continued to meet for a coffee or déjeuner after the class she was auditing. Was I flattered by her attention? I don't deny it, yet my attraction to her was not overtly sexual. It was an undefined sensation, the mystical pull of an inherently unattainable romance—but remember, I am proficient in the art of self-delusion. We had contrasting visions of reality: how could we not, given our ages and different life experiences? Never did we end up in her rue Bonaparte apartment, even when I walked her home. As a non-tenured ACP teacher, I was careful enough, toujours la politesse, while she projected her young innocence not like a lure, more like the accidental beauty of some anodyne wildflower hidden in the wilderness. Or so I believed. Some days I sensed her moody innocence was a little studied—yet most of the time it seemed remarkably, utterly sincere.

She asked me once, as we lingered on a cold December afternoon in a clean, well-lighted café across from the Sèvres-Babylone station, "What matters to you? Little books of poems, looking at a Rodin sculpture, listening to gifted musicians play jazz, drinking a beautiful vin rouge, what makes you happy, Darneau?"

"Your choices are all good, Melissa, but why do they say

nothing about sharing or giving? Do I seem so self-centered to you?"

"Sharing and giving are not in my répertoire. They are not components of my bonheur. They are too demanding, too intense, too perfect."

Then with a curious expression, "Darneau, why have you never married? Are you afraid of love?"

"I am afraid of hunger, which is the same as love. It can kill you if you don't satisfy it, and it can kill you if you do." I told her, "Nineteen years ago I was not afraid of love—to you that is a lifetime—though it is not more than a moment in the life of this city. I loved a girl then, a student at the Sorbonne like me. We were together for a while, inseparable. Then she suddenly left, and I was alone and crushed. There was no happy ending. Durrell wrote . . . but never mind."

"But I do mind. I'd like to know at just what point you became so pessimistic . . . perhaps when I started feeling a little more optimistic?"

"No. I disclaim the connection."

A long silence ensued, and she fixed her eyes on me like burning silver-blue stars—until a new, altogether unrelated personal literary conundrum fired up in the volcano of her mind. She was the princess of non sequiturs.

"Darneau, why did Tolstoy have Pierre say to Natasha, 'Je vous aime,' instead of 'Je t'aime'?"

"Did you read the novel in English or French?"

"L'anglais. Je ne lis pas le russe."

"Pierre switched into French from his own language just as you do. For him it was out of respect for love. For you it is to confound me. Perhaps Pierre put Natasha on a Russian pedestal and tried to reach up to her with his formal French amour. Maybe his noble Russian respect was stronger than his tender French love. Does that make any sense?"

At that perfectly ordinary moment, out of an appalling, blinding oblivion, Julie herself walked quietly up to our little table. She stood there as motionless as a Greek statue, staring down at us. Time went by—it felt like ten minutes, ten hours, ten days, or ten lifetimes—with her still not saying a word. Like a black cloud blotting out the sun, her shadow fell over our table in an indescribable, mortifying silence.

Finally she spoke. "Mon cher Darneau, salut! And you, my dear, must be Melissa Artemis. I'm ashamed to confess that I barely recognize my own daughter."

To say that Melissa and I were at a complete loss for words does not do the scene its stunning, breathless justice. We were absolument accablés, bludgeoned speechless, battered into mute incoherence. Melissa turned ghostly pale, visibly shattered. For a while she didn't move, staring first at Julie, then back at me. Finally she got up from her chair, shuddering desperately, grabbed her coat, her books, and like some livid Sarah Bernhardt stormed out of the café into the cold heartless Paris afternoon.

DIARY OF MELISSA ARTEMIS

January 11, 1983

You would think I'd know my own mother, but at first I didn't. She was different in some way, not looking sad or depressed exactly, but resigned, quiet, less fearsome. How long has it been? She must be thirty-eight now, yet surrendering nothing to those years, I have to admit, still wearing her blond hair long, her smile flashing white in her golden California tan.

I looked at Darneau as he stared at her, initially with shock and disbelief in his eyes . . . but profound recognition, too, and something more. He sat absolutely still, his face bloodless, ashen, mesmerized by my mother's sudden appearance. It wasn't until after I studied the look on his face that I felt it, that I knew. I have never seen him so lost, struck wordless, like a doomed, accused prisoner in the courtroom an instant after hearing his guilty jury verdict—but I've perpetrated enough bad similes for now. This is not the time for them.

When I stood up to leave, my mother said we must talk or something, but I shook my head, "There's no need." I picked up my book bag, walked home and fell on my bed, head spinning, wracked with unspeakable, unbearable thoughts. Darneau and Julie! The history of a deep past liaison was written unmistakably on both of their faces.

Please don't tell me Julie was the love who crushed him. I remember his exact words to me: there was no happy ending. And yet, they must have long ago separated forever. Why was she back in his life, in my life? I felt a shiver of horrifying fear and I cried then, which I never do.

Less than an hour later Darneau knocked on my door. For the first time in my life I threw my arms around him, holding tight to stop the trembling, and fought to blink away my tears. He came in, threw off his jacket, sat on my couch, and began to unravel the star-crossed tale of his student affair with Julie. How much of what he said was the truth, how much he left out, and how much were facts deliberately altered to soothe my feelings, I couldn't tell. In the end, I had the impression that he was telling me as little as possible. At no point did he mention the possibility that he could be restarting his relationship with Julie, but I understood now that this was his tragic lost love, and I felt an ominous, deathly threat gripping my heart.

CHAPTER 10

After Melissa had bolted out of the café, Julie sat down at our table, ordered a cup of tea, and never touched it. She began her melancholy epiphany by confessing (with a hint of characteristic ambiguity, it seemed to me) her regret for following Melissa and me from the college. She wondered how I could have missed seeing her standing by the entrance, looking right at us, but I didn't tell her that a conversation with Melissa required one hundred percent concentration—if your attention wandered, she considered it a betrayal. But it didn't take long for Julie to come to the point.

"You know now she is my daughter: Audrey Melissa Artemis. Not only did my ex-husband rescue her from me, he renamed her as well. I hope you're not falling in love with her, but you likely aren't. Melissa, on the other hand, looks at you like a teenage Sainte-Thérèse gazing at Jesus, except that Jesus wasn't her college English teacher and I was no Mater Charissima. And may I ask if she has any idea that you and I were living together in the Hôtel St-André des Arts, or was it Hôtel Delavigne for a while? I can never remember."

I sat there thinking how I remembered almost every minute, every hour, every night. Instead I said, "Melissa's last name is Artemis. Greek, I suppose—nothing like yours."

"She took her stepfather's surname after I left. I think Nico had it all done by court order. Our divorce was quite amicable, if that isn't a contradiction in terms. He ended up with Melissa and her sweet childhood; I got my freedom and my bitter self-delusions."

"But that was your choice, wasn't it?" A pause, then, "Why are you back in Paris, Julie?"

"Isn't it enough that I want to see you again?"

"To stir up old emotions? Or scrape away at old wounds."

"Okay, yes—but I wanted to see Melissa, too. I finally tracked her down by harassing my ex. Melissa has some of Nico's traits in her, I think, less of her real father somehow, except for their eyes, strikingly similar as I recall, though I haven't seen him in twenty years. Deep-set and brilliant ice blue, like steel knives—they looked right through me in that café. She is too young to have that look."

"Who is her father, Julie? Have you ever told her?"

"No, I never saw the point. I knew him even less than I knew you. We were just kids, really, living in different worlds: lovers one night and that was the end of it. We were never truly in love. But I told you, I don't want to talk about it.

"You, Darneau, on the other hand, are more dangerous than ever. I don't trust you with Melissa, because when you care for someone, your love draws you out of yourself and spills uncontrollably into someone else's life, unlike mine which is the reverse."

I answered immediately. "I have no idea what you are talking about." But, of course, I did. And her words hurt, like all truth does. I stumbled on. "Now that you have found her, what will you do to her?"

"I notice you didn't say for her."

"No. I suppose those days are gone."

"Are they? Maybe I should tell her that you lived with me, made love to me every night, and wrote poems to me about eternal love."

"No."

"And why not?"

"Because I will tell her first—perhaps she won't care. It was a long time ago."

"She will be devastated, and you know it. Darneau, you cannot be blind to what she feels for you. Give yourself a chance to do what's right before you get in any deeper. Otherwise, Melissa will be the one to suffer, and that is the godforsaken truth."

"I will have to be careful, won't I? Or maybe not."

"You are being cryptic again, making no sense. You have not changed at all. You want the world to be what you wish it to be, not what it is. That's the definition of despair. Unluckily for you, to wish something does not make it true."

I looked across at Julie and thought I saw, for once, perfect honesty in her eyes. It turned out that I was wrong again. I got to my feet, a little dizzy, wondering what to do. And I felt my beclouded heart splintering into a thousand harsh, unforgiving shards.

I left Julie at the café and walked directly to Melissa's building on rue Bonaparte, rang the bell and she buzzed me in. Like most student apartments it had poster-covered walls, mostly from old movies, and an avalanche of books, magazines and journaux on every dusty inch of the floor—with candles everywhere else, their floral scents, orange blossom, lemon, and Spanish lavender, filling the space with the aroma of youth. Her books were a disorganized mix of new publications and classics, including some old French editions with their uncut pages. Was it Pursewarden who said he would not want a reader too lazy to use a knife on him?

But I was looking at Melissa, not at her books, and I could not help but see the threatening glitter of her tears. She grabbed and held onto me as if she were a little child in danger of falling off a cliff, then finally kissed me on the cheek, let loose her arms and said, "I hate myself when this happens, when I lose control."

"Melissa, sit. We have to talk."

"There is no need. I know what you will say."

"Do you? And what is that?"

"You are reaching back to Julie—I saw the look of hope and desire on her face. When she watched me get up to leave, I felt her jealous eyes . . . She knew I loved you more than she ever had."

Melissa and I talked for the rest of the afternoon, a cheerless winter day with the blue-gray slate rooftops searching in vain for what little failing light survived somewhere out there in the sky. The weakened pale sun had surrendered, the dark cold tightening its night grip on the city. It was like the old French saying: il fait aussi froid que la charité. Melissa made tea and we talked on and on, strangely like lovers, which of course we weren't, moving from one topic to another, but always coming back to Julie, the tension of emotions overpowering the quiet words.

"Listen to me, Darneau, my mother wants you back. That's the only reason she is in Paris. She cares nothing for me, she never has. Look how she trailed you from the school to the café. It was not by chance. She wants to relive her dream of being young again, loving you with your long dark hair and bookish charm, she with her southern California looks and cool savoir faire. But I need you, Darneau, more than she wants you. Do you see that? She is going to try and drive me out of your life and cheat me out of your love."

She was again coming close to the fraying edge of tears, though Melissa almost never succumbed to outbursts of emotion—quite the opposite. I wanted at that very moment of agony to have the courage somehow to reach into my own mind, to find and examine the complete truth, how I felt, what Julie still meant to me (as if I had any chance of understanding that) and get to the most dangerous question of all: how could I avoid falling in love with the daughter of my first great love in this beautiful, treacherous city?

If Melissa was worried about the flame of that old liaison being reignited, I was just as worried about loving Julie's daughter, a student where I taught, almost twenty years younger. It did not seem realistically possible. But when I looked into her accusing eyes glistening into the dusk, full of loneliness and fear, there was no way that I could batter her now with the story of these confounding, conflicting emotions.

Yet I took a deep breath and tried. "Melissa, you are young and deserve to be happy. I am your mother's age and the years have altered my own concept of happiness. There is something that I have lost and cannot get back."

She shook her head sadly. "All you need to do is peel away the layers of time. I will help you. It will be easy."

"Melissa, you make it sound like everything will turn out perfect. But I never think about perfection because I know I'll never come close to reaching it."

Her unerring senses zeroed in on my weaknesses, as I suffered from the doubts and feelings that Julie had resurrected. I told myself then that we didn't really know what would be best, what we could do, or what would happen, that we couldn't see the whole picture. Lâche! I was somehow not acknowledging my own mixed emotions, not exactly denying them, but worse—not admitting to having them at all. Melissa herself had no trouble sensing my unspoken, hidden love for her. I felt the fierce honesty and power of her eyes fixed on me, appraising, absorbing—she saw into my heart like shafts of sunlight piercing through cracked, ruined castle walls.

She told me, "Darneau, if you're trying to make me feel better, you're failing spectacularly." Then she smiled sadly and spoke so softly that I could barely hear her words. "If I make you happy sometimes, it's not my fault."

Only later did I begin to see clearly what Melissa had meant, what she had immediately perceived without needing to judge or evaluate. I said nothing, reflecting shamefully that there would be a better time to go back through everything, even though I knew that was a lie. And mostly I feared the inevitable day Julie would sit down with Melissa and recount all the intimate details of our past—or worse, set it all out in a menacing, soulless letter from California.

But it's not strictly true that I said nothing. I asked her if she thought of her mother from time to time with any sense of regret or hope, those rival emotions splayed across the spectrum of time.

She answered quickly with her usual pitiless candor. "She is my mother, yes, but when I looked at her in that café there was no tenderness in her face. I think of her as often as she thought of me. We are connected by blood not love, and it is too late to start worrying about her." Then with her characteristic maddening volte-face: "Darneau, if you could choose any time in your life to live over again, when would it be?"

I stopped to consider this simple sweeping question. Until recently I would surely have chosen my first few blissful weeks and months in Paris—when I began to muddle along in French, getting to know the city, especially the Latin Quarter, making new friends, discovering new teachers, and then meeting Julie. Nostalgia has always been my greatest weakness: it can flood my heart with sensations of both deep joy and profound, bittersweet pain, and everything in between. I thought of the famous François Villon line: Où sont les neiges d'an- tan? Where has the past gone? But now I answered Melissa truthfully. "I'm not certain I would want to go back in time, back to relive any part of my life."

"You're lying, aren't you." I could not help but see the beginning of her irrepressible smile, though she made an attempt to stifle it as she said, "I would choose right now."

She lapsed into a poignant silence, then gazed up at me

with her dangerous sapient eyes, the corners of her lips turned slightly upward. I felt drenched in the winsome tenderness of her love, which was like soft rain falling on my bewitched arid soul. There was no chance I could speak truth to her then. My mind was numb, as if I were living in the confines of a dream and desperately attempting, not to escape it, but the opposite, to remain inside it—to avoid going outside to face the bitter possibility of having to leave Melissa just as Julie left me.

How could I ever allow myself to be the one to walk away this time, to break a heart into pieces, as Julie did to me? Or, to put it more honestly, to risk breaking two hearts into pieces, Melissa's and mine.

I left her apartment with a vague promise to see her at school.

And I felt irredeemably sad.

CHAPTER 11

I TRIED TO PHONE JULIE WHEN I GOT HOME, BUT SHE HAD checked out of her hotel. I was getting accustomed to her untimely, unannounced disappearances. She seemed immune to most people's sentimental partings. She never minded not saying goodbye.

Did her sudden departures still have the power to wound? I couldn't deny it. Julie will always, whether I like it or not, hold on to some part of me.

I did receive a short note from her a couple of days later.

Cher Darneau,

I'm wondering if you have the courage to talk to Melissa, to give her the whole truth of our love affair. I do not, and I don't envy you the ordeal. Nevertheless, I have changed my mind. I could not abort her then, and I cannot unravel her life now. You must do it yourself—she is your responsibility: you are the one who unlocked the door to her heart.

Adieu, J.

P.S. Darneau, I confess (although I tried not to show it) that I was utterly stunned to see you and Melissa walking from school together, sitting close to one another in the café, oblivious to everyone else, talking intently while I watched from across the room. What are the miserable odds that my teenage daughter would find her unlucky way to my old love?

I sat in my apartment for a long time, rolling around a myriad of bleak thoughts in my mind, deciding that there was something grotesquely unfair about this rapidly unfolding surreal histoire. I had no idea what I should do. No, that's not quite right. I had no idea what I was going to do. We were trapped in a ruthless triangle, Julie, Melissa, and I, blindly drawing our fates from the subconscious life forces of the city of Paris as we were carelessly manipulated over two decades. And in such a triangle someone is always denied happiness—sometimes all three. And there was no doubt that in this heartless triangle, I was the weakest of the three sides.

Late that night I fought to fall asleep in my dark, unhappy bedroom. I could suffer or I could sleep, but unfortunately the choice was not mine. Nevertheless, hours later I must have finally dozed off, not from counting sheep or moonbeams, but from having exhausted myself after a long night of wrenching, shifting thoughts, as I tried, with little success, to see my way through a chaotic tangle of feelings for a mother and daughter, dangerous feelings that were improbably joined and separated by my lifetime in Paris. And the burden of decision rested solely, painfully, on my own shoulders. My mind looped endlessly over a range of mostly desperate, some unthinkable outcomes: should I simply wait, explain nothing further to Melissa, do no harm, suppress all feelings, tell lies but carefully—remember that truth can kill painfully, just as love can? And when lies grow out of the truth, how can you tell the difference?

Every time I arrived at a decision to candidly lay out everything to Melissa, I suffered immediately from a mordant depressing failure of nerve. Was it fear, self-protection? I answered my own question: I simply could not face my own inevitable, unbearable, impending personal loss. I tried to take some solace from the maxim that we are never so happy or unhappy as we imagine we are. But as Melissa might respond: a shattered heart is beyond consolation.

Nonetheless, the days went by and with Julie physically gone from the scene, a sense of normality gradually returned to our lives. My images of Julie were slowly blurring again, though I could never totally escape the haunting old feeling of desolation and the lingering remnant of my love for her. She would always retain some threatening, unbreakable hold on me, no matter what happened and how much time passed. If Melissa sensed this, and I'm sure she did, she never mentioned it and, in fact, she began carefully to avoid any reference to Julie's crashing reappearance in our lives.

The next day I had office hours, and as usual no students dropped by to expose their misunderstandings or complain about their mediocre grades. Annelise came by and we left together for lunch. As we settled into a small table in a nearby corner bistrot, her German radar homed in quickly on my pathetic efforts to fake a friendly normalcy.

"What's wrong today, Darneau? You are not your usual harmless sardonic self."

So I looked everywhere but at Annelise and told her about Julie and Melissa's café encounter. I filled in the saga with a brief account of Julie's unconscionable maternal failures, her ex-husband's stolid support, and finally Julie's unannounced neurotic descent into my life after disappearing for nearly twenty years, mixing ancient memories with today's fresh emotions. I admitted to Annelise that I was intrigued by Melissa (a cowardly euphemism), that even before I knew she was Julie's child I had felt a vague connection between the two. Not that they closely resemble each other, it was something below the surface, perhaps just the feeling they each sparked in me. They could both be charmantes, they were both smart and stimulating, but they were not really alike. Julie could cheerfully walk away from responsibility, challenges, dangers. Melissa would confront all of them with unrelenting fearlessness, even if she had little or no chance to overcome them.

When I was done, following a painful silence when both of us struggled to think of what to say next, Annelise began carefully, "I have watched and listened to you lecture in class about great writers. You are sensitive, confident, the master of yourself, comme un vieux professeur bien-aimé. But now you are crossing into a different world and I'm afraid you could be slipping out of your normal self-control, not yet losing it altogether, but I am beginning to worry about you. Human hearts are treacherous things. Don't let Melissa take you past the point of no return."

I heard the honest chagrin and apprehension in her voice: "You must not damage her with even a genuine, sincere reaction to her feelings. I have seen her look at you—it is not with a student's admiration for a favorite teacher. You must take care before she throws herself at you or under a Métro train—does that sound too melodramatic? If so, I apologize. She is still so young, and you are just a hapless Parisian romantic. Let me ask you: how long did you know her before she stole your heart? Ten minutes? Remember it was you who told me that love is different in Paris—beautiful, yes, but more tenuous, more perilous. Life is not a stroll down the Champs-Élysées, as the saying goes. Because only a part of love in Paris is the person you are holding. The rest comes from the infinite, idyllic romance of the city: it is her gift to all of us. She brings out the deepest passions of the human heart. You taught me that.

"You don't want Melissa to be another victim, Darneau. The beauty of life here and the feelings of love often keep each other reckless company, but they can forsake a person in a heartbeat, like a moody shifting wind.

"By the way, Julie is running now, but I imagine she will be back. Whatever remains of her feelings for you, and for Melissa, you cannot create an ungodly rivalry between her and her daughter—that would be monstrous arrogance—and you cannot continue to evade the truth. If you do, you will destroy yourself, because at heart you are still an idealist. In this affair you can't win, and you can't lose." She smiled sadly. "So there it is—and what will you do?"

I could not think of an answer, at least not one I could live with.

DIARY OF MELISSA ARTEMIS

January 12, 1983

Sometimes when I'm with Darneau I feel short of breath, which is crazy. But I'm not ashamed to admit that I secretly followed him and Annelise from school to the restaurant where they had lunch. I hung back and they never saw me (too absorbed in each other?), but I watched them the whole time.

The thing I detested most was when she made him laugh once or twice. It's more than I ever do. The most I get are occasional rueful smiles during our regular exchanges of insults.

D. walked her to her Métro stop, Assemblée Nationale—nobody I know ever gets on or off there—but that's where I left them. He would walk home, I knew. He walks everywhere. Am I working my way down in this diary to petty jealousy? It's the most unforgivable sin, in my opinion. It should be one of the Seven Deadly, if it isn't already. Maybe it is.

CHAPTER 12

The next Friday Melissa followed me out of class, heaved a sigh, and announced that what I had said about Stendhal's crystallization theory of love was bollocks, I believe was how she phrased it. We walked together toward le Pont de la Concorde.

"You don't actually believe it makes sense, do you, Darneau? Know what I mean?"

"I don't."

"I think you do."

"Melissa, I will not tell you what I believe or disbelieve. You can figure it out for yourself. You usually do."

"D'accord et merci quand même, Darneau. I can picture you as a student at the Sorbonne, jeune, intelligent, un peu sentimental, naïf, soaking up all your literary perversions."

"Well, it is too long ago for me to remember, or even imagine."

"Forgive me, but that is a lie. You remember everything. We are different that way. I forget what I don't like, which is almost everything. You not only forget nothing but you remix the memories into your life, into what you teach, into images and stories and lines of poetry. Sometimes I think you do this to keep all those memories from staying inside you, to keep them from getting into your heart."

I thought back to Stendhal for a minute, reflecting on the wonderful flaws in his writing, his philosophy, and his famous dictum: One always chooses to be in love—it is rare to find a man complaining that life has no meaning if he is in love.

But Melissa persisted, unstoppable. "Forget Stendhal and his theories. Look at me. Do you see yourself in this mirror?"

"No, never," I lied.

And I looked into her eyes, shimmering like the surface of rippling sea water under a crystalline sky, her hair flailing haphazardly in the breeze off the Seine, looking as if all the mirrors in her apartment were broken. She pushed on. "When you are old, do you think you will regret the chances you took and then failed, les affaires ratées, or the chances you didn't take at all?"

"I am not allowed to regret both?"

"You must choose, and there is no point in telling me anything but the truth."

"Then I choose neither. I am still waiting for my chance. Young people like you go out into the streets of Paris every day, thinking perhaps this is the day they will fall in love. Et pourtant, others, smarter, know it won't happen that day."

"I hate you when you talk like that." A pause. "Look at me. I'm telling you how I hate you."

"Do you know what you hate, Melissa? You hate the truth because it is not beautiful enough for you. It is not what you want to hear."

"No, what I hate, Darneau, is that you find beauty only in the past, your old dead poets, the ancient royal buildings overlooking the Seine, the memories you refuse to let go. Why can't you see beauty in the present? I promise you, the stars will shine the same tonight as they did when you were young."

I answered her. "Melissa, you know there are no stars visible in the skies of Paris, except maybe in your eyes."

"Then look at them there, Darneau. It's better than nothing."

By now we were approaching the abandoned Gare d'Orsay as a raw gust of wind knifed up the quai which was nearly empty of flâneurs. The river's turbid waters kept churning by, licking the cold stony banks. Melissa's face shone vibrantly with the invincibility of her years, casting off a beguiling rosé glow. Yet the beauty of the moment struck me with a singular sense of melancholy, that time itself was hunting me, threatening my happiness . . . though I realized Melissa felt none of that sadness herself. Her eyes and voice were lit with joy.

She huddled against me and pulled her coat tight against the chill of love. Trapped in her infinite, unthinking tenderness, I could not look away from her, and I clung precariously to the edge of tears myself. I prayed that the great passionate bells of Notre Dame would not begin to ring the hour—the cadence of that melodic tolling sound would have nudged me over the edge. If I ever wanted time to stop, even for just a few moments, that would have been it, ce temps-là de mon idée folle. But it was Melissa herself who provided the nudge.

"Darneau, I was born to love you." Her soulful eyes, now soft blue like the color of Wedgewood china, were languishing in her own unaccountable tears. She held onto me for a time and then laughed. "Darneau, you have lost your train of thought—that never happens."

I told myself I could not be honest with Melissa because it

would ravage her happiness, but I knew that was mainly a lie. It was the illusion of my own unimaginable happiness I was defending.

Then she laughed again, quietly, and said, "Why was your lecture on love and Stendhal's philosophy so perplexing today?"

"I don't know, Melissa, but you are going to tell me."

"I will, yes. Today your mind was not on *La Chartreuse de Parme*. It was on yourself. It was on your past. It was on your lost love for Julie. I could see it in your face. Stendhal may have believed that one's first love is the deepest and lasts the longest, but you, Darneau, should not live in the past. Turn the page."

"And if I can't, what will happen?"

"Everything will be lost. You will have nowhere to go because even you cannot turn back time."

"Melissa, I wouldn't want to."

Then with a fleeting smile, in the truest, most beautiful way she said, "Tell me you don't love me."

I broke the desperate silence, my voice falling to a whisper. "I cannot."

We walked slowly back from the river in perfect, mindless, indefinable bewilderment. In the west the Tour Eiffel was outlined against a blue and orange sky, and Melissa's eyes were shining like those of some medieval saint who had just glimpsed the Promised Land.

The next day, bags in hand, she knocked on my door.

CHAPTER 13

I FORGOT TO MENTION MY SUSPICION, IN PERFECT TUNE with Annelise's, that I hadn't heard the last from Julie, and we were right. I slit open her blue airmail envelope with my little pen knife like I was cutting apart our old affair. But the real knife was in Julie's hand.

Darneau—

I have been pondering the débâcle you are creating now. I will always believe you loved me, in your own starry-eyed way, but in the end I had to leave you because practically, not emotionally, I was afraid to accept that love, to receive it on your absolute terms. As time went by, some days, admittedly, I felt profound remorse; most days I wallowed in selfish regrets and endless guilt. You were the first of my life's disasters, I think the greatest and saddest. But I was young then, not knowing I was designed to attack life with insensitivity rather than love. And yet, even now I will offer you some advice which I am in no way qualified or entitled to give.

Darneau, you are older than the boy I loved in Paris, but in essence you haven't changed at all. I know, I know—you are rolling your eyes and humming my song: still crazy after all these years. But look: young foreign students in Paris, as you and I once were, as Melissa is now, they are always on the brink of falling in love. They dream of it, they get ready for it, they are bored without it, and for some of them, for you and me certainly, the love can arrive, then unexpectedly vanish, seemingly without a trace. But later the memories of it trickle back little by little, remnants of everything they might have forgotten, until those memories have grown back deeper and truer than the original affair. (Now I'm beginning to sound like you.) Can that second wave of love be more beautiful in the end because memory by itself doesn't require engagement with the actual physical beloved, a real liaison? It requires just a recollection, a souvenir. Didn't you like to say that nostalgia is the most perfect of all sensations? And nostalgia, too, doesn't need an event or a person or a real love. It needs nothing more than a memory, even if the memory is a chimera. But then along came Simone Signoret, older and wiser than both of us, who remarked, "La nostalgie n'est plus ce qu'elle était." Nostalgia is not what it used to be. It sounds better in English, doesn't it? But my mind is wandering.

I hope Melissa's wild adoration for you will wear away in time, but if it doesn't, you will learn, as I have, how guilt can ruin your life. When I think of a first love, I wonder if it isn't in some ways better and purer than all later loves, simply for the reason that it didn't last. It can even make you happier because the infatuation, if you want to call it that, doesn't come with permanent unbreakable iron chains. And its inexorable transience, the ever impending threat of the end, only deepens the passion. The one tragic thing about infatuation is that it only happens to the young, like Melissa . . . and like you, Darneau, because you have never grown up.

I met you when we were both nineteen, and we became happy, didn't we, you and youth and I? Who wrote that once you have been happy in Paris, you can never be happy anywhere else—not even in Paris. (I'm sure you can tell me.) Before you throw this letter in the poubelle, let me get to the final point: Melissa's infatuation versus your self-deception. And don't delude yourself. She's way out of her depth, and maybe you are too. You have been bewitched by an orphan. It can't go on without a bad ending. Am I jealous of her? Of course. Is my pride hurt by her hold over you? Yes. But shall I hate her because she is like me?

Still, I am not on trial here. You are.

Bonne chance—

Julie

I read the letter twice, at first resenting Julie for diminishing love by calling it infatuation. But the truth was more complex, and I was gradually learning and relearning more about Julie. Her lies, spoken and unspoken, were utterly contemptible, yet I think I have come to understand her frantic sad rationale. There are different shades of love. Julie's was bluish-violet, mine was reddish-orange, and they clashed. Or did they? What color was Melissa's? I wasn't sure I wanted to find out.

One day Julie could be deeply caring, another day she

moved on to a different contradictory mood, swinging like a pendulum. She had been a little like that when I first knew her; she was more like that now. Julie had a knack for hurting you, but she was not merciless. She could not kill. And mostly, like all of us, she hurt herself.

⚜

Five minutes after Melissa showed up at my apartment, I sent her home. Or I should say, I picked up her bags and walked her home, her eyelashes wet, her hands clenched, her strained voice suffering in protest.

She lashed at me: "My advice to you is to forget my mother and remember me."

I said softly, "I am always grateful for good advice." Then I made some other desultory remark about preferring not to lose my job.

She responded, "Paris is immense, how would anyone know we were living together? No one will pay any attention to us or even notice it. This is Paris, not the Vatican City."

We reached her apartment door and I stood there, looking into her blaming eyes now darkened by humiliation and defeat.

"Darneau, I never used to feel loneliness on a day that I saw you." Then her last stabbing words as she went in. "But you don't deserve my love."

I walked down her steps into la rue Bonaparte where Paris life continued at its usual frenetic pace, as if nothing had changed, people hurrying by, unaware that in my life, every part was self-destructing, especially my conscience. Sometimes you cannot help who you love, who loves you. You can lose your heart or have it stolen, and maybe not know which it is. You cannot even foresee which unfortunate person you might meet. You cannot prevent someone from following you—the choice is not yours and perhaps it is not hers.

I knew, of course, exactly what I should do: end this impossible, dangerous relationship. I had known that for some time, but not exactly what I would do or how I would do it. I walked down the cold gray streets toward the Luxembourg gardens, thinking I needed a hot brutal sun to burn away the fog of my irresolution, and where in this bleak winter landscape was I going to find one? I wandered through the disconsolate streets, trampling the dead brown leaves, the old torn newspapers and grimy discarded wrappers scattered in the breeze, giving myself up to the indifferent overcast city. I promised myself once again that if I did not have the courage to tell Melissa how deeply I had loved Julie, how my life had belonged to her mother, then our relationship must end today. Because if it didn't, we were racing down a blind cul-de-sac with no way out. It was the kind of mistake I had been making all my life. Melissa's history with her mother was terrible, yet perhaps not beyond redemption, and what kind of role could I play in that? Julie had come to Paris, the city of our love affair, but also her daughter's home. What was she searching for? I had no idea, and maybe she didn't either.

Other demented thoughts were turning around in my fatuous mind. Forgetting Julie for the moment, which I knew was impossible, Melissa and I were still a generation and a world apart. In theory, two people can love each other with equal passion, I suppose, especially when both are young. But even then I suspect it doesn't happen often. It's not just that one person's love is greater than the other's, but that they love differently, leading different lives, wandering in separate directions among different stars. This doesn't necessarily sabotage the love entirely, but it can stunt its growth by injecting doubt about the future. Eternal love: the greatest oxymoron. Was it Kafka who said: *L'éternité, c'est long . . . surtout vers la fin.*

Love is impossible, say poets, because they place the demand on love that it last a lifetime. Mine never last a year; sometimes they don't make it through the night.

I was still walking aimlessly as the cold city descended into darkness. I began to feel the weight of guilt that Julie foresaw. In a way I despised her for the silent years of her exile, her evasions and lies, her crashing reentry into my life. As for Melissa, who could predict what she would do? Her approach to life was unencumbered by rational thought processes. I felt the lingering sting of her last accusation, and how could I tell the truth to someone who refused to listen to it? Still, I swore to myself that I would.

But I knew I wouldn't.

It had begun to rain again, heavy drops coming in from the northwest rim of the city, vengeful pounding rain lancing through bare trees, splashing against dark buildings, collecting into sad rivulets that ran along the curbs as they pleased, threading their way down toward a final ending somewhere, taking the easiest path like me, but mine more riddled with gut-wrenching twists and unforgiving turns. It was growing late, and the lamplight and neon arc-en-ciel reflections shimmered on the puddled sidewalks and in the shiny vitrines, trying to compensate for the encroaching gloom. I went home and finally slept, dreaming of the irretrievable Paris when I was young, always my age in dreams, elusive dreams from the remorseless, distant past.

DIARY OF MELISSA ARTEMIS

February 13, 1983

Why is it that just when things seem to be going well, something always comes along to empêcher mon bonheur? Darneau once asked me about my name. "Wasn't Durrell's Melissa Artemis a pathetic, tragic figure in the end?"

Yes, I told him, a perfect name for me.

This morning my step-father left a message to call him. I searched the sky for omens. I couldn't find any, but the fateful black thunderbolt was to be fired by Nico himself, and I would be the sole casualty—even I can't come up with a dreadful enough cliché to account for it. He wants me to go to university in Switzerland, the most boring country in the world. I know, I have lived there. Her only redeeming features are chocolates and fondue. Nico and Julie clearly want to get me out of Paris, but, I told him, that's not going to happen. I tried to hide my feelings from Nico, but he's a perceptive bastard. I guess you can see where this is going.

No doubt Julie has been poisoning the well, fixating on Darneau's age and lying about how he's taking advantage of me. Has she lost her mind? I will see Darneau tomorrow and . . . and what?

I suppose I should not get used to being happy. I can go back to feeling angst-ridden like all my crazy depressed friends. Darneau will know what to do. Switzerland would be ghastly, horrific, épouvantable.

CHAPTER 14

Melissa and I walked out of the ACP building together, just as we had so many times before, but I could tell by the tremulous sound of her voice that some intolerably painful words were coming. And they did.

"Nico told me you might be my mother's old lover from her time at the Sorbonne." She was talking to herself really.

"I think you knew that, Melissa."

"That doesn't really answer my question, does it?"

"I thought it did."

"But did you ask her to marry you?" A long poignant silence fell, full of fearful self-pity.

"I don't know. It's not impossible. We talked about many things."

"Perhaps impossible is the wrong word."

"Perhaps it is."

I looked directly at Melissa and finally filled in the whole sad truth, which surprisingly didn't take long: "Yes, we were lovers, living together like young romantic dreamers, replete with all the emotions except common sense and good judgment. Then suddenly, without warning, in the midst of this idyll, Julie abruptly left Paris. She never told me about a pregnancy, never told me about anything, until she returned last fall. She did leave me a letter when she went home to California.

It didn't say much. Time went on. Her life went on. She never mentioned a child, ever. She never wrote me a word about you, or anything else."

"What are you thinking, Darneau?"

I saw Melissa was fighting to hold back tears, and I could tell she was going to lose that battle. The tears were not yet in her eyes, but they were already in her voice. I didn't feel too calm myself, but I took her hand and said, "We can't relive the past, Melissa, and we can't deny it."

"I can, Darneau. I will not allow Julie to infiltrate my life, to steal what I have found. You cannot know the extent of my love."

"No, I cannot. Yet you know this love is impossible madness."

"Yes."

"Then we will end it."

She answered in almost a whisper. "No."

I didn't know what more to say. I wanted to hold and protect her but I realized I couldn't. I thought how the bitter, pitiless circle was closing in on us: I was again losing hope for love in Paris, just as I had when Julie left and took it away from me the first time. I think my reticence was hurting Melissa in some unintended way, because she turned and walked away without saying another word. Inside of me I felt fear and emptiness where I should have felt love.

DIARY OF MELISSA ARTEMIS

Valentine's Day, 1983

I left Darneau in the street without saying goodbye. I wanted desperately to stay, but I did not want him to see me break down. He should have come after me, he should have told me nothing matters because he loves me, but he didn't. What he said to me was pointless, but at least it wasn't a lie. I thought to myself, mon dieu, why am I being crushed by all these unchosen, unwanted forces born of long forgotten sins and passions, when I did nothing to bring them on? Life's sad iron rack is breaking me into pieces, and I wonder how you can ever put yourself back together again.

But I have reached a decision. I have changed my mind: I will go to Switzerland and enroll in the University of Geneva. It's better than exile on Elba, I think. Maybe Darneau will learn a lesson when I leave him. I will call Nico in the morning, and at least one of us will be happy. Then I can petition the Swiss government for emotional asylum.

CHAPTER 15

June 1983

It has been four months since I last saw Melissa, months of profound malaise with no letters, no phone calls, no contact at all. And the same from Julie: perfect silence. I had plenty of time to mull over the unfortunate truth that one's greatest love often comes into his life too early—or it arrives too late, if it arrives at all. The window of love opens, you have your chance to win or lose, and then it slams shut for good. I could still feel the power of Julie's raw instinctive passion, in contrast to Melissa's innocent heartfelt love, both pure and vulnerable in their own ways.

How do you spell love in Paris? M-I-S-È-R-E.

A brief message had come early on from Nico explaining that he had moved Melissa to Switzerland for her own self-protection, given her history of emotional ferment, that he understood how a young student can idolize a favorite teacher, fall under his sway, etc., etc. He wrote that Melissa's moods and feelings are like an iceberg where you can't see ninety percent of them, and those are all the hazardous parts.

After a perfunctory closing, he signed the letter formally with his full name.

⚜

It was nearing the end of June in Paris, the gold sun flaring in this heated city of passion and profanity—her sidewalks, streets and parks drenched by the summer light, some days hazy and pale, other days glittering as bright and clear as a glass of perfectly chilled Sancerre. And the long evenings went on and on with dusk not extinguishing the fading light until almost 10:30. There was a fresh invasion of tourists, most speaking English, some German, but others chattering in incomprehensible dialects, families with scrapping toddlers, older students from everywhere—on back-packing trips, auto-stoppeurs hitchhiking around, all soaking up the usual sights, sounds, and aromas. They crowded into little hotels, pensions and youth hostels, meandering day and night up and down les grands boulevards and winding ruelles of the left bank, drifting in and out of boulangeries, pâtisseries, and ethnic restaurants, hanging out in cafés and bars, hitting on each other, looking for love and romance.

I was teaching just two classes at ACP during the summer term, with no trenchant young auditeur slouching in the back row. Was I hurt by Melissa's disappearance without a word? What do you think? But I had been through this cruel siege before. My life now was tranquil, slow-paced, placid, not quite morbidly so, but strangely, inexpressibly muted. At what point did I realize, or rather did I come to appreciate, that I had to be close to Melissa or I would not be happy? I suppose many men, especially when they are young, believe they are accomplished lovers, adept virtuosos of love. Others understand they will always be novices. I put myself in the second camp.

I would sometimes wake up after a night of broken sleep, half hoping to look out and see rough overcast skies to match my mood, wishing for an opaque, gothic morning to pair with my expanding sense of futility. As I grew older my students seemed to get younger, smiling, laughing, still confident of their paths to future success and happiness. The reality, I understood, but didn't want to tell them, was often less beautiful than their faërie castles in the air.

I would take long random walks through the age-old centre-ville that I had come to know so well, comme ma poche, as the French say—pacing around like a man in a prison yard, losing myself like some literary vagabond in the Paris that had birthed and nurtured her own geniuses, or had magnetically drawn them in from the ancient provinces: gifted artists, poets, philosophers, novelists, her sublime wordsmiths, their names now immortalized with bronze plaques marking the shabby lodgings and cheap hotels where they lived and drank and worked in poverty and pain—and then died in silent anonymity. It would not be for generations, sometimes centuries, until they would be remembered and honored by future readers and voyeurs whose forebears never spent a sou on their poems or paintings while they were alive. These masters, these légendes disparues, have to console themselves now by reading their names chiseled on Père Lachaise tombstones.

I saw Annelise from time to time. We mostly avoided talking about Julie and Melissa, though Annelise had admonished me again—this was shortly after she had left for school in Geneva—that Melissa's vision of life was impossibly, fatally romantic, that I must not play with her delicate dreamy emotions. She looked at me sadly and said, "You can probably control your own feelings, and you must. She cannot—she is too honest to keep herself from falling in love."

I said it didn't matter, regardless, because I was sure Melissa was not coming back any time soon. Annelise didn't exactly smile as she said sotto voce, "Espérons," without a trace of hope in her voice.

"Don't count on her not coming back, Darneau. There is a bond linking the two of you that extends far beyond the kilometres between Paris and Geneva. Still, I am surprised she hasn't written to you. Perhaps I'm wrong . . . but I don't think so. And I hope you know what you're doing."

"So do I."

To tell the truth, I was also baffled by the total silence, month after month, though in the event Annelise was not wrong. A few days later, toward the end of a warm sunlit afternoon, I found Melissa sitting on a big valise, waiting alone in the little courtyard of my apartment building.

I barely overpowered the urge to run and throw my arms around her, but she fixed me with her most implacable smile and said, "At least you didn't grow a beard. You need a haircut; you look like a sixties hippie." She raised her arm and brushed the hair back off my forehead with her fingers.

"You came all the way from Switzerland to make fun of my hair? A lesser man might take offense."

"It's longer than mine, Darneau."

"It's had longer to grow, years longer."

I dragged her bag up my four flights of steps and unlocked the heavy wooden door with my old iron key. It was Melissa who wrapped her arms around me then, trembling and sobbing before I could do or say anything. Those frozen sea-blue eyes you could get lost in melted and poured into mine. She said in her most serious tone, "Remember when your friend said to always listen to your heart? I listened, and I have come back."

She sought refuge in French to speak her simple truths: "Écoute-moi, Darneau, je ne te quitterai plus jamais. J'appartiens à toi, je t'aimerai toujours."

Never was Melissa so beautiful as when her eyes were filled with tears, eye water she called them, laughing, while my own mind was breaking down into indescribable, irrational sensations. I thought how perfect to be Melissa's age again, standing there so certain and straightforward. I shuddered under the oppressive burden of my own age and my own vapid past, bleaker and darker than night, falling back from the indestructible light of Melissa's youth. Her triumph was open-and-shut. Yet I did love her, unthinkingly, desperately, I would say. The feeling of despair was the hard-earned legacy of my own years of fumbling through this city's cycle of hope and rejection—which could exhaust emotions and destroy love. You wait and wait for some kind of petit bonheur and when it finally appears, it comes in on tortured illusory broken wings.

But I asked Melissa hesitantly, "Why no letters, no phone calls, nothing but silence, day after empty day?"

She answered like the enigma she was. "It was a trial of love. How can I tell if you'll miss me, if I don't go away?"

"That sounds like the title of a bad country song, Melissa. But not even a postcard?"

"Don't judge me on my habits of communication, Darneau, and don't try to take the temperature of my soul."

"I don't judge you at all."

"Ah, but you do. When I was in Geneva, were you miserable, happy, or something in between?"

I waited before answering. "Truthfully, there was no way to tell, because I was disconnected from everything, existing by myself in a world of strangers, isolated, alone."

She told me about her visits to a psychiatrist in Switzerland. "After a while the doctor told me, how did he put it, that I was standing in my own way, just going through a phase. I told him the phase had lasted for years, all my life, really. When he started asking personal questions about your affair with my mother, I got up and walked out. The last thing I said to him was that I was not mentally ill, that I was just another sad human being blown off course by the world's delirious, ungodly winds."

I can picture Melissa frowning, then half-smiling, as she flung her final metaphor at the psychiatrist. Later he reported to Nico that she needed therapy, but not with him, as he didn't trust anything she said about herself—it was all fabrication.

Melissa finally fell asleep on my couch, her face submerged in a big French down pillow, the tears that had streaked her cheeks now dried, her eyes that could peer into your soul with unforgivable audacity now closing, just before the slight smile had time to disappear from her face. I watched her lying there, a young heart-thief, her quiet breathing occasionally broken by a sigh like the hush of a soft summer breeze. I looked outside through my two little windows. We were entrapped by the falling Parisian twilight, as it turned slowly from rose to lavender-gray to deep purple to darkness, its lurking shadows wrapping up the city and the day. What dim light lingered was only a mirage seeping out of the city, and as I looked at

Melissa, her lips slightly apart, sleeping in utter peace, I felt as if I were part of a beautiful Renaissance painting, just a minor figure, some anonymous religious acolyte gazing devoutly at a blessed, revered young saint . . . and I whispered softly to her, "Bonne nuit, petite étoile."

DIARY OF MELISSA ARTEMIS

July 2, 1983

I've been here at Darneau's for three days now. We've walked the narrow, cobbled streets down to the Seine, talked for hours, gazing at the massive palaces and other historic buildings outlined against the evening sky, crossing the thronging bridges which link la Rive droite and la Rive gauche. We watched the river flow by, an inexorable current of time floating toward Apollinaire's Pont Mirabeau and the great Citröen and Renault car factories, then past them into la grande banlieue. I wonder how many ancient treasures, artifacts, precious relics of the past still lie deep below the river bottom, lost in the mud and gravel and sand. We saw the 1910 all time high water mark of the great flood, the date chiseled into the stone wall of the quai, not far from where Paul Verlaine would walk by taking his poems to the printer after a night of drugs and drinking absinthe in Paris bars.

From the Pont des Arts we snapped pictures of the western sky, stained in blood from a wounded sun sinking through scudding clouds. Darneau taught me that word, scudding. He likes to sit at one of the outside tables of a little café in La Place Dauphine, sipping a cold drink, feeling the oasis of quiet among the vieux bâtiments. Once he said to me, "Gamblers and lovers keep playing till they lose."

I told him, "You are hopeless, Darneau. You have lost faith in yourself."

He said, "Yes, I know. I'm sorry."

I told him, "Don't be flippant. Save your caustic sarcasm for your sleeping, worthless students."

What was going on in his impenetrable mind, to say nothing of his bone-dry soul?

I asked him, "How old were you when you reached the age of reason? Three, four?"

He said, "Have I reached it?"

But my next question surprised him. I asked him whether he would rather love or be loved. He didn't answer for a while, then said, "Aren't they both the same illusion in the end?"

Later I said, "Darneau, do you remember when I was wondering if you believed in God?"

"Why do you bring this up now?"

"Because if you believe in God, I can't love you."

"All right, I believe in God."

"So I will hate you, because you are insufferable . . . tu es dégueulasse." A line I admit I stole from Belmondo at the end of *À Bout De Souffle*.

But I saw under his masked face the beginning of a smile. He made an attempt to conceal it, but he could not, and he knew that I had seen it. And I knew he was happy.

CHAPTER 16

The glimmering, splintered light of July was slowly passing us by, day by day, though the long summer evenings were still not ending till nearly ten o'clock. Often Melissa and I lazed away our time on the shaded benches of the Luxembourg jardin, watching the tennis players and listening to the little Parisian gosses, running, playing, and shouting in their effortless, naturally perfect French accents, having no problems at all with irregular verbs or the subjunctive mood that all foreigners struggle to master. Sometimes we wandered back to the quais where we studied the floating péniches, choosing which one we would like to live on. We did finally hear from Nico. Melissa reacted comme d'habitude by slipping into her withdrawal mode, and when I wondered about it, she vaguely apologized, then said so quietly I could hardly hear her, "Oh, I don't want to talk about it."

But I suspected Nico knew where she was. It was difficult for Melissa to hide the truth from him, though not as difficult as to conceal it from herself. It followed that Nico wrote to us both separately. To me he cautioned, "Melissa feels too much and thinks too little. Be forewarned: she will always act as she feels. She conjures up ideals and pretends to know what she wants, but she has no real clue. She lives in a different world than you or I, Darneau."

Still, Melissa and I went on, yes, living in our own fantasy, but deceptively content. In one breath she would ask me to tell her stories of the "old days" when I was a student her age: "What were you like then?" The next moment she would grimace and accuse me of living in the past: she said that was my fatal character flaw, that nostalgia was my favorite word. Perhaps it is. Remember as a little child how you would come home from shopping and proudly announce to your siblings your new bigger shoe size, because it meant (though you didn't understand this) that you were growing older, growing up. Later you came to learn the truth, that time is the enemy. It never slows down, never even hesitates, and it knows perfectly how to steal your youth.

She said, "My love for you has no beginning and no end. It was there before I met you and it will be there if I never see you again. Does that make sense?"

I thought about this for a minute, then answered, "Actually, no. There is no mandate in love to think about the future. Eternal love: it can last a day or a hundred years."

"Darneau, stop kicking my heart around."

"That's a song title. I've heard that old song. But I don't remember how it ends."

"I guess it depends on who's doing the singing. It's not a blues, you know, and I have a trivia question for you, Darneau."

"Fine, I'm ready."

"What do these three songs have in common? 'Basin Street Blues,' 'Birth of the Blues,' and 'Blues in the Night.'"

I thought about it. Then: "I don't know, what?"

"Not one of them is a blues."

"Melissa, are you the expert on sad music? Are you trying to impress me?"

"Yes, how'm I doing?"

One night she left her couch and came into my bed. I woke up and joked, "What took you so long?" But she didn't answer, so I said, "Melissa, it is insanity to continue like this. You will have to find your own place."

She looked at me through her soft wavering eyelashes and said at last, "Are you still thinking about Julie?"

"Not if I can help it."

"What if you can't?"

I had tried so hard to convince myself that everything would work out somehow. Yet most of my days began in self-doubt, continued in self-pity, and ended in frustration, not love.

I said, "Melissa, we cannot stay together like this."

She answered gently, "Darneau, don't worry about it. We can find ways. If we dwell only on the dangers of our situation, it will eliminate every possible beautiful outcome—we will be giving up all we have."

My voice cracked as I said, "Non, non, c'est impossible! You cannot forfeit your future like this. It would not be fair to you."

"So we agree—there is no fairness in life. It's not drawn up to be fair. But understand, Darneau, I'm not looking for fairness. It's nothing compared to love."

She stared at me. She had the simplest wish, but it could not be granted. Our drama, like her mother's, like all tragedies, could not end any way but unhappily.

"You know, Melissa, living in Paris you would have soon

fallen in love even if we had never met. You were born to be loved."

"I don't believe that. You belittle me when you say that. I didn't meet you by accident. I would have found you a day or a week or a month later. It's incomprehensible really that it took as long as it did. You see that, don't you, Darneau? If I had not followed you . . ." But here she stopped.

Curiously, we had never talked much about our age difference, though it was always in the back of my own mind. But I was now grasping blindly for any rational straws.

"Melissa, you are a teenager. I am nearly forty."

"You are using numbers again to destroy emotions. I never understood the connection between happiness and age, if there is one. We are all day-to-day, Darneau. Françoise Sagan's husband was twenty years older."

"And how long did that last?"

"Chaplin was happy with someone thirty-six years younger."

"He was a comedian."

"Catherine Howard married Henry VIII when he was over thirty years older—and she was a teenager."

"I see you've been doing some research, though as I recall that one ended badly for her. And Henry had six wives, I've had none."

"You're a pathetic defeatist, Darneau. I am the only positive thing in your life. I would kill myself except I wouldn't be there to see you grieve for me."

"Melissa, don't ever say that again . . . ever."

She turned silent as a churchyard. Finally, inscrutably, "Tell me what I did to deserve this unhappiness. Is it love that punishes, or is it life?"

"What is the difference?"

She didn't answer . . . because there could be no answer. But she looked up at me and said, "When I close my eyes I envision us together, but I can't see if we're happy or sad."

"My advice would be to keep your eyes open."

Then, as quietly as a prayer whispered while kneeling before the Pietà: "Promise me you won't see Julie again." Her untrusting eyes filled with tears marking time before they would fall.

"Promises are like chains, Melissa. They don't work if they're imposed on you from the outside. If you truly want to do something, you don't have to make someone a promise. And the worst thing is to make promises you know you cannot keep."

"Is that a no, then? You understand, if it weren't for Julie we wouldn't have any of these problems."

"If it weren't for Julie, you wouldn't be alive."

"You keep saying all the wrong things, Darneau. Julie's a quim."

"A what?"

"A quim, un con. Despicable. Unspeakable. A woman without a soul." She sat up and burned her fire-blue eyes into mine. "You won't leave me, Darneau, will you? What if I need you? Where will you be?"

A tear spilled down her defiant cheek. We could both sense the impending threat of loss as it ironically sharpened the blade of our love. We talked late into that final tender night. Not one word she said made any sense. She lived only in the present, and I could not escape the past.

"Darneau, have you turned out to be the person you wanted to be?"

"Not yet."

"Would you look at me?"

"No."

"Why are you afraid of me tonight? Your mind is too somber for me. Leave your past and your fear behind you for once. Look no further. Come to me."

I think that was the terrible, irrevocable moment I decided to run from Paris and my life there, where love was becoming a form of torture. I was learning that sometimes pleasure can hurt you far more than pain. But I said to her, "I do try not to keep looking back into my past. I know it's best to forget, best not to know. And yet while the past is a closed book for most people, it can't quite be closed for us."

"Yes, but better to slam it shut and throw it away, Darneau, better not to talk about it. Remember how Sainte-Thérèse answered the bishop, when he cross-examined her about what she said when she claimed to talk to Jesus?"

"No, I don't."

She said, "I don't use words—I just love him."

"Melissa, I would give up everything . . ." And I stopped in mid-sentence.

"To be in love with me?"

"Yes." I turned away hopelessly. "You will forget me someday."

"In my mind perhaps. Not in my heart. Forgive my sentimentality."

It was late, and Melissa was beginning to surrender to the hour and the heavy tired feeling that had fallen over her. She lay still, her thick dark lashes guarding her closing eyes. Finally she slept, forsaking the ruins of our conversation, hors de combat.

I thought to myself, she's vulnerable now (aren't we both?), but in a year she will change or even forget. As for myself, I knew we could not continue like this. It would gradually get worse—and I would go mad brooding and worrying about her sanity, and my own. Au revoir, adieu, farewell. The terrifying words turned over incessantly in my mind. Finally, I turned off the lamp and lay awake in the dark.

The next day I took advantage of one of Melissa's suburban shopping excursions to pack and leave. Like all self-contemptuous cowards I left her a letter, not unlike the one Julie had bludgeoned me with. The circle was complete.

DIARY OF MELISSA ARTEMIS

July 30, 1983

I have read it a hundred times, this tear-stained unconscionable letter drenched in Weltschmerz. I will copy it here, though I know every word of it by heart.

Ma chère Melissa,

I am leaving Paris. I am ashamed to say that you have forced me to run away, not from you, from myself. I will apply for une année sabbatique from the college and perhaps do a little writing and teach somewhere. I will be gone for at least a year. When I return, you will have forgotten about me. Go to your classes, read your livres, go to the cinéma, to concerts, galeries, librairies, to the Caveau to dance. Tu es jeune et jolie, ma poupée, forget me—throw me out of your life like yesterday's fish.

Listen to Nico: he truly wants what's best for you. You are lucky to have him. I will contact my landlord, hopefully to sous-louer my apartment. You can stay there as long as you want, though I'm sure Nico will want you out yesterday. Don't try to reach me. Truthfully, I don't even know where I will end up, London, New York, no not New York, maybe Italy or Spain. I hope to come back to Paris after this year of exile, to rethink, replan, rebuild. I learned long ago that I can leave Paris, but it doesn't leave me.

Melissa, in my heart I cannot wish to be forgotten by you, but in my mind there is no doubt that that would be best for you. As Kafka put it many years ago: "There is hope . . . but not for us."

We are the unlucky ones, the defeated. This world was not meant for our love.

Je t'embrasse—
Darneau

So that's it. Who has the power to control my life now—Nico, Julie, Darneau, myself? All of us or none of us? Nico will never understand my love for Darneau. It was my bad luck to be so much younger, though D. never made me feel immature, or that I was in over my head, that I didn't belong with him. I will always trust him. If I had not met him my life would be indescribably different, directionless, a disaster. I told him that. Does he expect me to hang out now with some young self-important student in love with himself? Or some naïve American expat? It is not something I could endure, cet amour-propre. To get through this time I will need strength, skill, will power, and better luck; without them I won't have a chance. But in my heart I know what Darneau needs, and what I need.

There is an absolute, unbreakable link connecting us. It may stretch or bend, but it will not come apart. I will find him. And if I can't, I will wait for him and count down the days. He once said that the deepest love comes before you grow up. I will not celebrate my birthday. I will not live in a future that does not include him. And I will not move out of his apartment, though

I don't belong in this city without him, or anywhere else in the world.

Une année sabbatique dure longtemps, je le sais, mais pas toujours. He will not be able to stay away from Paris for the whole year, if he cares about me. You are not alive if you are not in love. Yet sometimes love alone is not powerful enough to stop someone from leaving you. I will defeat his awful loneliness—isn't that the raison d'être of love? I will have to recapture his heart . . . if I want to live without tears.

I know you can't speed up or slow down time—it does both on its own. I think Pursewarden wrote it is the only fabric that does not wear out . . . time.

Alors, je fabriquerai un calendrier, jour après jour, dont le premier est presque fini. I will cross them out every morning when I get up, one by one, day by day, like this. Only for a year. I'm not interested in eternity.

~~365~~ 364 363 362 361 360 359 358 357 356
355 354 353 352

PART TWO

Un Anno a Firenze

CHAPTER 17

I ARRIVED IN FLORENCE IN THE FURIOUS HEAT OF AUGUST, the air heavy, humid, and stifling. I said to myself: It can get no worse. I had caught the late train from Paris-Gare-de-Lyon, tried to sleep off and on, then upon arrival found a small hotel as far away from the long lines of tourists as possible. It was blessedly air-conditioned. Why Italy, after all? I suppose when you are fleeing from yourself, it doesn't matter what direction you take or where you end up. You just follow the tracks to any distant oblivion, and forget the roads not taken. I did have a contact in Florence who was able to get me an interview for a teaching position. The headmaster was kind, or he sensed my despair, or both. At any rate he offered me a job. It was in a small anglophone school a few kilometers outside the city, originally founded by Americans after the war and now catering to an international student body, mostly expats or children of local businessmen or academics. I was contracted to teach two French classes, an English lit course, and a humanities class—it was only my French that got me the job. It was not quite full-time, but included room and board in a little pensione affiliated with the school.

Once classes started in September, my life there fell into a comfortable routine: teaching mostly in the morning and early afternoon, usually followed by long solitary walks beneath the quiet sky, a time to think and later to write about the traumas of Paris and other forlorn stories. I was able to begin studying Italian with our Upper School language teacher, called Gina, actually the daughter of the school's headmaster. She was one hundred percent Florentine and drilled me nonstop in an attempt to impose the pure local accent onto my Franglais-flavored Italian. Fortunately for me, her tolerance level for a stumbling beginner was high; I tested its limits on a regular basis.

As time went on and I got to know her better, she would often join me on my walks through the nearby countryside, along dusty unpaved roads through shady cypress groves and little vineyards with their ripening sangiovese grapes. As my Italian vocabulary slowly grew, we were able to have real conversations, moving beyond the weather, school matters, and her favorite topic: the Tuscan cuisine. She taught me amicizia . . . friendship. Like any young, curious, affable Italian (and I was learning that all Italians are easy to talk to), she eventually reached the subject of my life in Paris, especially my social life. I knew she would get there at some point, and I wasn't sure if I dreaded it or, in some way, was thankful for the chance to talk about the past: old memories, and some not so old.

It came on a sunlit fall day during one of our after-school walks as we enjoyed the tenuous warmth of a dying Indian summer. After a few gentle probes and a few gentle evasions, she asked, "Darneau, are you running away from something?"

"What makes you say that? Do you read minds in more than one language?"

"If I could read yours, would I see a fugitive from a great loss or from a great love?"

"Yes."

"Which is it, or aren't you sure?"

"I am sure of nothing."

"If you are looking for love, Darneau, you have come to the right place. Italy is famous for two things: saints and lovers."

"What about pasta and pizza?"

"There you go, turning a serious conversation into a joke about cibo. I think that is what you're good at, masking sensitivity with irony."

"I'm not really that good at it. The truth usually survives my irony, unburdened by any self-awareness."

"Darneau, do you believe that you are unlucky?"

"Cowards like me are never lucky, yet they don't need luck because they take no risks."

"But the odds are against you?"

"Yes, they've never been worse."

Sometimes I sensed that Gina was, how shall I put it, not falling in love with me—because why would she?—but becoming attached in her own flirtatious, sensual way. If Italy is known for saints and lovers, Gina firmly belongs in the second group. I did feel an affinity to her, yet at the same time I felt an incalculable distance between us, not at all due to any resistance on my part, there was no intentional effort involved . . . simply the subconscious after-effect of everything that had happened in Paris. And how could Gina's perfectly candid sincerity ever penetrate beneath the surface of my deranged self-deceit?

Writing down these thoughts at night, as I sit back in my little camera da letto, has given me a sense of peace that I welcome, even as it comes with memories that I cannot ignore, let alone escape. So I will remove them from my heart and put them into words on these pages: joys, sorrows, even the little things. Like the time, not long after I had met her, when Melissa remarked that I was misspelling my name, that in France it was d'Arnaud. I told her it was not my fault that some New York immigration clerk wrote it a different way when my ancestors came through Ellis Island, as he was recording names in the ledger for witless illiterates. She then advised me I should change it in court, that Nico's lawyer could take care of it. But after pointing out the spelling error, she was apparently satisfied and never mentioned it again. Melissa didn't need to win; it was enough for her that I was wrong.

Gina and I would occasionally have dinner in a local ristorante she favored called Da Michele; in fact, she seemed to know everyone who worked or dined there. I told her I was surprised that the Florentines didn't always twirl their pasta, but Gina very patiently explained the correct methodology, which occasionally involved cutting or separating the noodles with a fork, rarely using a knife, and never twirling them against a big spoon. Spoons are for zuppa, she said. It is difficult to joke with an Italian about food. In their solemn minds they live in the sacred gastronomic mecca of the world.

I did appreciate Gina's affection; she was the perfect companion for me, her francese-americano fuggitivo, as she described me. Gina had a little of Melissa's innocent charm, and something of Annelise's sensitivity. She, too, had the gift of listening, unlike most people who invariably are just thinking ahead about what they're going to say next, usually something about themselves. But then she was fundamentally unlike both of them because she was never stubbornly rebellious like Melissa or full of savvy, prescient forebodings like Annelise. Gina was more naturally at ease with herself, entirely comfortable in her soft golden Mediterranean skin.

Speaking of Annelise, I received a letter from her a few days later.

Mon cher Darneau,

It was good to hear from you at last, and that you have found a place in the international school. Don't be too hard on your high school students—they are all younger than our ACP misfits.

Speaking of students, Melissa Artemis has been the star of my German literature class, still abusing Goethe, and her new favorite poet is Heinrich Heine, a romantic dreamer like herself. And like you he was a longtime expat in Paris, died here and is buried in the Cimetière de Montmartre. Melissa has taken flowers to his grave and also advised me that he had a beautiful love affair with a much younger Française.

She does ask after you, tactfully, I will give her credit, but I have told her nothing. She did mention that she has sent letters trailing after you to international schools in all the capital cities, including Cairo and Beirut! They have all been returned, of course, addressee unknown. She has not yet unearthed your little school in Tuscany. So her letters are unanswered, sadly, like her hopes and dreams.

The other day she asked me what year I passed the Abitur, a not too subtle way to guess my age, so I pulled the date forward to make me almost ten years younger, but she was not fooled and not amused. She's still living in your rue de Sèvres apartment, paying the rent herself, or should I say conning it out of her stepfather. She asked me what to do with your mail, but I told her I had no forwarding address, which I didn't at the time. I suppose you've notified La Poste by now.

Darneau, I can understand how Melissa walked off with your heart. She is the best German student in all my classes, she is a charming, enchanting girl, jeune, jolie, fraîche and more dangerous than ever. She is still young, but she is growing into an attractive, even beautiful woman . . . and her mind is more beautiful than her face. It is clear that she misses you now, yet who knows how long that passion will last? As you like to say, "L'avenir nous le dira."

The letter concluded with a bit of other news, an affectionate goodbye, and left me with the staunchly unyielding impression that nothing at all had changed since I left Paris. That wasn't true, of course, because I had excised Melissa out of my day-to-day life, but what hadn't changed was her unyielding, subliminal hold on my sorry, emotional, sentimental frame of mind.

I didn't answer Annelise's letter for a while: what could I add to her perfect time will tell . . . other than life was passing me by; and I realized that I could not elude anything that had happened in Paris, nor could I forget any of it, even as the days in Florence slipped by.

CHAPTER 18

Occasionally on our free days, Gina would take me into the centro città and give me the local cognoscente's tour of Renaissance churches, monuments, art and architecture. She knew what days and times were best; as in Paris during the busy months, tourists in the streets of Florence can outnumber the natives. One of her friends, a young history professore, guided us around the great Florentine cathedral, the Duomo, its magical religion perhaps a sham, but its architecture bedazzling, unadulterated beauty. The climb up to the fifteenth century cupola with its frightening high walkway fired up my acrophobia. But mostly Gina and I patrolled the little country roads where she would quiz me on Italian grammar and attempt to enrich my still limited vocabulary. She particularly enjoyed drawing ruthless distinctions between her Italian words and what she called my false French equivalents. She would finish her example and invariably add, "Make a note of it."

Other times we would just talk about nothing in particular and savor the last of the mild autumn weather, the landscape sprayed with touches of Tuscan fall colors. These walks, however, were not helping me evade memories of my life in Paris. If anything, they stirred up thoughts and recollections of walking along the Seine while talking, arguing, and laughing with Melissa, mostly Melissa laughing at me.

Gina told me that our little international school had its American beginnings in Rome, but it didn't work out there financially. She complained that Romans always brag (vantarsi: I'll have to remember that word) about how they live in the Holy City. "But in Florence," Gina said, "we don't need the pope ... we have already been blessed simply to live in la bella città." She was smiling, but then looked intently at me. "Darneau, I have seen you walking alone at night, under the stars, down empty roads ... what are you searching for?"

"I ask myself the same question."

"I think I might know. People like you come to Tuscany to find an alternate universe, a distant, serene refuge where they can write books or compose music or just live through some great sadness. What is your Holy Grail, Darneau? Perhaps to write the elegy of your own personal sadness, inspired by Petrarch and Boccaccio? You are a lover of words and profound poetry. In that way we are different. I am simply looking for ordinary love and the gift of children. We could not be more different, could we? I trust everyone, Darneau, and you trust no one."

I said, "That's not true, Gina."

But I knew it was.

⚜

One day she mentioned that her father had received a phone call from an American named Julie, asking about me and if I were teaching here. "Who is she, Darneau?"

"An old friend. I knew her in Paris years ago, but she lives in California now."

"If she is an old friend, why is she calling my father instead of you?"

"That's a good question, Gina. Maybe she doesn't know where I am."

"Maybe you don't want her to know where you are."

She asked me one or two more questions about Julie, and I told her one or two more lies, not really knowing why I was once again enshrouding the truth. It was becoming my specialty, not the lying, but the not understanding why I needed to lie. Gina let me gently off the hook, as I knew she would, in her naturally mellow, laid-back manner.

"You don't owe me anything, Darneau, least of all the truth about your past. We Italians have been fabricating lies to cover up grandi storie d'amore since the Middle Ages."

When I returned home after saying fino a domani to Gina, sitting alone in the lobby of my pensione was a phantom from California, my great lost love, resplendent in a little red, white, and green sundress shining like the Italian flag, looking good I had to admit, obviously having left far behind the French tricolore of her 1960s.

"How are you, Darneau? Do you like the dress? I'm wearing it in your honor."

"Julie, you look like a fresh pizza Margherita."

"I knew you would say something mean like that. I wore this for fun, to make you smile. Instead you use these pretty colors to try and hurt me. Which is okay, I guess, it's what I deserve."

"How did you find me this time, in a new city, a new country?"

"You probably should have at least changed your name, a new nom de plume, or nom de guerre, perhaps. I did have to hire a French detective. He was good, better than good. Do you know how many letters of recommendation were sent to your new school?"

"Two or three?"

"Three, Darneau. And he got copies of all three."

I sat down and looked at her for a long moment. "So why, Julie, why come all the way to Italy? Are you looking for something you couldn't find in Paris? If so, you didn't give yourself much of a chance there. You always run away the day after you arrive."

"I run when I don't know what to do, Darneau. The last time, seeing you with Melissa, it was more than I could cope with. I felt possessed by a jealous, maddening love, I felt deranged, and you were no help."

"You have never given me time to help, Julie. And I'm sorry for making fun of your dress."

⚜

Julie had flown in from Paris and found her way to the school by hired car. She had no hotel reservation and there was no room in our pensione, even if I had wanted her to stay there. So I called Gina and without going into great detail, asked for help. Fifteen minutes later she arrived at the pensione and I introduced her to Julie. She asked me sarcastically in Italian if this was my old friend, la mia vecchia ragazza, and, in fact, she continued to speak only Italian the rest of the afternoon. Julie later mentioned that I had told her Gina was a teacher, and wondered that she didn't speak any other language. I answered that her English was perfectly fluent, if you don't mind a bit of an American accent, and her French was as good as her English.

Julie smiled and said, "Touché, then, Darneau. She was fencing you away from me, wielding her mother tongue like an Italian branding iron: no barbarian Californians allowed onto her Tuscan ranch."

Gina did find her a hotel room a couple of kilometers away and dropped us off there herself. When we were alone, Julie looked at me and sighed. "Darneau, if you were parachuted into some Bulgarian wasteland, you would still land near a good looking woman. And you would be speaking her language in a month. I expected to find you stranded like a clochard under a lonely bridge, but instead you are safely in the care of a young bella teacher of romance languages."

"Gina is the daughter of our headmaster who was nice enough to give me a job; and she herself was nice enough to find you a room and a ride."

"I'm only kidding, Darneau, but be careful. She may turn into another lost dreamer searching for you, and you may turn into the lost soul waiting to be found."

I thought to myself, she has found me already, but I said nothing more to Julie. Jealousy appears every time Julie comes back, but it doesn't always disappear when she leaves. It makes people dislike her. She usually ends up with more hate than anyone deserves.

We made arrangements to have dinner together in a local trattoria suggested by the hotel concierge. Needless to say, I was not taking her to Gina's favorite restaurant, for many reasons, but mostly in deference to my perfect, bottomless cowardice.

JULIE'S JOURNAL

October 21, 1983

This is not a bad hotel Darneau's Italian friend has found me, clean, quiet, décor hopelessly outdated and a bit forlorn, matching my mood. It was odd signing the register Julie Artemis. I hadn't used that name in so many years, though Nico had bestowed it on me in the divorce decree. As I told Darneau, it was about the only thing he gave me.

I haven't written in this journal in months, but tonight's dinner with Darneau was supposed to be my crossing of the Rubicon—I wonder if that river might even flow by somewhere near here?

What I had planned to be a nice dinner of hope and renewal of old affections morphed into a sad rejection of my efforts to make Darneau love me again, not a rejection really, more a shrug of confused indifference. Reflecting on that Parisian Sunday morning when I chased him down the steps of Saint-Sulpice and on our later conversations during that same trip, I am struggling to understand why I ran away from him for the second time, why I felt afraid of him and his secure, contented place in his beloved city, a place where I no longer belonged. And this fear gripped me even before I found out about his devastating relationship with Melissa. I must have been trying to rekindle something of our old affair, enhancing it by creating an aura of mystery and nostalgia. Did I love him again? I thought I did. But maybe I just wanted him to love me again.

Talking to Darneau in Paris, I could tell immediately that

for some reason he was holding his emotions in check. I was surprised and disappointed by his coolness. Of course, it didn't help that I admitted I was pregnant when I met him and when we became lovers, and that I had later essentially abandoned my now twenty-year-old daughter. My lies, some silent, some spoken, reach back all those years, unforgivably and painfully senseless, still following and condemning me today. Yet I know how Darneau feels. He said, "You betrayed me. You lied to me." He told me this in Paris, and he told me this again tonight.

I said, "Darneau, I kept my pregnancy a secret from you because it had nothing to do with you; I was the guilty party, not you."

His answer was full of disdain: "Julie, you are talking about guilt while I am talking about love."

I said, "Yes, that is how we are different, isn't it? But if I had told you in Paris that I was pregnant by another man, you would have thrown me out of your life. Maybe I lied to you to protect myself."

He looked at me with that sad expression he has perfected. "Julie, you stole that decision from me, and if you think I would have abandoned you, then you don't know me at all."

Now here I am, writing these thoughts down in a quaint, out-of-the-way Florence hotel room, after failing again to recapture even a little bit of Darneau's heart. I asked him after our dinner, "Do you think you could ever love me again?"

He said softly, "I have loved you for almost twenty years. I could not stop if I wanted to, which I never have."

"Then you will walk me back to my hotel and let me be close to you again."

But he shook his head and smiled. "Not tonight, Julie. Romance is not in our cards tonight."

I returned his smile: "Maybe if I loved you less, you would love me more."

"You're quoting Nat Cole now, Julie. I know that tune. A little later, didn't he sing 'Maybe I'll be left with no love at all'?"

He did kiss me goodnight, at least, then left me standing alone in the doorway of my sad little bedroom, sadder than a silent, empty nursery.

Of course, Darneau and I couldn't avoid talking about Melissa at dinner. (I am beginning to forget she was ever named Audrey.) Even here in Italy, hundreds of miles away and months after the event, I cannot blot out that terrible afternoon when I followed Darneau and Melissa and they blindsided me in that ghastly Paris café. Watching them from across the room, I suspected immediately that they were not just casual friends. I saw with my own eyes what was going on right in front of me, even while at the same time my conscious mind refused to accept that what was happening was real. Like a crystal clear image from the past, burnt into my memory, I recognized Darneau's look of love; and Melissa's beautiful eyes were fixed on him as if never to let him go. It didn't take an expert analyst of romantic affairs to see that they were falling in love, and I am an expert. I will never get over the shock of that horrific day.

But I left them in Paris, lay low for a while, and now I have followed Darneau to Florence, chasing a memory, God only knows why. I listened tonight to his anguished account of deserting Melissa in Paris, with no warning to her, just as I had left him when we were both her age. You wouldn't expect a woman with my years of self-centered, shallow California living now to start feeling sorry for Darneau, and perhaps I wasn't. Well, maybe a little. But my deeper feelings, of course, were for myself. Yet I hate feeling jealous of my own daughter.

In the end Darneau sat back in that little Italian restaurant, looking at me with his deep sad eyes. And in those eyes I saw both his own personal distress and the selfless protective citadel he had built around Melissa. He ran from Paris, the city he loves, because he wasn't able to love Melissa there.

I think in the end I probably hung on to a glimmer of hope that he would understand, if not respect, the reasons for my abandoning him in that shabby little 1960s Paris hotel room he had found us, with my pitiful goodbye letter left on our tousled, unmade bed—and that he would understand, after all, the reasons for the following long years of evasion and silence. I hoped he would now perhaps appreciate my ultimate honesty and find a way to forgive my past pathetic deceptions, but I knew truly all that was impossible. I had to face the reality that Darneau could never forgive me any more than I could forgive myself.

And yet . . . and yet . . . perhaps the passing of time will help me a little—for Darneau and I were impassioned, inseparable young lovers once, living in Paris, holding onto each other madly. I was a spineless, insensate fool to fear Darneau's love, to flee from it, and then obliterate him completely from my life. That was shallow, ignorant, cruel, noxious, though not as contemptible as neglecting my daughter . . . Audrey, now Melissa, now my young rival. For in some unthinkable way I am competing with her for Darneau's love . . . how is that possible?

Perhaps it was Melissa who tapped into Darneau's soul

and even enabled me to better see his true character after all these years. She has spent more time with him in Paris than I ever did. I can see him reflected in her soulful, guileless eyes, while all I see mirrored in my own eyes are false pride and true shame. After so many years of smiling into that mirror, who would have ever guessed that I could begin to feel sympathy for Darneau, or for Melissa, or for anyone other than myself? I ended up looking inside my soul, seeking a memory of a better time. But like the old Benny Carter song: all I found was a broken heart among my souvenirs. I think Darneau said it best: we can no more revive our youthful love than we can revive our youth itself.

I was surprised when he told me that he thinks Melissa deserves to know who her father is. I never thought it would do any good, but maybe I was wrong. If Darneau believes it's a good idea . . . I'll have to give it some thought. But I will not stick around Florence. Maybe he will not hate me, or maybe he will. Yet maybe he will not forget me, I hope. I will leave tomorrow.

CHAPTER 19

The next afternoon was my regular Italian session with Gina, but I was tired and called her to cancel. There was no answer at her number, so I decided to meet her as usual, and she began by fiercely drilling me on her favorite subject: abolishing all pernicious anglicisms from my Italian conversation. Finally I conceded the battle and begged her to ease off.

"What's the matter with you, Darneau? You are a little slow, not at your best today."

"I don't know. Maybe the gears of my mind cannot shift into Italian today."

"Maybe your gears have shifted into Californian instead. Your old friend is not as old as I pictured, Darneau. She is absolutely lovely, but at the same time, how should I say it? Focused, serious, intensa in Italian. She came a long way to find you. Yet you didn't seem to be overly celebrating her arrival."

"No, it was less a celebration, more a confrontation."

"And what exactly is that supposed to mean?"

"I will tell you someday, Gina, but not today. I am not in the mood to ruin this nice afternoon."

"Fine. I will hold you to that promise."

She sounded disappointed. Maybe she had reason to be,

and maybe not. But she smiled up at me. "How long will your friend be here? Should we have a festa for her?"

"How long? Let me tell you something about Julie. She could be getting on a plane somewhere this very minute and nobody anywhere in the world would know. She doesn't do farewells. No festa for her."

"Let me know when she gets on the plane. I may have the festa then."

"Gina, someday soon I will tell you Julie's strange story, when we have the time and I have the willpower. For now, let me simply say that in the last twenty years I have seen her on just two occasions, both in Paris . . . until yesterday, when she stormed back into my peaceful life, pillaging my quiet pensione."

"Maybe her love for you has lasted twenty years."

"In Italy do they have love that lasts that long?"

"Eternità is an Italian word, Darneau. Put it on your vocabulary list."

⚜

That same night I sat alone in my room and tried to set down on paper the confounding narrative of the past few hours and days, this insidious, gothic fairy tale. I started over several times: the words would simply not come to express the inexpressible. I acknowledged to myself that there was no reason why my tired hands should not be shaking as I wrote these tormenting words, but the nervous trembling came from my mind, not my fingers. I understood so little of what was happening, and worse, why it had happened. I could not think rationally, I could not see through anything at all, while I felt the fierce tug of love that still existed between Julie and me. Each inconceivable time she dropped back into my life, I felt it. Yet the stark revelations about how she had treated her daughter, brutal slashes back at the truth for her, to be sure, cut even more deeply into my life. For me they affected nearly everything: how could I ever feel close to Julie again, when she had mindlessly shattered the young life of someone I was falling in love with? Julie was still beautiful, but she trailed unhappiness behind her wherever she went. And unlike me, she was fearless. She was afraid of nothing except perhaps growing old and less beautiful.

I tried to turn away from the illusory mirror of my life, one that I had stared into all this past year, day after day, looking at pale, cowardly reflections of anxiety and despair . . . until I had finally completely capitulated to them. Unlike Melissa, who never flinched in the face of reason, conceding nothing even when surrounded by adverse facts and arguments that she knew were true; unlike her, I had given up. Worse, I had run away. Somehow Melissa could always see the faint shaft of light far out in the sea of darkness. She retained unshakeable faith in me, had unmitigated hope for our future, and had endless, powerful belief in her love. Faith, hope, and love: I had not a shred of any of these three great Biblical virtues. And Melissa knew which was the greatest of the three . . . she overflowed with love.

The next day I saw Gina again after school. Actually, she was waiting for me by my classroom door, like a jumpy paparazza anxious for a picture and the rest of the story. Outside, the weather had turned dark and windy, unusual for October in

Tuscany, with a squall full of harsh tears blowing up the Arno river valley. We had to forgo our usual walk and instead hurried over to the local caffè. We found a corner table and sat there for an uncomfortable minute or two, completely silent. Gina was smiling, waiting for me to begin; I was not smiling, waiting forever for the words to come.

She looked up at me and said, "Have you forgotten what you promised?"

"I think I have."

"Let me refresh your memory: the strange story of Julie Artemis played out in Paris and California."

Finally the words started to come. Three espressos later I had finished telling Gina the true, if somewhat abridged, joint life histories of Julie and Melissa, and my two improbable, hapless episodes of love, loss, and heartache in Paris—separated and connected by almost twenty years, a full generation of isolation and failure. The story ended, of course, with the last dramatic scene at the local trattoria: Julie's sad epiphany, her final descent into truth, and her disquieting, unforeseen appeal for love and forgiveness.

Gina sat there motionless and incredulous. "You mean a nineteen-year-old student young enough to be your daughter, and you, a sentimental American wanderer teaching in Paris, fell in love? And this girl turns out to be the daughter of your first great love, who suddenly, mysteriously disappeared from your life and then rose from the dead twenty years later? This didn't really happen, did it? It's just a sorry fictitious libretto that Verdi would compose a tragic opera for. The only question is which character will commit suicide in the final act."

She waited for me to speak, but my thoughts and my words had vanished entirely.

"So, Darneau, what should you do now?"

"I was going to ask you the same question."

"I think you will return to Paris and let things work out naturally, like Michelangelo's life: agony or ecstasy."

"He was an artist and genius. For the rest of us it's always something in between, isn't it? Usually something closer to agony."

"Nicely put, Darneau. Your rhetoric never disappoints. But you remind me of someone. Who was it who said, 'Cheer up, the worst is yet to come'?"

"Mark Twain, probably. Maybe Oscar Wilde."

"Doubtless a cynic like you. I promise you it wasn't a Florentine. You need more time here, Darneau, to work out of your black humor. Yet I predict you will go back to Melissa in Paris, and you will not return to Firenze."

"No, Gina, I may travel to Paris for the Toussaint holiday, and then I will come back here for two reasons. First, I will not break my contract and leave my students high and dry in mid-semester. Second . . ." But here I fell silent. I was looking into the deep wells of Gina's dark brooding eyes, and for a brief moment I could not put my thoughts into words. "Second . . . I like it here." It was one of my many evasive lies, a harmless one for a change.

"Darneau, it appears to me that you and Julie both paid heavily through those endless years, and your penance lasted a long time for such a short period of love together."

"Are you saying we were cursed and punished for our sins?"

"I didn't know you believed in sin, Darneau."

"It's just a figure of speech."

"Well, you know what the great Marcello Mastroianni said about sin."

"No, tell me."

"It's not technically premarital sex if you don't get married."

It was so typically Gina, to bring out the guns of her Italian humor to blow away my chaotic, ragged sense of reality. Like Annelise, she understood things about me that I had no awareness of, though without providing Annelise's insightful explanations or reluctant, flawless advice. That was not Gina's style. Still, she could see into my soul, no matter how hard I tried to cover it. I wonder what the Italian word for percipience is . . . I could read it in her soft brown eyes, which were looking right through me. Whatever their word is, she was born with it in her heart.

I asked her, "Gina, what's going through your mind after hearing this storia bizzarra?"

"I'm thinking how two months ago you could not ask me that question in my language."

"You are taking great pains to teach it to me. I'm very grateful."

"You are a fast learner, Darneau, and you never forget anything."

"Yes, that is my most unforgivable weakness."

"No," she smiled. "You have others, worse."

"Name them."

"Self-pity is one. Sentimentality is the other."

"I thought all Italians were sentimental. Even Fellini has Paola wave to Marcello at the end of *La Dolce Vita*."

"Mio amico, that film is a withering parade of grotesque and delirious scenes put into focus by a master storyteller and satirist; yet what you remember is the sad final wave by a pretty teenage waitress from a romantic seaside restaurant."

"Precisamente. Fellini was smart enough to understand that people walking out of a movie theater remember the last scene after everything else."

"So what will you remember of us, if you go back to Paris and never return?"

"I told you, that's not going to happen."

"But pretend it does happen. Indulge me, Darneau."

"I will not forget an Italian tutor who was not happy with my perfectly acceptable accent, so she drove me to insanity trying to force me to sound just like her."

"That's all you'll remember?"

"You didn't ask me to itemize every single memory of Florence. That wasn't the question."

"I thought you might say that you would remember our walks down Via del Carota . . . because those were the only times I knew you were happy."

"You have been a true friend here, Gina, I think more than a friend."

"I'm not digging for compliments, Darneau, or for your affection."

"You're not? Then it is not fair to play with my feelings in the language you are teaching me to love."

"Did you realize that you used all three languages when

you recounted the tragic, twenty-year Paris love saga? When you described Julie's role, you spoke mostly English. When you talked about Melissa, it was only in French. When you were finishing, when you were finally talking about yourself, you spoke nothing but Italian. Not that you didn't include a few egregious anglicisms."

"Gina, I was not going to mention it, but Julie pointed out to me that you spoke only Italian when the three of us were together."

"Yes, and she understood me perfectly, didn't she? She needed no translation."

"Do I detect a whiff of feline feminine intuition?"

"Julie è un serpente. She sees nothing but her own way. On the other hand, I think I would like to know Melissa. She is vulnerable, even more than I. As for Julie, let me know in any language when I can drive her to the airport."

"I don't see your vulnerability, Gina. It doesn't slip through your Italian syntax or your Florentine bonhomie."

"Perhaps you haven't looked closely enough. I said you were sentimental, not sensitive."

CHAPTER 20

Friday was the last day of school before the All Saints half-term holiday. I waited for Gina to finish her final class, then we joined her family for an aperitivo at her father's centuries-old villa, located on a windy hillside not far from the school he had run for over twenty-five years. Gina and I begged off their dinner invitation, and we settled for a quick snack at a caffè near the Stazione di Santa Maria Novella, from where I had train reservations back to Paris.

Gina's first question surprised me. "Darneau, did you get a one way or round trip ticket?" And she added, unnecessarily, "Just kidding!"

"I told you, I will be back in a week, or less. You seem to be in a good mood for a farewell scene."

"Yes, I love this holiday and the cool weather it brings. And not all people cry when someone they love is leaving."

"Actually. I don't recall ever seeing you cry, Gina. Tears don't come easily to your unblinking dark eyes."

"But they do. Just never in public, and never around you."

"When was the last time you remember crying?"

"Ask me that next week. I may have a precise date, time, and place for you. But enough about tears in Firenze. Soon you will see Melissa in Paris and tell her the good news about her mother's visit to Italy."

"She deserves to know the truth, Gina."

"Yes, and what will happen then? If the two of you fall back in love, it will be stranger than ever. She will see in you the fugitive outlaw that you are, who betrayed her love. And you may never be able to look at her again without remembering that you left her in Paris because you loved her mother. The intrigue will just be beginning."

A pause followed, as an unsummoned touch of melancholy fell over the two of us. I finally broke the moody silence.

"Tell me something helpful before I have to get on my train."

"Okay, I will. You must never decide what you're going to say to Melissa until you say it to yourself in Italian, to make sure it doesn't hurt her. English has too many cruel words that cut, and French is full of lies. You will hear music when you think in Italian, forgotten melodies."

"Yet I never envision Melissa when I think in your language. The two conceptions don't fit together."

She stared intently at me. "When I'm looking at you, Darneau, before you utter a word, I know that you love her."

"You have a talent, Gina. Not only do you read minds, you read sad faces as well, or is it the same thing?"

"No, I can read only your face. You are too skillful at camouflaging your mind somewhere beneath your dark heart."

"I believe I asked for final words of advice, not a critique of my inborn pervasive dishonesty."

"There is an old Italian saying: Never follow advice unless it shouts what you've been thinking all along."

"Yes, I know that maxim. It has been my guiding star, and it has never failed to get me in trouble."

"Then one last thought, mio caro. Don't promise the impossible, because it might end with everything in flames. And it will be you, not Melissa, who has lit the match."

⚜

When my train arrived in Paris, it left me at the Gare de Lyon on the same voie where I boarded the eastbound train to Italy three months before. I wondered why in some years time seems to rush by, but these days I didn't have that feeling at all. The half-term of teaching, the Italian lessons with Gina, the months in Florence had been filled with contentment, good food and wine, and beautiful autumn weather, even though the spirit and memory of Melissa Artemis reached stealthily into every hour of every day.

But I was tired after the long ride. I got to the Métro Ten line, avoiding the nasty Châtelet correspondence with its long exhausting corridors, and sortied at Odéon. At the top of the steps I felt the north wind pricked by an early season frost. Then, like a wily veteran homing pigeon, my steps retraced a familiar path to the Hôtel Saint-André des Arts where Julie and I had lived together in a different age. I took a small single room, coincidentally on the same étage as our old chambre double, which had featured an antique clawfoot bathtub with a built-in seat at the end. My new room, with no tub, no shower, just a low bidet, was down at the end of the couloir which, I suspected, had not been painted since we stayed here twenty years ago.

I wanted to rest for a bit, and truthfully the last thing I wanted was to show up at my old apartment at some odd hour, not knowing who might be there or what changes were going on in Melissa's life, assuming she was even still living there. In any event, I couldn't fall asleep, so after a while I went down the hall, showered off the dusty kilometers of my voyage en train and left the hotel. I walked slowly west through the heavy November gloom, down the rue St-André des Arts, crossing the Boulevard Saint-Germain toward rue de Sèvres. I gave myself plenty of time to consider what I would say, thinking, in spite of Gina's heart-felt advice, that I would not rehearse it in Italian, even though I risked losing the harmony of her version.

I arrived at my old address, entered the code which let me into the courtyard, and climbed the steep steps to my door, on which a scribbled note was taped: "Liam, leave poem under mat. I'm at the American Library wasting time."

Liam? I vaguely recalled a friend of hers named Liam. At least he didn't have a key to the place. My own spare clef was probably still behind the brick in a crevice halfway up the steps, but I couldn't quite bring myself to barge in, wait around, and scare her senseless when she returned. So I decided to wander over to the library and see if she was still there.

I headed out into the septième arrondissement past the École Militaire and over to the rue du Général Camou, where, a generation ago as a young college student, I had first discovered the American Library and kept up with its collection of *Sports Illustrated,* impossible to find anywhere else, and other English language periodicals.

When I arrived at the library, I opened the outside door, walked through the entryway, and saw her immediately, sitting at a far table across the room, reading intently, the only way she knew how to read. The room fell completely silent, as if there was no one else in the whole city. A little rectangular band of autumn sunlight splashed through the high window and fell across her eyes, and I remembered Yuri Zhivago catching sight of Lara Antipova's sunlit face captured forever by David Lean's camera, in another library, in another time. Melissa didn't notice me right away, though she glanced in my direction. I thought: she doesn't recognize me, or is blinded by the light shining in her eyes, forgetting that I had the advantage of knowing she was at this library while she thought I was living in a different world, she had no idea where. I never moved, stood there for what seemed an hour and was probably only a minute or two. Then she dropped her magazine, walked directly over to me, reached out with both hands as if to keep herself from falling, and said, "Am I hallucinating, monsieur?"

We went outside and her next words were, "You're a bastard, Darneau."

"Then why are you hugging me?"

"Because you're my bastard. But you should never have left me like that. You duped me. It was criminal. It was sinful."

We huddled together there by the library steps and the words gushed like blood from Melissa's quavering voice. "You know, Darneau, I've had no dreams since you left. And the nights are long."

"Maybe you aren't thinking before you fall asleep. Empty minds are dreamless."

"But I am thinking, I'm always thinking. I never stop thinking of ways I can get back at you. Revenge fills my mind. Hours later I fall asleep."

DIARY OF MELISSA ARTEMIS

November 2, 1983

I was reading an old *New Yorker*—all the American library magazines are months old, like the tasteless, stale dated American corn flakes sitting on the Monoprix shelves. For some reason I glanced up and saw, standing inside the entrance near the reception desk, a man whose long dark hair reminded me of Darneau. He didn't come into the reading room where I was sitting, just stood there looking around, but I knew he had seen me, and I knew who it was. Our smiles crashed together across the room like a barreling head-on train wreck—why am I writing this effroyable prose? I haven't written like this since he abandoned me alone in his apartment three months ago, comme le salaud qu'il est.

Yet I rushed over to him like a moron and could barely stop myself from embracing him right there in front of the most stoic librarian in Paris. After we got outside I did hug him, moronically, totally forgetting my book bag which I had to go back inside to retrieve.

My first words to him were, "You're a bastard, Darneau."

And of course he agreed. He had to.

"Yes," he said. "Do you want a written apology? I think I could come up with a pretty good one for you."

Then he said simply, "Melissa, let me start at the end of the story. I have just seen Julie in Florence where I am living and teaching at the international school. She tracked me down there, found me at my pensione, and we talked about everything. She finally confessed to me who your biological father was, not his name precisely, but it was some foreign student she knew before me. She was pregnant when I met her and pregnant when she returned to California, with no warning, with no explanation, leaving me alone in our Paris hotel room, bewildered, stunned, heartbroken. She told me nothing and never contacted me in any way for years and years, until last fall."

There was more to the story, but that's the bitter gist of it. I told Darneau I knew all along Nico was not my father; I couldn't have such a smart, savvy businessman as he is for a blood relative.

I said, "I told you she was a lying quim, but you didn't believe me."

"Truthfully, I suspect I did, Melissa. I just didn't know what a quim was."

"Well, now you know."

"That's true, but I didn't really know what to believe then or what to do. So I left."

"Yes, Darneau, you are known for your decisive irresolution."

I asked him how Julie had found him, he told me, and our conversation meandered on as we walked back to 50, rue de Sèvres. It was fall, and les feuilles mortes were drifting down—demonstrating again that the cycle of life is short and sad. I don't need any more proof.

We climbed the steps together, I unlocked the door and invited him into his own apartment.

CHAPTER 21

After Melissa opened the door, she stood aside and let me go in first. I would not have known where I was if I hadn't seen my name on the boîte aux lettres. The living room was unrecognizable. Not only was my old couch gone and replaced with a new one in a plush dark red fabric, it was moved to a different position, now facing a large screen TV that she must have brought over from her rue Bonaparte apartment. A floor to ceiling built-in bookcase took over the wall where my couch used to be. Flowers, real, artificial, or imaginary, I had no idea, were everywhere.

"Well, what do you think of your old bachelor pad, Darneau? It took me three days to scrub the crust off your bathtub."

"I never take baths. And showers are self-cleaning."

"In your world, maybe. How do you like your salle de séjour?"

"Intéressante. Non, incroyable. It can't be your apartment. No books kicking around on the floor. No scented candles glimmering everywhere."

"The books are on the shelves, not alphabetically arranged like yours, I'm not sorry to say. Actually, not arranged in any way. And the candles are in the bedroom where I watch them burn down and flicker out when I should be dreaming."

Then I remembered Liam's poem. "Melissa, you forgot to look under the mat."

"For the poem? I did look—it wasn't there."

"Who is your poet friend? Have I met him?"

"Probably not. He's just an old friend."

I remembered using that same expression before Gina's tough appraisal of Julie in Florence. And how old could Liam be, twenty-one, twenty-four?

"I have a lot of friends, Darneau. You were gone. Do you want to meet them? Liam composes long poems about plagues and death, la condition humaine. He gives them to me to edit . . . there are too many words. Once you get rid of half of them, you might have a poem, so I slash and cut and hand him back twelve lines about mountain pastures and shepherds looking up at stars. Are you jealous of Liam? Trust me, he is not someone you would envy."

"That's probably true, Melissa, because jealousy is an emotion of the young. It is a habit that has passed me by. What replaces it is not envy of any other person, like your friend Liam. It is replaced by an awareness of loss, not of defeat exactly, but the absence of personal bravado. Does that make sense?"

"Darneau, I've missed your asking me if your scrambled thoughts make sense. They never do. You usually stop talking just before I have a chance to say, 'You're kidding, right?'"

I'm writing down these oblivious remarks and ideas as I lie back on the bed in my tiny hotel room. Melissa asked me if I was learning to speak Italian. A little, I said. Why was I diminishing the truth again? It is becoming worse than an addiction. But I knew I feared truth because, contrary to the Biblical teaching, when you know the truth it does not set you free. It usually does the opposite.

I realized I was losing my concentration, so I put down my pen and let my mind roam through the three tenses, past, present, and future. Melissa plays a role in all of them, wielding the vendetta of her convictions with enough power to frustrate, even unintentionally destroy, my capacity to live. She asked me how long Julie had stayed in Florence. She pretended not to be surprised when I told her that the day after our first dinner together Julie left in her usual manner, without the slightest hint of an au revoir. Melissa explained that she did that to intrigue me. It's part of Julie's contrived mysterious persona. I wasn't sure I agreed with Melissa this time. I had seen Julie's tears—they may have been driven by frustration as well as remorse, but they were not staged. Melissa was unswayed.

"Darneau," she countered. "It's one of her tricks. You are falling for it like the sucker you are. Her sudden, mystifying departures: mon dieu, why do they never last?"

"The first one did."

"That's true. So now she wants you back, though that desire may be no more honest than her remorse. She once told me that when her parents took her to church on Saturday afternoons for confession, she would lie to the priest, make up a bunch of sins, then never recite the penance he gave her. She would walk right out of the church the way she walked away from you. Neither exit involved an act of contrition. Julie's heart is selfish, hollow, empty. And now she wants you to fill it back up."

It was not easy to withstand the intense sincerity of Melissa's outpouring. And I couldn't deny that it still deeply hurt to recall and to feel the unbearable weight of Julie's deceptions, even after her earnest crusade to find me in Florence. It will take time, I told myself, and then we'll see what happens. I'm not optimistic.

So I'll try and sleep now, and in the morning I will have time to think about facing the uncontrollable future. I'll get up early, when the day is still full of hope: November dawn. Tonight perhaps I will dream of some helpful little Florentine scolaro volunteering to clean my classroom chalkboard, to wash away all the thoughts and words and marks left there at the end of the day, to expunge the scattered traces of my emotional bedlam. Buona notte, amico mio.

DIARY OF MELISSA ARTEMIS

November 3, 1983

Darneau and I walked over to the little Italian restaurant we both like on rue du Cherche Midi. I have to admit I was impressed when he ordered for us in what sounded to me like pretty fluent Italian. The chef Tomaso was even more astounded because he didn't know Darneau had been teaching in Florence, and they had communicated for years only in French. I asked Darneau how he could have picked up the language so easily, so quickly. He just said that he had a good tutor.

I nodded. "Who is she?"

He said, "What do you mean . . . she?"

I said, "Men teach science and technology. Women teach languages and the arts."

He told me that remark was not worthy of a response.

Tomaso insisted we have his seafood pasta dish, the specialità della casa, and it was probably good, but I couldn't taste a thing. Still, our conversation was not as strained as you might have supposed. We didn't exactly pick up where we had left off last summer: those emotions were scattered in the cold dark gap of our separation. But we caught up on three months of our lives, our schools, our classes, what we were reading; both of us kept away from any talk of our feelings or the future. We stayed well back from the edge of that cliff. Even I was not brave enough to go there.

He did tell me that he enjoyed his teaching in Italy more than he anticipated. I told him, Darneau, you are a born teacher.

All you need is one good story and a couple of good students and you're soaring. He said he would be in Paris for just a few days but mentioned the possibility of my visiting Florence over the Christmas holiday. He mentioned it, I say, because it didn't come without a slight bit of hesitancy, or am I imagining this in my suspicious little mind? So I didn't commit, even though I think I would follow him anywhere.

At one point I asked him if he knew Julie had never told Nico who my real father was.

He answered, "That doesn't surprise me, though nothing about Julie could surprise me."

I said, "Nico even thought it was you who might have gotten Julie pregnant, but I told him I could not be related to such a cold-hearted bastard."

"Thank you."

"She still hasn't told Nico or me who my father is, not that I'm losing any sleep over it. Nico is father enough for me." But D. didn't say anything more.

We lingered over tiramisu and coffee, not wanting to reach the end of this reunion dinner, prolonging the evening until we were the only patrons left, just sitting there, talking, building a campfire as serveurs like to complain. Nonetheless, the end had to come, and Darneau finally walked me back to rue de Sèvres, past the darkened Bon Marché, and said, with perhaps a trace of indecision, that he wouldn't come up to the apartment, though I invited him. After all, we had lived there together for most of July. I told him that I wouldn't want him to have any inappropriate sexual thoughts, and he answered with his usual sad smile. "I've been having them all my life."

Then he said, and I want to record his exact words: "I have never felt this mélange of love and fear. It is paralyzing." I could sense the fierce intensity of what he said, and I wondered if he could foretell which of those two emotions, love or fear, would win in his heart.

One could argue, I suppose, that the three of us, Darneau, Julie, and I, have been cast into insupportable roles. Julie wants to slip back into Darneau's life. Darneau wants to change everything for the better. And I want Julie to be struck by a guided missile.

CHAPTER 22

THE FOLLOWING DAYS OF TOUSSAINT WERE FILLED with what seemed like a reenactment of our pre-Florentine lives, albeit without any classes at the college which was closed. One day Melissa and I walked around the Jardin des Plantes, visited their little zoo whose animals, including their two elephants, were all eaten by the starving Parisians during the Prussian siege of 1870-71. We strolled through the Natural History Museum and pretended we had all the time in the world to waste away, when in reality we knew we had so little.

The last night before I was to leave we had a farewell dinner at Le Fouquet's—Melissa insisted on treating me, said Nico could afford it. Nico had inspected my apartment in the early days after I left for Italy. Melissa admitted that he was responsible for the new built-in bookcase after tripping over a stack of books she had left on the floor. At Fouquet's we went upstairs to the formal dining room which was dimly lit and quiet, perfectly suited for melancholy conversation while we ate our soles meunières.

"Darneau, the strange thing is that even though my mother flees back to California every time she sees you, I feel somehow that there is still a barrier between you and me, but different than before."

"I feel it, too. I think it's the lingering wreckage of Julie's hold on me through all those years, ending in the inconceivable news that she is your mother. How could it seem right or proper or natural that I was falling in love with a young student who was the daughter of the great lost love of my life? It seems impossible. Although Julie may have been a brief, youthful love, she is still burned into my memory, worse, into my consciousness, irrevocably. As time went on, the tensions and pressures became unbearable for me. So I left."

"You know, Darneau, throughout the whole past year we have been apart for most of it: my long semester in Geneva, your exile in Florence. No phone calls, no letters, no goodbyes even."

"Yes, you took French leave, Melissa."

"Et toi, mon ami, tu as filé à l'anglaise."

"What is the difference?"

"It is less polite to say it in English, I think. One would think we were mortal enemies, Darneau. What are we?"

"Truthfully," I said, "I don't know. But this time, at least, although I am going back, no one is sneaking away."

"It's still a separation."

"But not a long one. The Christmas holiday is not far off. The churches in Florence will be beautiful."

"Darneau, did you really want to invite me to come to Italy?"

"Do you have to ask?"

"You don't absolutely have to go back to Florence at all, do you?"

"Melissa, I signed a contract, I have classes stranded in midterm, and I have no job here."

"Then I will come to visit you after my exams, but I will fly. I'm not riding on that filthy train which takes forever."

"Fine, I will reserve you a room where Julie stayed."

"That's not funny, Darneau. You are never amusing when you joke about Julie. Actually, she came to mind the other day during my astronomy class. Neither light nor love nor truth can escape from the black hole of her starless heart. I put that one in my diary."

Then she pulled out a little wrapped package and said, "I have a going away gift for you." I opened it and found an old 45 RPM record by Ketty Lester called "Love Letters."

"This is very nice, Melissa, but I don't even have a record player."

"You don't need to listen to it, Darneau, it's a mnemonic device. I want you to prop it up in the middle of your desk so you see it every time you sit down to study your Italian. Ketty Lester is not her real name, you know. Her real name is . . . I forget. It doesn't matter. What matters is it will make you want to write to me. It's a spark of love. You get the point?"

⚜

I felt a little guilty, well, not guilty, but a little selfish for not making more of an effort to see Annelise—there was so little time. I did phone her from my hotel one night, and no one answered. She may have left the city for the holiday. So I wrote her a short letter recounting Julie's surprise attack on my Florentine hideout and a few details of my trip back to Paris and Melissa. I didn't have to explain what prompted this to Annelise; she would know immediately that I missed both of them, even if I wouldn't admit it to myself. It would have been nice to see Annelise and get her take on everything, but it didn't happen. Nevertheless, I can picture her calm reaction and hear her sage advice: "Darneau, Melissa is still young and her love is a wild heart-fire. Don't let it burn out of control again. She loves without thinking. So do you." Of course, Annelise would never have phrased it so melodramatically. Her style is Germanic, rational, intelligent, cautious, level-headed. How did I ever get involved with her?

As my train pulled into the Firenze Santa Maria Novella station I found myself agreeing with Melissa that it was a long boring ride. I could fly if I had to, but I don't have to. It's not that I have a deep phobia about flying, but trains are so damned safe. If something goes wrong with a train engine, at least you're already on the ground. Still and all, I was tired and dragging my bag slowly down the steps, only to see Gina waiting at the gate. She spotted me and waved, flashing her wide unabashed smile, her ubiquitous zest for life on full display. I smiled in spite of myself and then asked her how she knew which train I would be arriving on. She started to laugh and said she had met all possible Paris connections that day and finally found one with me on it.

I thanked her profusely, but she added, "Non c'è problema. There weren't that many. Believe it or not, Darneau, I half-expected you to have Melissa on your arm as you got off the train."

"No," I said, "but you may meet her over Christmas. She's planning to fly in during her winter break."

"That will be nice. I think I can find her a room in the Santa Maria Convent guest house not far from our school—a good place for daily Mass and to attend to her spiritual duties."

"What about my spiritual duties?"

"I don't think I've ever heard you express any interest in them."

"Maybe it's time I did."

"No," she said. "Don't start going to church, Darneau. It might further damage you mentally."

We found her Fiat in the parcheggio and I slumped back into the passenger seat as she navigated through the city traffic toward my pensione.

"Darneau, I'm anxious to hear your Paris stories, but for now you should get some rest. Your students will be waiting for you first thing in the morning."

So I thanked her for meeting my train, said good night and soon collapsed onto my familiar little bed . . . but not before placing the "Love Letters" record carefully in the middle of my desk. Yet it was Gina I was thinking about as I fell asleep, about her warm and generous spirit, maybe not more than I expected but more than I deserved.

⚜

The first day back in school after a holiday is normally half filled with rejuvenated kids ready to learn, the other half of them dazed and still a million miles away. It felt good to be back in the classroom, though I already missed the flow of Paris life and the challenging repartee of Melissa's capricious banter. After our last class Gina shanghaied me outside my room and we slipped back into our usual student-tutor roles.

"I see you have not completely forgotten your Italian, Darneau. You are prattling right along, doing better than I would have expected. If we can only get rid of the annoying French rhythm of your sentences, and replace it with good undulating Italian dynamics."

"Gina, I did get to use my new language in a little ristorante near my apartment, or should I say, Melissa's apartment. I've been going in there for years, and the chef was shocked to hear me speaking to him in his native tongue. If you come to Paris, I will take you there; the food is excellent."

"Yes, there is no city in Europe where you find yourself more than a bus stop away from good Italian cuisine, even if it's just the best cheesy pizza in town. So, Darneau, you are back in Firenze as you promised, a bit to my surprise. Tell me the news from Paris."

"To be brief, I found Melissa in the American library and she immediately called me a bastard for deserting her last August without even saying goodbye."

Gina looked up and said, "Well, for sure she was right about that. Did she then fall into your arms and stop your heartbeat with her love?"

"No, to tell the truth, we resumed the same tentative—I was going to say demoralizing—relationship that I had forsaken last summer. It was as if we were afraid of each other and the deep waters in which we had been shipwrecked. We weren't exactly sinking, but we weren't getting anywhere either . . . floundering, for sure."

"Then you are lucky the Seine is not a wide river."

"Have you spent much time in Paris, Gina?"

"Yes and no. I've been there a few times, but honestly I have never been seriously tempted to stay. Paris is like Milano or Roma, immense, noisy, full of speeding cars and fashion statements and businessmen running around chasing money, evading taxes, hiding their mistresses—too fast and loud for me. There is no time for contemplation in these great cities."

"Next time you go there, Gina, you must boycott la Rive droite. The soft charm of Paris is on the other side of the river."

"Darneau, I have an idea. Would you like to come to Sienna with me for a weekend? It is just about my favorite city, even though it fought many battles against Firenze and has a few too many churches. You know how Italians have always loved to pray and eat, but they have never liked to walk very far, so they first built churches and then restaurants on every other block. Our specialty is laziness . . . pigrizia, did I teach you that word?"

"No, and don't tell me. I can already hear you: prendine nota."

I finished telling Gina about Paris and Melissa, and she talked me into the Sienna trip, which really wasn't more than an hour away and, she added, is practically empty of tourists in November. I say talked me into it, but truthfully it sounded like a nice idea right away, and I had somehow missed Sienna in my first life as a student vagabond.

⚜

Our excursion coincided with the American Thanksgiving holiday, which was half-heartedly observed by our international school in deference to the many students from the States. As one of my Cornell professors once put it: "It's not a bad holiday, even if it was invented by the Puritans." So we drove down there on that Thursday and checked in at an old Sienese hotel that Gina said was famous for romantic weekend getaways.

"Is that what this is?" I asked her.

"Life is like this weekend," she answered. "It is short, but it can either be depressing and meaningless or it can be joyous and unforgettable. The choice is up to you."

"Is this a choice or a test?"

"You are a teacher. You know there is no difference."

"Some days I wonder if I have a choice."

"Darneau, if there's one thing I learned from reading Machiavelli, it's that we always have choices, and we must take advantage of them because there is no way to avoid them."

After that daunting beginning she walked me down to the Piazza del Campo, the historic town square and home to the famed Palio, a horse race on brick pavement for brave imbeciles.

"Why do you call it a square, Gina, when it is clearly an oval?"

"Basta, Darneau! You will not quibble away this weekend with thoughtless semantics. You will be chivalrous and forgiving."

"But those are Italian virtues. Remember, you were the one who designated me your francese-americano madman."

"I didn't say madman. You tacked that on to make me look unkind and to give yourself an alibi for your erratic behavior. Nonetheless, I will take you to the Cathedral. If you brighten up your outlook, they might let you in to look around."

Actually, they didn't let either of us in as it was closed for their intervallo del pranzo, so we decided to follow their schedule and settled into a little Greek taverna featuring savory, spicy food and chilled white wines. The cathedral could wait, Gina said, it's been there for eight hundred years.

The lunch was excellent, and the Cathedral was admittedly a beautiful lesson in medieval art and architecture, though I was shaking a bit as we climbed to the fearsome top via the endless, twisting bell tower steps.

Nothing slips by Gina, of course. "Darneau, do you suffer from claustrophobia or acrophobia? You are definitely showing your nerves."

"Yes, I have many phobias. The worst of them is gynophobia, fear of women."

"Yes, but I know the remedy for that."

"Do you?"

"Senza dubbio. I will cure you later, if you want. It won't take long."

The afternoon was almost perfect, marred only by brief forays into two or three of the local boutiques where Gina, like most women, shopped enjoyably without buying a thing. Eventually we traced our way back to the little hotel Gina had picked out.

"Darneau," she began, "I reserved the only room in this place that has two single beds—the receptionist said we could push them together or move them farther apart. She also believes in the concept of choice."

"Thank you. But what if the choice is made for us, not by us?"

"That's absurd. You don't know how senseless that sounds, Darneau. You need some guidance, some direction in your life. You need a consilium vitae. It's time to do something meaningful."

"Perhaps that time has passed, and I was fooled again."

"Perhaps your time is still coming."

"You are ever the optimist, Gina. Do you know the expression: is the glass half-full or half-empty? I believe you always see it half-full."

"I believe if it's a good vintage, drink it. Although I admit that everything in life doesn't turn out the way I plan, including some of the wine I choose."

We were both tired after the long afternoon of flânerie, from traipsing over nearly every medieval square metre of Sienna's centro città. So we decided to have a light meal, una cena leggera, as Gina put it, in our hotel dining room. Afterwards we had coffee and amaretto in the little sitting room and I found myself for the first time, really, asking personal questions about Gina's past.

I began shamelessly. "Gina, have you ever been engaged or

married? You are what, twenty-six now? I always thought that Italian men went for youth and Italian brides wanted to have their first bel bambino while la nonna was young enough to take care of it."

"Yes, there is some truth in what you say, Darneau, although not enough to outweigh the effrontery of your question, phrased in your usual artless style which I am getting used to: impolite, rude, a dire il vero. Not Florentine at all."

"Yes, I know. . . . I'm living in Tuscany but I don't abide by all their customs or etiquette, at least, not yet."

"Bene. To answer your question, I have never been married, which is not so rare these days with more Italian girls going on to university. I got engaged while taking classes at the Firenze education college; at least I had a fede ring which I can show you if you need proof. The marriage wasn't meant to be. He graduated and went to work for a big bank in Rome; I graduated and stayed home waiting for you. When you finally showed up, you had left your heart in Paris with a young ladra who will never give it back. And here we are, sharing a camera d'albergo in Sienna, an Italian tutor and her heartless student."

"Chapeau! You are nothing, Gina, if not open, amusing and honest. Not things I am good at."

"Perhaps not, although your bizarre life this last year probably does not lend itself to unmasking your emotions. And is there any natural law that mandates emotional honesty? If there is no duty to tell the truth to another person, why should guilt alone require it?"

"Is it guilt I suffer from or merely dim-witted lunacy? Blindly loving a twenty-year-old Parisian student escaped from the pages of a romantic Victor Hugo novel?"

"No, Darneau, from the pages of Shakespeare. You are like Othello—you love too well, but not wisely."

"It's true I've never understood much about love, or why I'm here with you tonight."

"I think you're confusing my affection with Melissa's love."

"Am I? What is the distinction? Maybe there isn't any."

"There is, but you will have to draw the line. Just don't wake me by calling out Melissa's name in the middle of the night."

We finished our drinks and climbed the old stone steps to our room, which, Gina laughed, were probably not steep enough to trigger my phobia, though truthfully my nerves were rattling me a bit as we unlocked the door. The beds had been turned back and shoved together by some Eros-inspired cameriera.

Had the choice been made for me? Before I could think of an answer, Gina had put her arms around me and raised her lips, which still tasted of amaretto. I felt the kiss and her peerless Italian bosom pushing faultlessly into my chest. How should I put it? Finito.

I could describe the act of love that followed, but what would be the point? Others have done it better . . . D. H. Lawrence, Henry Miller, James Joyce. Sex between nineteen-year-old lovers like Julie and me had been passionate and beautiful, life imitating art. For me now, it was still beautiful but less about art—still passionate but now drenched with remembrance and reflections. Of course, I said nothing of this to Gina. She was not an analytic lover. It was enough for her to feel it, express it, share it.

She sighed. "Did you hear bells ringing, Darneau? Was it because of me or just the cathedral?"

Before we fell asleep, I thought ruefully that if I meant to be loyal to Melissa, I should never have come to Sienna, should never have walked with Gina down the Via del Carota practicing my Italian, should never . . . should never . . . why torture myself like this? I had been making love to Annelise and others for years. What was the difference? But I knew the answer. The difference was that Melissa would look at me with her deep blue eyes frozen on mine and say, "You slept with her, Darneau."

Gina had told me, "I almost didn't kiss you, not because of Melissa, but because of you. I didn't want that slice of guilt separating us. Maybe if I knew Melissa in person, I would have held back, or maybe I would have tried to wait for you. It's complicated, love is, but it's not meant always to punish us. I'm not into guilt that much anyway. It's an overrated emotion. It's not even a mortal sin, is it?"

"I'm not an authority on what sin is, Gina. I think I know it when I see it, but I'm not seeing too clearly right now."

"Then don't worry about what happened. Remember the most important, most elemental lesson."

"And what is that?"

"That there are no lessons." She shrugged slightly, a familiar mannerism I had gotten used to. "So, Darneau, will this change Melissa's plans to come to Firenze?"

"Should it?"

"Is it my call?"

"Let's say it is."

"Then she will come. I deserve to see my competition. I deserve to meet la jolie fille qui a enchanté son professeur, n'est-ce pas?"

"Merde alors! Vraiment, ça fait mal en français."

"Mais ça va, Darneau. If you take the sex out of it, what's left? That's what's important to me."

I think Gina drifted off first, sinking into oblivion, her long curly hair tumbling darkly all over the pure white pillow. I'm not sure what prevented me from sleeping, guilt or love? There was room for both in my unraveling psyche.

The rest of the holiday flowed peacefully by, now that the parameters had been established. We ended up spending just two nights at the hotel, perhaps because that was enough for Sienna in November, or possibly we didn't want to push our luck with a longer stay. There was no overt tension, we never felt ill at ease, yet we both felt by Saturday afternoon that it was time to leave. Gina said it best: Forty-eight hours of bliss is perfect, maybe even a few minutes too long, even in paradise.

CHAPTER 23

When I arrived back at my pensione, still a bit addled from the tumultuous emotions of Sienna, there were two letters waiting in my mail slot, one from Melissa and the other from Julie. Which do you think I opened first?

Mon cher Darneau,

When you first saw the return address on this envelope, you were probably deathly worried that I'm writing to cancel my trip to Florence. Au contraire, mon ami, my plane should arrive December 19th and my travel agent has booked ground transportation to your pensione. I'll phone you when the plane lands so you know when to expect me, late afternoon hopefully, if the pilot somehow makes it over the Alps.

I have not reserved a hotel room; can you take care of that for me? I trust you know the area better than my agent who suggested some big old hotel near the train station. You can do better.

I'd like to have a little kitchenette or at least a fridge to keep the champagne cold (that you will bring me). Make sure they speak one of my languages, something more intelligible than Italian. I'm not sure I trust you to interpret for me.

And, Darneau, get a haircut for Christmas. If we go into a church, I don't want the nuns mistaking you for Jesus.

Je t'embrasse,
Melissa

The other envelope was thicker because it contained both a letter from Julie and another from her to her daughter in Paris, that one still sealed in the unopened envelope marked "Return to sender".

The note to me was brief.

Darneau, if you see Melissa, can you give her this letter? That will provide her a second opportunity to ignore it. She has always been good at rejecting me. I think the address is current; I got it from Nico.

I have been wondering lately: what would have happened to us if I hadn't left you in Paris all those years ago? I guess we're not allowed to know what could happen in life, if we don't give it a chance. I remember telling one of my profs at Berkeley that I could have gotten an "A" in his course if I had wanted to. His response was quick: "No, you couldn't have, because you didn't." So now he would tell us that I could never have stayed with you, because I didn't. I suppose he's right, but it's pretty depressing.

Darneau, I'm not seeking forgiveness from Melissa—you know better than anyone that that ship has long sailed into the dark night. Yet one thought has crossed my mind: I'm wondering if I should try and track down Melissa's biological father. Then she could decide if she ever wanted to contact him. Maybe she has a little half-sister somewhere with China blue eyes like her natural father's; I remember his eyes, deep set, bluer than forget-me-nots . . . but then I not only forgot him, I never once talked to him after I met you. He has no idea that he has a daughter. What do you think?

Julie

What did I think? What did I think? My first thought was to burn both of Julie's letters and scatter the ashes off the Ponte Vecchio. Yet in the end I decided to save them for Melissa, in case she ever did become curious about her natural father who, when you come right down to it, was like the rest of us, a victim of Julie's far-flung pitiless deceit. I didn't open her letter to Melissa, which I figured would probably never be read by anyone, anytime, anywhere in the world, and of course I didn't have much of an inclination then to write back to Julie. Our ship too had disappeared over the farthest horizon.

A few days later I was surprised by a message asking me to stop in and see Gina's father in the headmaster's office. All the locals call him Pietro or just Signore, but when he had originally interviewed me in English, he told me to call him Pete. Actually, he had been born and raised in Brooklyn and didn't move to Italy until the 1950s—his English still carried a definite Brooklyn accent, not quite to the extent of dem bums or ax me anyt'ing, but it was there nevertheless. In a way it added to his charm, and maybe he preserved it intentionally, like Maurice Chevalier and his French-flavored English. Everyone at the school liked

Pietro for the simple reason that he liked all of them. He once told me that he hired teachers not for their academic credentials, but those whom he suspected students could bond with. He said, "I always studied harder for teachers I liked and admired, so that's been my recruitment M.O." In any event, I dropped in to see him after lunch and it didn't take him long to get to the point.

"Parlerò italiano, I think. I've heard you conversing with Gina. You've made remarkable progress in so little time."

"I've had an excellent teacher."

"Yes, she is good. That must be why every anglophone teenage boy signs up for her Italian classes. Not so many girls, though."

I rolled my eyes and thought to myself: where did he refine his male chauvinism, Brooklyn? Italy? I suppose it could have been anywhere, but I said nothing.

"Darneau, I would have to be blind not to notice how close you and Gina have become. My interest in this today is not so much as her father, but strictly as the director of this school, because you are two of my best teachers. Your personal relationship is none of my business, of course. So what's going on with it?"

This, needless to say, was perfect circuitry. The last thing I wanted was to plunge Pete into the turbulent waters of my past life in Paris, yet with Melissa arriving in a few days, how could it be completely buried? Easily, I surmised, if one is a complete, abject, lying coward.

"Pete," I began, "you don't need me to tell you that you have a pretty incredible daughter—una su un milion—and she has turned what I feared would be a difficult, lonely semester into one of deep satisfaction, not only teaching me her language but giving me a taste of your culture in her unique, gently teasing style. She saved me, Pete, to tell you the truth."

"So you will stay on for the second term? Our contract gives either of us the option to terminate it." He smiled. "If you decide to leave, just give me a week's notice, two if you're taking Gina with you. I won't be able to find anyone with your ear for languages—vous qui n'avez aucune peur de l'imparfait du subjonctif français—but maybe I can find someone who will never break my daughter's heart."

⚜

December 19th, a Monday, was the first day of our Christmas vacanza. True to her promise, Melissa called me from the airport and soon was pulling up to the pensione in a noisy private taxi, a Fiat, naturally. It was late afternoon and the pallid sun was struggling gamely in the west. The early winter season had begun to bite, with a touch of light, but no heat.

Melissa jumped out of the car, wearing a dark red French beret, a soft burnt umber leather jacket and high boots. I stopped the driver, who was already unloading her bags, and asked if he would take us to her hotel which was only a few blocks away. He quickly reloaded his trunk and smiled his 'va bene' at us.

The hotel was, as Melissa put it, perfectly absurdly Italian, from the old washed-out brick and lime stucco exterior to the dimly lit lobby with its venerable divano and dark wood receptionist's desk. But Melissa's room was brighter, with a window overlooking the giardino, and it did contain the requested little refrigerator humming softly in the background.

After the porter's buona serata, Melissa hung onto me and sighed, "I like Italy. I even like to hear you speak Italian now. Actually, I've been working on it, too, with tapes and my pocket dictionary, though mostly it's all about ordering food and asking directions to the museo or chiesa. Maybe I'll move here and study art history—there are a bunch of programs for foreign university students. And maybe I can take Italian lessons from your tutor."

"You will meet her tomorrow," I said. "We're invited to dinner at her family's villa up in the hills. It is beautiful there."

We ended up walking to a nearby family ristorante for dinner where Melissa ordered the entire meal for both of us in her new language, featuring Bruschetta Florentine and Filetto di Vitello Arrosto. She also featured heavy French intonation on her Italian which prompted the server to ask her in French to clarify her wine order. Blushing slightly, she switched to English in an attempt to throw him off his game, but he came back without missing a beat, "No problem, Signorina."

The vitello was delizioso, the time flew by and we were once again the last two customers lingering in a little Italian restaurant. On the walk back to her hotel she held onto me and said, "Darneau, I will love you forever."

I answered, "But what about tomorrow?"

"You've been saving that line, Darneau, it's not bad. Where do you get all your bons mots?"

"Why is it that whenever I say something clever, you always think I'm quoting someone?"

"Because you are a shameless literary thief. Where do you find them?"

I shrugged. "I steal from everybody, but mostly I steal from Pursewarden."

Her eyes shone with playful disdain. "Do you know the difference between love and truth?"

"Tell me, I'm listening." And I braced for one of her fearful verbal flourishes.

But she explained seriously. "Here is the difference: truth is the same no matter what time it is. Love changes every minute of every day. You can't describe it—it has no definition. Love shouldn't even be listed in dictionaries. It isn't in Larousse."

She looked at me, expecting me to laugh or at least smile, which I eventually did. There are two ways to lift Melissa's spirits. One is when she realizes she is amusing me; the second is when she sees she is aggravating me. She is unrivaled at both.

At her hotel she suggested I come up to her room in case I was too tired to walk home.

"Not tonight, Melissa, maybe tomorrow."

She shook her head. "You may not be invited tomorrow."

⚜

The following day broke blue and wet and cold—the mist was so thick it fell into the river like snow. Gina had offered to pick us up and drive with her to the villa, but I figured she would be needed early to help with the dinner, so I thanked her and said we'd get a taxi, but might need a ride home. We were to meet our driver at Melissa's hotel, and I have to admit I had never seen her so stylishly dressed. Stylish is not the right word, of course. Can a twenty-year-old sarcastic, recalcitrant college student dress elegantly? She wore a scoop neck short satin dress as bright green as good luck, with her high boots and high hair. I suspect stunning is the right word. She crushed it.

So I said, "I didn't think Melissa Artemis was an Irish name."

She came right back at me. "So my name makes me half Greek. The rest may be Irish, what do you know? Don't stand there with your mouth open, Darneau. We're going to a holiday dinner party, a soirée! Green is the perfect Christmas color."

"My apologies for the jaw dropping—you do look festively beautiful. My only regret is that I don't have an outfit that rises anywhere near your shimmering femme fatale benchmark, but you of all people know the limitations of my closet."

She nodded. "Yes, you do have many sartorial challenges."

We rode up the winding road to the Pietro Lorentino family villa, and I tried mentally to prepare myself for the imminently threatening social and verbal conflicts. In a few minutes Pete's house would be full of Italian humor and French irony, dangers everywhere.

Nevertheless, the introductions at the entrance went smoothly enough. Gina was dressed entirely in what I believe fashionistas call winter white, contrasting to perfection with her Mediterranean coloring and dark hair, her smile blinding like a sunlit Venetian morning. Was it Lacoste who said a woman is never more beautiful than when she is dressed in white? If

Melissa was too young to be elegant, perhaps Gina was not too old to be enchanting.

She asked Melissa whether she preferred to speak French or English. Melissa answered blithely, like the casual language dilettante she is. "Whatever. Ça m'est égal. Sto imparando l'italiano."

"So is your escort. He is practically a fluent paesano now. He has a gift for languages. Perhaps you do also?"

"Darneau has many gifts, some he's not even aware of."

"So he lacks the gift of self-perception?"

"I'd have to think about that one. I really don't understand him too well. We speak the same languages differently."

The six of us eventually filed into the impressive sala da pranzo with its ancient planked oak table covered with holiday dishes. The dinner party included Gina's brother, Alessandro, an engineer working in Milan, the quintessential nerd, according to Gina, and of course, her mother. But Melissa was clearly the brightest star. Standing there in her luminous green dress, she shone through the candlelit dining room like a blazing emerald torch.

When he saw that we were ready, Pete announced, "Sit wherever you want—this is not the King's High Table. Anywhere except, naturally, at the head of the table which is my . . . wife's place. Melissa, you will have the place of honor—next to me, I think. You others, sauve qui peut."

I noticed that on the far wall above an antique sideboard the four famous infinitives were emblazoned: OSER VOULOIR SAVOIR SE TAIRE. I asked Pete if he had first seen them in Anacapri, on the wall of Axel Munthe's Villa San Michele.

"You have been there, Darneau? But these words were not written by Dr. Munthe—they go back many centuries in the original old Latin. A pity we no longer have students studying Latin. We used to offer it in our school. In fact, I taught it."

I looked at Pete. "Sunt lacrimae rerum."

"Exacte." He smiled.

For me the rest of the dinner passed in a fog—much of the family conversation dominated by Gina's father, mostly in English, which her Florentine born mother struggled with. Pete asked me at one point whether I had taught *The Sun Also Rises* in my Paris college literature course.

I said, "I used to, but now I avoid it, if possible. It is too bleak. Hemingway is no longer one of my heroes. He still appeals to students, though—not so much to critics and professors. Students love his style, both in his life and in his writing. Yet I do sometimes assign *For Whom The Bell Tolls*. It is long, but it is less bleak."

Pete remarked, "Yes, the door is not closed to romantic love there, even if the best writing in the book was by John Donne. But how could there not be a fall-off after that opening passage? Do you do any writing yourself, Darneau?"

Like a bell ringing on cue, it was Melissa's turn to chime in. "He's writing a roman d'amour about Paris. He had to come to Florence to get it right."

"Va bene," Pete said. "How long have you been working on this Paris book?"

I smiled. "All my life. I will not go down in history as one of the most prolific literary figures of the twentieth century."

For some reason there did not seem to be much tête-à-tête

conversation between Gina and Melissa, other than a little on run-of-the-mill subjects like school courses, vacation plans, learning Italian. Yet I detected absolutely no tension (not that I have any expertise in that regard) and no veiled remarks other than Pete's gentle teasing. He turned to Melissa and said, "Your dress is poetic: a sonnet in green satin. It's not often I have a chance to flirt with a young and pretty Parisienne—may the Good Lord pardon me on His birthday."

Gina and I laughed, and Melissa had the good grace to join in.

Gina explained, "He's only joking."

But Pete responded, "Am I?"

Melissa looked back at him and confided what she claimed were Heine's last words: "God will pardon me. It's his métier."

Pete nodded. "Does that extend to all of us?"

Melissa answered, "Not all of us ask to be pardoned. Some prefer to guard their guilt like a precious jewel. It is one of life's priceless, intolerable misconceptions."

Pete looked at me. "Darneau, you have brought to my house a young philosopher, a Simone de Beauvoir, only beaucoup plus jolie. And I don't understand either of them."

DIARY OF MELISSA ARTEMIS

December 20, 1983

We hung out pretty late at the Lorentino villa, the family all sipping the local grappa. I tasted it: beastly—it was turpentine. Darneau and I stuck mostly to coffee and a little Cointreau.

The conversation wandered everywhere: politics, the cold war, education issues, books we were reading. I was gratified when Pietro swung to my side in our old argument over the role of spontaneous inspiration versus studied craftsmanship in the creation of beautiful poetry. I asked him if he liked the style of Robert Frost's New England poems. He said, "Yes, I can understand him. He uses plain language that even students in Brooklyn can understand."

Darneau couldn't help himself. "Yes, Frost was the ultimate craftsman, working carefully, patiently, through his perfectly balanced verses, musical, mathematical, forme fixe."

I answered him. "Darneau, stop. Admit that Frost was sublimely inspired. Didn't he say a poem begins as a teardrop in the heart's eye?"

But D. just laughed. "I think Melissa Artemis said that. Frost said free verse is like playing tennis without a net."

I went on. "Then Carl Sandburg wrote an essay proving tennis was a better game without a net. And he said words in a poem should leave little cuts, like blades of invisible sawgrass."

But Pete brought us back to the Italian Renaissance. "You understand, Darneau, Michelangelo wasted no time on drafts and revisions of his poems."

As usual, D. got in the last word: "Michelangelo was dreaming of Carrara marble, not the lyrics of his love sonnets. Do you think that great poems are written while the poet sleeps? Je pense que non. Although they probably do appreciate a burst of inspiration, especially if it comes at the same time every day when they sit down to work."

It was late by the time we left and walked out to Gina's car—the temperature had dropped and a harsh wind knifed down through the hills. Gina, of course, offered to drop us off separately, but I will give Darneau credit for getting out and coming with me to my hotel. I was thinking to myself: I knew Gina's surname would start with an L—like Lavinia, Loren, Lollobrigida. He walked me up to my room where I closed the door, threw off my coat, kicked off my boots and sighed, "Let me down easy."

He was silent, but I read the question in his eyes, so I answered it.

"I could tell after five minutes that you had slept with Gina."

"Why would you think that?"

"Darneau," I said, "Why would you not? She's too old to be your student. And look at her: God made her to be loved."

"And why did he make you? To humiliate me?"

I said, "She does have nice bubs."

And he said, "Where do you find these words?"

But he never denied making love to her. I felt as shattered as on the afternoon Julie walked into that star-crossed café in Paris and poisoned my life. Darneau always acts the part of a noble penitent . . . he is good at it, but I still wanted to kill him . . . and love him. I could have used a little less penitence and a little more noblesse oblige. I just need someone to watch over me, and I hummed the tune sadly to myself.

Before he left, I reminded him that he had told me there are no do-overs in life.

"Did I say that?"

"You did, Darneau."

"But maybe there are second chances."

"You didn't say that. You never said that."

Afterwards I felt sorry that I had come to Italy, though I can't stand myself when I let self-pity take over my life. It's the most horrific, stifling emotion. I realized there was no valid reason he should not be with Gina, but it hurt deeply anyway. This is not the same as his relationship with Annelise, because she was there before me. Gina is a betrayal. I'm going back to Paris tomorrow.

Speaking of Annelise, I remember now the words of her warning. "Think twice before you fall for Darneau. I didn't and sometimes still regret it; but I'm German—I got over it."

Maybe I won't return to Paris tomorrow. Maybe I'll tell Darneau you can sleep with anyone you want as long as you don't fall in love with her. It doesn't matter. And then I picture him with Gina . . . but I'm beginning to think like Julie. I wonder if jealousy is hereditary, like hemophilia?

Will I compete for Darneau's love like a schoolgirl with a crush on him? Or perhaps I should attend midnight Mass at Santa Croce and pray for better fortune. Michelangelo is buried there, and Rossini, who lived and died in Paris. I could shoot an arrow at an apple on Darneau's head, like

William Tell. Or is there a pagan ceremony somewhere honoring Jupiter, the King of the gods, a philanderer like Darneau. That would be more appropriate.

What did Scarlett say? I'll think of some way to get him back. You have to have a plan. Demain est un autre jour.

CHAPTER 24

THE DAYS AFTER THE DINNER PARTY WERE TAKEN UP by sightseeing and Melissa's Christmas shopping. She bought me a pair of Florentine leather gloves. "To keep your hands warm," she said, and added, "I couldn't find anything to fit your heart."

Melissa seemed her normal self, which is to say perceptive and absent-minded at the same time. She was easygoing and affable until suddenly she wasn't. Occasionally she faltered into one of her dark moods, questioning her fundamental existential being, then interrogating me about my own raison d'être. Although we sometimes ended up in her hotel, relaxing with a drink in the little bar area, we spent almost no time together in her room, and none in her bed.

One night she patiently explained to me how I had retained a distressing father-mentor complex about her, a new psychological concept she had just invented.

She went on, "I'm not that innocent, Darneau. I'm in my twenties now."

"When I met you a year ago at the Caveau you were barely nineteen."

"Life is like a race. Maybe you met a sprinter that day."

"Yet the year did not pass quickly, Melissa. And we had no idea where we were going—nor do we now. Would you agree?"

"I agree that you need a good therapist."

"Yes, one might be helpful, especially if it could be St. Jude, the patron saint of lost causes."

It goes without saying that I couldn't bring myself to tell Melissa anything about the Sienna trip, let alone confirm any of her painfully insightful suspicions. What purpose would that serve? Honesty for its own sake is a dubious virtue. A more useful virtue is the ability to limit damage with acutely sincere hypocrisy.

We went to Midnight Mass with Gina's family, not one true believer, I surmised, among the six of us, unless it was Signora Lorentino, kneeling there with her hands clasped in prayer, gazing dreamily at the flower-covered altar. Several priests participated, sending out mercifully short sermons to us in various languages aimed at the linguistically diverse holiday faithful, or as Gina pointed out, the same nonsenso in all the ones she could understand. Still, the mystical setting—a thousand flickering yellow and white beeswax candles, the choir singing Latin and Italian hymns, and the thundering organ: beautiful superstitions everywhere—it was enough to stir sacred childhood memories among even our jaded company.

Sitting together in the same pew as Gina and her family, with my godless mind roaming inattentively, I was thinking of Melissa and myself almost as two passionate adversaries, verbal rivals playing our instruments and mentally fine-tuning in French and English for the next cutting session. Whereas Gina and I, steeped in her old Italian traditions of cortesia and gentle mockery, fell into more of a noncombatant status, no fighting words. As my friend Klaus might say, "Gina's the kind of woman you want to sit down and weep with." Her face could tell you the whole story without her ever saying a word out loud. Melissa, on the other hand, you want to sit down next to, gaze into her mesmerizing eyes, and let her go on talking forever about her all-time favorite poem that she first discovered half an hour ago.

Two young women, indescribably different, yet both entwined in my life like trailing bittersweet vines that you could never tear yourself away from: one, heartbreaking, menacing, vulnerable, completely believing she is in love or entirely imagining it; the other, a little older, a little wiser, sensuous, alluring and inspiring, completely believing . . . what? I had no idea.

I recall admitting in Sienna: "I don't think I can give you what you need, Gina."

Her response: "You don't know what I need." It could have been a remark stolen verbatim from Melissa, actually.

Such were some of my desultory, irreligious thoughts during the celebration of High Holy Midnight Mass in Santa Croce as I bowed my head in a pastiche of devotion, playing my ambivalent role of God's fool . . . again.

Melissa's aller-retour ticket was for just a week, and the time went by in a blur. On the last day I helped her pack her gifts and clothes, putting on my sunglasses as I picked up her resplendent green dress.

"Good one, Darneau. But you are running out of time to make fun of me."

"We have time, Melissa. I will be back in Paris before you are ready for me."

"What if I told you I was considering staying in Florence, going to school here? Your boss said I could be a teacher's aide in your school."

"Did he? That was the grappa talking."

"You don't want me to stay, do you?"

"I want you to be happy."

"Why?"

"Because I love you."

"It took you seven days to say that."

I paused. "Do you question the emotion?"

"Yes, I think I do. I suppose I should let you work it out with Gina. You have trouble working out things with one woman at a time, let alone two. So I'll go back to Paris. You say you love me. On verra. Annelise told me that when you left Paris you were not running away from me, no matter what anyone believed. She said, 'Be careful of following him. He is running from himself. He is not made for happiness; he does not know where he is going.' But I do, Darneau. I am going to Paris."

Sometimes loneliness or pain can suppress a woman's beauty, like shadows darkening a rose garden. But not Melissa's. Sadness seemed to enhance the color of her face; it lit her up like the pale rose afterglow surviving a burnt-out sunset. She looked up through her fierce tears and smiled at me, and I wanted to never let her go, not back to Paris, not anywhere.

I'm sitting at my ink-stained old writing desk in the silent pensione, now emptied of people by the winter holiday, recording these thoughts just hours after Melissa's plane took off. I can still see the anguish in her glistening eyes, their threatening, deep pure color shaming the skies she was about to fly through. (I'm thinking to myself as I write these notes: how many different ways will I have to come up with to describe Melissa's troubling, violet-blue eyes?) At the airport she could not say goodbye or adieu—she barely got out a whispered au revoir. I hugged her, and she held on to me so tightly that her meaning was unmistakable: in your heart you should not be able to let go of me.

I didn't think Melissa's departure would leave me as depressed as it did—although by now I should be accustomed to the chaos she brings into my life. I was torn between a mad desire to rush back to Paris after her and there run out the treacherous emotional race she had envisioned or, alternatively, to hide away in the peaceful hills of Tuscany, teaching, writing, daydreaming, and walking the quiet country roads with my perilous Italian tutor. Florence was a dreamworld, certainly, yet still one of unsettling confusion and omnipresent temptations.

Of course, Gina was not just a bystander in this strange disquieting drama. She understood every nuance of the long, tortured Paris history which had led to Julie's deceptions and to my (and Melissa's) misery. Gina understood it but felt apart from it, confident in her own brash ability to live life as she liked, seeing bright beacons of light in the gloom, guilt free . . . the polar opposite of me. And the opposite of Julie, whose love for me was profane and egocentric, while Melissa's love was sacred and demanding, and Gina's, in her own way, perfettamente altruista.

How can I put this? Gina wants me to be happy. Melissa wants Melissa to be happy. No, that's not entirely fair. Melissa thinks only Melissa will make me happy. And I don't deserve any of their loves . . . well, perhaps Julie's.

I picked up the record Melissa gave me in Paris, "Love Letters," and looking at it I felt the same kind of deep emotion that overcomes me every time I teach Salinger's only novel, when I go back and reread the haunting pages he wrote about Phoebe Caulfield—not simply drawing out sadness, but infinite, unending pathos . . . feelings too profound for tears.

In those few rare hours when Melissa was not terrorizing my mind, I could sometimes imagine myself living in Florence with Gina, perhaps even having children. I could never envision myself married to Melissa, settled down in a relationship endorsed by a printed state license or sanctified with an embossed church certificate. How could the links of her outrageous love ever be forged into the official chains of a legal marriage? They couldn't. It would be a crime against nature, or a sacrilege. Once I asked Melissa if she ever thought about the future, wanting to settle down, to live a normal life. And her answer was, "My life will never be normal. Maybe nobody's is."

CHAPTER 25

1983, L'ANNÉE CHINOISE DU DIABLE, WAS running out of days to persecute me. Gina had invited me to a party that one of her friends was giving, but I demurred. "Thanks, but I don't think so. I don't know whether I'm coming or going, to an end or a beginning."

"Maybe it's neither, Darneau, but I'm not going to let you sulk alone in your lonely room on Capodanno. I will reserve us a table at Da Michele's and we will enjoy a beautiful cenone and unravel your endings and beginnings. They know you there and will not hammer you. And you don't even have to wear a tie."

So that's where we went to say addio to the old year and its storms of unhappiness, or as Gina optimistically put it, to say benvenuto to the new. Michele's had outdone themselves with brilliant seasonal decorations, glimmering lights in the traditional Christmas colors set high along the restaurant walls like flashing embedded jewels: rubies, emeralds, sapphires, diamonds. And the candlelit tables were fragrant with fresh sprigs of alpenrose. The feast started with capesente and finished with the traditional lentils and sausages. The Chianti flowed and two guitarists alternated their jazz manouche with Italian love songs. It turned into a perfectly enjoyable evening as, I had to admit, would any in Gina's spirited company.

She asked me if I was wearing red underwear for good luck in the coming year. "No," I said. "I've heard of the custom, and I certainly could use the luck, but my wardrobe fell short again."

"No, Darneau, to wear it, it must be a gift. Next year I will wrap up some nice red boxers for you, if I still know you then."

Gina herself wore a forest green sweater dress which clung to her like a baby hugging her mother. "You know, green is the color of true love, Darneau."

"Yes, it is in the Italian and Irish flags, not, unfortunately for me, in the French or American."

I thought to myself again how fundamentally different Melissa and Gina were, yet they shared one trait in common: neither of them ever evinced the slightest trace of vanity. They must have been aware of their attractiveness, but you'd never know it from how they acted. They didn't seem to fuss about their looks, though I have to admit Melissa came close to disproving that dictum when she rose to the occasion at the Lorentino soirée.

Midnight was approaching and Gina said we must tell each other's fortunes for the new year. She went first and predicted I would be offered a position at the Sorbonne teaching English literature and conversational Italian. I then pronounced that she would become director of the International School as her father retired to the life of a country gentleman. Neither of us said a word about amore o felicità. And not a word I spoke after that came out anywhere close to how I intended it.

At the stroke of twelve we kissed and toasted in the new year with wishes for luck and success. I tried not to wonder what Melissa was doing at precisely that moment, far from me on her life's journey into another world. I was thinking good luck is a caprice, unlike bad luck which is more dependable. Gina did not miss my mood change. She never does.

"A cloud is hanging over you, Darneau. Shake it off. Be true to your better self. Let the rest of the world suffer if they prefer—there's not enough time to worry so much as you do. You were not born to lose. You did not take all those university courses to become an anxiety specialist."

"My universities offered no courses on happiness."

"When did you come to believe that you are not meant to be fortunato? Happiness is not rare like old Florentine gold ingots. There is enough felicità to go around and make everyone rich."

"Maybe not all of us are born to share your trove of happiness, Gina. Perhaps for some of us it requires special luck or special vision."

She sighed. "I think you see no more than what you wish to see. You miss the true essence of felicità which is invisible to your rambling, wishful thinking."

"Yet I should be happy now. Julie has told the truth and vanished. I am free. Melissa is free. And you have always been and always will be free. So why am I not happy?"

"Do you really want to know?"

"Yes, unless it will extinguish what hope remains for me."

"Darneau, you are not happy because you choose not to be happy. You revel in self-despair. You search every day for sympathy. You are afraid to cross your Rubicon. Nevertheless, at some point I believe you will learn how to change your direction and get off your road of disappointments. There's an old

Italian saying, it was even the title of a Pier Angeli film: Domani è un altro giorno."

⚜

January came in cold and fierce like the cruelest month it is everywhere except in one poem, although the shortened days did not pass quite as quickly and darkly as in Paris. Students in the Upper School were focused on their exams, at least some of them. The others were focused on their long ski weekends in the Dolomites. Gina and I had talked about going skiing at the Abetone resort in the Appennini, but the older kids all made fun of the easy runs there. Anywhere else was a long drive and neither of us owned a pair of skis or boots anyway, so what sounded like a good idea didn't quite gel, which was the fate of most of my good ideas.

I was doing quite a bit of writing, not spewing out glittering prose, just recording the minutiae of daily existence. I had never really been disciplined enough to keep a regular journal—but the thought processes of my current sporadic scribblings did help me see into the mêlée of my life, not with blinding clarity, but I was trying to understand how I truly felt about Melissa, whom I loved in my own luckless romantic way and wanted to reach out and protect. Of course, I can hear her derisive voice: "I don't need your protection. I need more." And then Gina, whom I was usually not honest or brave enough to admit I loved, though she certainly inspired no need or urge to protect—she was more likely to protect me.

Can I truly love them both? No. By definition, logically,

that must be an impossibility, a philosophical absurdity, which would mean that I really love neither of them. For sure I could not win a battle with either of them. No one in the world could love Melissa enough to breach the pure stone walls of her innocence: they are impregnable. Yet Gina was just as invincible to me, an insurmountable Florentine cittadella of love.

I asked her once if she expected to tire of me someday. She answered, "No, my expectations are not that precise, not well defined at all. You'll never even notice them, because I will never mention them. And I remember, Darneau, when we were in Sienna you told me you always hurt the one you love."

"I think, Gina, that I was simply quoting a song I liked, because the truth is you just as often hurt yourself or hurt both lovers."

It had not taken her long to grasp the essential nature of Melissa's persona. "She is beautiful, Darneau, with sublime eyes like blue mountain wildflowers. She is your Helen of Troy. Yet unlike Helen, surprisingly, she is not obsessed with her beauty, is she? That's part of her allure. When we met at the dinner party, I was prepared to hate her, that fiery green miniabito, her perfect French, how easily she captivated my cynical father. But at the end of the night, I already completely understood why you loved her. Of course, I still hated her."

Yet the admiration Gina felt shone through her gentle Italian mockery, and I wrote later in my notebook: If Melissa is like the pounding high sea waves of my roiling emotions, Gina must be the placid, sought-after shoreline.

DIARY OF MELISSA ARTEMIS

January 1, 1984

Bonne année, tout le monde! It was not good for me last night. A boring student dance party at a forgettable Rive droite club, mediocre warmed-over food, cheap champagne, execrable music—you get the idea. I left Liam there shortly after twelve and was lucky to find a ride home, because the métro was impossibly jammed, with gridlocked lines just to get down into the overflowing stations. I thought of Darneau in peaceful Firenze, sipping whatever they drink there for New Year's, some cappuccino maybe, then more grappa to kill off the old year once and for all. He was doubtless in some romantic spot with his Italian tutor. May the plague return to Florence and chase her away, far up into the mountains—an exile like Dante—that would be a Buon Anno. He probably didn't give me a thought at midnight.

9 a.m. already. I will walk down to the boulangerie for a fresh breakfast baguette and look up through the clear blue cold of the January sky and make my plans for 1984, Orwell's sinister year. I think I must stay in Paris—Darneau will return, that is a given—he loves this city more than Florence, more than Gina, more than me. He could have asked me to stay with him in Italy. I thought I saw the words forming on his lips before he said au 'voir. His hesitance was like a great blackened sledgehammer pounding on the iron anvil of my soul . . . the first cliché of my 1984 diary!

I cannot exist without him, yet I will leave him there with his lovely Florentine tutor—maybe she turned into a pumpkin last night at the stroke of twelve. That was my final New Year's wish.

CHAPTER 26

In Florence, the January days limped slowly by, the inclement weather cutting into my walks with Gina, the heavy moist air off the Arno cold to the feel. Despite this, she was still working dauntlessly on my Italian. You reach a moat or perhaps a plateau when learning a foreign language. I remember arriving at it in French. Gina said the secret is to force yourself to think in the new language and close off as much of your mother tongue as you can. I recall when I was a young student in Paris, waking up one morning thinking for the first time in French to brosser les dents. Little by little the words and phrases start to permeate your mind, until they're all wrapped up in there, soaking your verbal brain, and you don't need to take the time mentally to translate into French your initial English thought. Yet Gina would still stare me down when I slipped a French expression or an abysmal anglicism into our Italian conversation, as if it violated the sanctuary of her holy, treasured language.

One afternoon she surprised me with a compliment on my improving fluency and accent, although quickly adding several qualifications: not bad for an American, decent for just six months of lazy effort, still too much bland French intonation, and the ultimate slur . . . you'll never be mistaken for a Tuscan.

About a month after Melissa returned to Paris, I received a

letter from Annelise. Melissa herself was not an assiduous correspondent, though she wrote occasionally, sent a card or two, and telephoned once. I think she believed I had to be looking at her for her to communicate anything meaningful. I recall only too well, when she was at the University of Geneva for last year's spring semester, I never heard one word from her. It was not that she was being coy; Melissa never thought in terms of feminine wiles, strategy, tactics. Whether she absolutely loved or hated you, you would know it in less than ten minutes, not that this is necessarily a virtue.

Annelise's letters were different—she needed no eye contact to make herself perfectly clear. She wrote stylishly in French or English, and if I could better read her German, I'm sure that would be even more persuasive. Her letter brought me up to date on college news and gossip; her winter classes were going well and she had even picked up some new German-speaking students for a more advanced literature seminar. She concluded the letter with an account of a meeting she had with Melissa.

"One afternoon she dropped by unannounced during my office hours, plopped down, looked up at me, and started talking about her trip to Florence over Christmas. Her chief concern seems to be your Italian friend and tutor, Gina Lorentino, whom she went on to describe in detail as only Melissa could: unspeakably beautiful in a menacing Italian way, a dark curly haired nightmare, a ruthless clever devil disguised as a saint. Those were the highlights, as I recall. Melissa's usual winsome smile was nowhere to be seen.

"I talked to her for a while, as I would to the little sister I never had. Yet how could I know what she wanted when she usually doesn't know herself? I said, 'Melissa, Darneau has never subscribed to the doctrine that all of us are meant to be happy all the time, yet he himself is always out looking for it—das Glück, you know the word—it is inseparable from the word luck. He lives his life searching to be happy, as most of us do, but he believes he is always caught between his bad luck and no luck at all. The potential is often there, but he finds a way to miss it. This all started with Julie, of course; and since then in his own mind der Regen has been constantly pouring on his parade. It's almost impossible to contemplate. Yet he doesn't complain, at least not to me. He faces down his discontent with irony, or he runs away from it and learns a new language with a pretty Italian teacher he can be unhappy with.'

"Melissa asked me if I thought you might stay in Florence. She said her whole life consisted of people abandoning her. I said I didn't know anything specific, had never even heard of Gina, but I finally provoked a smile when I told her, 'Paris is the one immutable factor in Darneau's life; the city has given him twenty years of her history—he is more Parisian than a fleur-de-lis or la Tour Eiffel.' I said, 'Melissa, you have been at his side, you have watched him, you have walked with him many times along the ancient quais, the Seine flowing eternally through his heart. Do you think he could ever forsake this for even the glories of Tuscany with its matchless Italian cuisine? Das glaube ich nicht. Paris is an omnipotent lodestone. For Darneau, she is irresistible. So don't be despondent. Morgen ist ein anderer Tag.'

"When Melissa got up to leave, she thanked me in German, and said, 'Annelise, Darneau is the first thing I think about when

I wake up in the morning, and even if I forget about him all day, he is the last thing I think about at night.'

"So that's about it, mon ami. What I have always admired about you is your instinct to protect, to never hurt anyone, if possible. That's why you ran to Italy. You like to mock and tease, Darneau, but the minute you sense hurt or pain, you draw back. And you have always been good at forgiving and forgetting, although sometimes you don't forgive yourself. And it's usually because you don't know what you're doing, or why you're doing it. Je suis désolée si ça ne se comprend pas."

The affectionate closing was also in French, though the letter had mostly been in English. There was not one question in any language about Gina, not a trace of idle feminine curiosity. Annelise: always the adult in the room.

⚜

The second semester was shifting into high gear even as the Tuscan winter was easing down. The March mornings were cool and damp, much like April in Paris. Gina and I had settled into an affectionate routine—with no repetition of our Sienna passion. After she had met Melissa, I think she felt, not sympathy, certainly not guilt, but when Melissa returned to Paris, Gina was aware that some kind of vague, almost melancholy peace fell on me, somehow enveloping her as well, demanding time to work out its fate.

For myself, I wondered a bit anxiously if my feelings for Melissa were too much about wanting to reclaim the time in my life when I was like her, young and curious, wandering around the halls of the Sorbonne. She reminded me of what I had been, perhaps what I still wanted to be: what I should have outgrown, but hadn't, what I should have forgotten, but couldn't.

And from time to time I thought also of Julie: would I ever love her again like before, like Paris? She's shameful, she's terrible, but she's still captivating, intelligent, and beautiful. Could I be happy with her again? Probably not, but when did that ever stop me from heading down the wrong direction on the wrong road?

⚜

One rainy afternoon Gina and I sat in our little caffè near the school, sipping chilled Trebbiano and munching on salted almonds and olives. She asked me if I was happy with the way the second term was unfolding.

I said, "I've decided never to answer questions with the word 'happy' in them, especially my own questions."

"Bene, I'll try and rephrase it for you then. What are your plans for the Easter break? Are you going to Paris to bring me back some happy chocolate bells?"

"Maybe I will—it's not out of the question. I would guess you have no Easter bunny in Italy? In the States, Jesus has to share his holy resurrection Sunday with a pagan rabbit. But to answer your question, I have to go back to the American College at some point and see if I still have a job."

"You will see Melissa then. Does she write to you?"

"Not very often, actually. I hear more about her from her German professor, my friend Annelise Petermann."

"Yes, you have mentioned her." And Gina gave me one of her rare serious looks. "I know Melissa loves you and she is sensitive and vulnerable in a way I could never be. I'm not trying to foretell the future, Darneau, but listen to me: I may not be there in fondo alla strada, if and when you need me. No woman ever wants to finish second; the silver medal is not quite worth the race. Capisci? On the other hand, maybe someday I'll come visit you in Paris. If you marry Melissa, you'll need a godmother eventually, or a shoulder to cry on."

"Matrimonio . . . in English the word is marriage. Take out an 'a' here and an 'r' there and pretty soon you have mirage."

"Yes, that's clever, Darneau, but you know, I don't think about it much. Did I ever tell you one of my brother's friends proposed to me last summer, the same week I first met you? But he did not bring me felicità."

"You were doubtless more than he deserved—as you are to me."

"Is it too late for us, Darneau, or too early? Or both?"

"I could not put into words, in any language, how I feel about you, Gina, because—how do you say it in Italian . . . è ineffabile? My feelings go beyond anything you might be thinking. After Sienna, I felt lost when Melissa came to Florence over Christmas, though when I was with her in Paris last November, I was lost then too."

"You owe me nothing, Darneau."

"I owe you the truth, cara mia."

Then she whispered, lowering her eyes. "I won't be hurt if you lie to me; just choose your lies tenderly. I realize Melissa staked out her love before you and I even met. She was first—I can live with that. And believe it or not, I still want to be with you, especially when you are talking about truth and trust and not making any sense. You know you often go beyond reason."

"I have never denied it."

"And some days you slip into your laconic self-absorbed mood, saying ciao to no one, slinking back to write alone in your room."

"It's true I am chiefly known for my debonair charm."

"Darneau, can you ever utter one irony-free sentence to me? I am being serious, and you are trying to create a molehill out of my mountain. What am I going to do with you? What do you suggest?"

I stared at her. "Suggest? Let me help you: assassination is the word you are looking for."

"Yes, I will dig up my grandfather's dueling pistols. Mine will be loaded. Yours will be empty. We will meet at dawn."

We had finished our wine and left the caffè. The sun's golden streaks were fighting through the spring breeze and making a brave attempt to dry off the wet façades of the old buildings. This time I did say ciao to Gina and walked slowly back to my pensione. By the time I got there I had nearly succeeded in forgetting how dejected I felt rambling on in the caffè about Melissa and Gina and our illusive, precarious emotions. Back in my room I glanced at the open notebook sitting innocently on my desk. The last sentence written there was, "Love can redeem you or it can just as easily destroy your soul."

I scribbled beneath it: Cheer up—tomorrow is another day.

DIARY OF MELISSA ARTEMIS

April 2, 1984

Got through April Fool's Day with no fish on my back, but did receive a letter from Darneau. He's coming home for the Easter break, which is late this year. Maybe he'll stay at the apartment this time, or will he be back hiding on Saint-André des Arts? His letter was tenderly reassuring—he's good at that, expressing poignant sentiments. Whether he means them or not, it's impossible to tell, that's how good he is at it. He is also the master of emotional non sequiturs, ranging from humorous to grim to senseless, yet his soul is filled with poetry.

When I talked with Annelise about Darneau, she seemed to think he would come back to Paris for good—she of course has not had the misfortune of meeting Gina Lorentino. Our conversation turned to his long years of living here, starting with the bitter loss of Julie, later his careening from one affair to another, some short, some (not many) longer, with occasional intermittent stretches of peaceful Bohemian solitude.

Finally she asked me, "Do you think you can change him, change his way of life?" And I answered simply: "Yes."

I remember watching Darneau and Gina at her father's soirée, feeling a wild crush of emotions: jealousy, of course, but later a measure of pity for all of us. I sensed the way Darneau felt about Gina was different from the way he felt about me. With Gina, there was affection, laughter, admit it: there was love—she couldn't hide her feelings, didn't even try, and why would she? Yet I detected a sense of control there. Darneau and

Gina could control their feelings about each other. He could never control how he felt about me. He felt loved by Gina, I'll give her that, but he felt possessed by me, absolutely, irrevocably owned.

Or am I the maestro of my own willful delusions, living alone in a world of myths and phantasms?

CHAPTER 27

Un bel giorno Gina grabbed me between classes and breathlessly announced that her father had given her two box seat tickets to a weekend performance at La Scala in Milan of some opera I confess I'd never heard of.

"Pack your dark blue suit and this time you will need a tie."

"Shall we drive or go by train?" I asked.

"Which would you prefer?"

"Train?" I suggested.

"Okay, we'll drive," Gina said with her challenging smile.

So we drove north through the scenic countryside up the crooked spine of Italy, arriving in Milan conveniently in time for the worst rush hour traffic. Nonetheless we finally found the hotel Gina had booked us into, decent looking, with free parking, and just a ten minute walk from the theatre. We checked in this time without any facetious discussion of the number of beds or their configuration.

The opera was a romantic tragedy, though I had difficulty understanding the Greek soprano's lilting Italian accent. Afterwards, we had a drink at the hotel bar and then headed nervously (at least on my part) up to our room.

Gina started the conversation. "Darneau, if you read the newspaper long enough, maybe I'll fall asleep and you won't have to make love to me."

"I don't have a newspaper, Gina, but I noticed a Bible on the bedside table; maybe I can read that aloud until you fall asleep. But how can you think I would not want to love you?"

"That's not quite the same question, is it? Not the one in the script. However, I will answer it. Your desire is deep, but it does not reach the heart. You may have left the spirito d'amore on the Teatro alla Scala stage. Or you left it in a Rive gauche apartment in Paris."

"I think you know, Gina, I have never made love to Melissa. Perhaps I never will."

"Shall I weep for you, my friend? Tragically, I believe you were born in the wrong century of the wrong millennium. The problem is you came along a thousand years too late. You excel at playing the chivalric role of Sir Galahad, the perfect knight. I think I should prefer Sir Lancelot, also gallant but less pure. He would fight and win my flower."

"Gina, when the knights were not jousting, they composed verses to their paramours. Some of their bad poems have come down to us. I could write you one."

"Darneau, have you been wanking off a lot?"

"Why do you say that? And where do you pick up your British slang?"

"I haven't seen you with a woman since Sienna, other than Melissa's Christmas intrusion."

"It's true I haven't been a good advocate for procreation. Closing in on forty and yet to father a child."

"Yes, a pity to waste your charms on a life of celibacy. Wasn't it Saint Augustine who prayed for the gift of chastity? Of course, he then added, but not yet."

I reached out to hold her, but after the initial embrace she drew back a little, watching me with her sad, questioning eyes. Her look was remarkably direct, softened by the steady, placid mood of her heart, untrembling. My eyes must have betrayed the tremors of my own torn soul, because she said, "I can't, Darneau. We could make love but the pleasure would be followed by your guilt, my depression, and both our lasting pain. There is an old Italian proverb: il gioco non vale la candela. Perhaps some day our game will be worth the candle. I'm going to sleep now, so don't wake me up. Read your Bible to yourself.

⚜

I decided to break with my habitual tradition and actually fly back to Paris for the vacances de Pâques. Gina remarked, "Welcome to the twentieth century," and offered a ride to the airport. En route she kept the conversation going, cheerful as always on her part, a little anxious on mine. She asked me if her father had ever told me why he didn't renew my predecessor's contract. Apparently he was funny and intelligent but erratic, good in English and American literature, but weak in French and had no interest in Italian. The final blow to his future at the school came when he assigned everyone in his senior English class to complete a limerick, the first line of which was, "There once was a girl from Nantucket . . ."

Gina told me I looked good next to him, then added seriously, "Papà would love to keep you on the faculty, but he knows how you feel about Paris, teaching and living there for so long. Here we are slow and provincial by comparison. I suppose we peaked five hundred years ago when we birthed the Renaissance. We can't compete with Paris now." There was no mention of the blue-eyed elephant in the room.

When we said goodbye at the Alitalia terminal, Gina warned me, "Don't do anything ridiculous in Paris. Your kids need you back here to finish up."

I answered, "I'll be back Friday—I can get a bus from the airport."

"No, I'll meet your plane. My Fiat specializes in Rides for Lunatics. Look for the sign."

My plane descended safely into Orly through a disconsolate amethyst sky, landing only forty-five minutes late. It was the trains Mussolini made run on time—he didn't survive quite long enough to perk up their air traffic. I took an airport bus to Montparnasse and walked the few blocks to my old apartment where Melissa was waiting for me. I can't say she was dressed to the nines, but she looked better than ever in her dark blue fitted jeans and dusky pink sweater. She gave me the once over too, remarking with approval that there was no trace of lipstick on my cheeks or collar, and for once didn't make fun of my hair.

"Are you staying here this time, Darneau?"

"I thought I would try out your new couch—Nico has good taste."

"Yes, except when he married my mother. And he had another marriage later that didn't last much longer. He always tells people that his life sentence as my stepfather compensates for his brief marital lockups."

We ate at a tiny Chinese restaurant on rue du Dragon because practically everything else was closed for the Easter Holy

Day. It was excellent and a nice change from my rich Italian pasta diet. After dinner we ambled through the Luxembourg park, breathing in the fresh spring air, oddly reticent for two people who had been separated for so many months. Back at the apartment the mood was different, Melissa suddenly more talkative as we sat around sipping Calvados from an ancient bottle she had unearthed somewhere, still smooth after sitting forever in her kitchen placard.

She looked at me expectantly, the passion shining through the prism of her eyes, breaking into all the colors of her young world. I thought to myself: anyone blessed with eyes like hers was sure to have caissons of good luck. A light breeze drifted through our open windows, bringing with it the evening sounds of la rue de Sèvres.

She asked me, "When did you change, Darneau?"

"Never."

"But you are still not free. You have been taken prisoner in Firenze."

"In your eyes, perhaps, I may not be free. But today I feel good, hopeful . . . happy, I think. And Paris is still my home, even if you have usurped my royal bedroom."

"Darneau, will you return to ACP to teach next fall? How long are you going to exist until you become who you're meant to be?"

"Why do you ask that in such a heartsick, frazzled tone of voice? If you're trying to arouse my sympathy for you, you're just wasting your time."

"That's probably true, but I can't help myself. As for my tone of voice, isn't the reason clear, even to you? You say you are happy today, yet you once insisted to me that happiness was not written in your stars. I wrote it in my diary."

"Consistency is the hobgoblin of little minds. It is not one of my virtues."

"Neither is commitment."

I had no answer for that. Melissa was like Gina in this respect: they both saw things in my life that I couldn't see myself. Or if I could see them, I wouldn't face up to them, the hopes and magic of our plans and dreams.

We did not speak any more . . . we had said all there was to say. Outside, slices of night slanted in through our little windows as I fell asleep on Nico's comfortable red couch, wondering if everything would be better, or worse, when I woke up.

The next morning when I did wake up on the couch, at first not remembering where I was, I still didn't know if anything would be better or worse. I couldn't help but recall how last summer our positions were reversed: I was in the bed and Melissa was crashing on my raggedy old sofa.

I had an appointment with Jack Roth, my friend and department head at the American College. I showered in my sparkling clean old bathroom and walked to the school, following the familiar route I had taken for years. Jack laughed at my interest in teaching conversational Italian, though he didn't rule out offering an Italian elective down the line. He essentially proposed I teach the same courses I had last year with the addition of a class on the twentieth century American novel, from Dreiser through Roth, a different Roth, talented, no relation to Jack. We reached a tentative agreement in fifteen minutes and, like all good Frenchmen, adjourned for lunch. Later that afternoon I also put in for a part-time stringer's position at the *International Herald Tribune,* covering local events with a chance to run occasional pieces in the New York editions. I had reviewed novels and collections of short fiction for them in the past. So at the end of the day my prospects were looking good. I wouldn't be buying a seaside house in Deauville, but I wouldn't be playing an accordion down in the métro either.

Melissa was pleased with all this but later lapsed into her accusatory mode. "Darneau, you realize I worry about Gina every day you're in Italy, so why don't you ever worry about my love life? I think I will re-introduce you to my poet friend, Liam. Would you like to read his latest bleak masterpiece?"

She handed me a single typewritten page of verse entitled "An Irish Elegy." I vaguely remembered Liam from ACP, young, earnest, with literary ambitions, though I never had him as a student in any of my classes. I think occasionally he came with Melissa when she was auditing my European lit class.

I was stunned when I finished reading his poem—juvenilia, to be sure, but exquisite juvenilia, with a gift and feeling for language that I had never come across at ACP. It was also, I had to admit, far better than anything my peers or I had produced at his age. I told this to Melissa, who did not seem entirely happy with my reaction.

"Did you edit this, Melissa? I know you were working with him last fall."

"Not really. On this one I simply told him to cut to thirty-two lines, no more, no less. He is my best friend; he follows my advice. Are you jealous of Liam for being the better poet?"

"Is that a real question?"

"Jealousy is an honest emotion."

"Should I be jealous? Are you having an Irish love affair?"

"Don't be an imbecile, Darneau. It isn't the sixties any more. And wanton sexual energy is not necessarily hereditary."

"Then excuse my curiosity. It comes along with my poetry criticism at no extra charge, a fringe benefit."

"Fine. I do have another document for you to evaluate—it's not in verse, however."

She handed me the following letter.

Dear Melissa,

As the old warning goes, you better sit down before you read this.

My name is Anders Bak. I believe I am your father.

Please forgive my English, though it is better than my French or, I would guess, your Danish.

Let me start at the end of the story. Literally out of the blue, out of the most remote, long forgotten past, out of nowhere really, your mother, Julie Artemis she calls herself now, telephoned me late last night. And she gave me this address for you, courtesy of your step-father Nico, she admitted. At first I did not remember her. Of course I did not recognize her surname, but when she started filling in details, dates and places, it all came back to me, like a faraway fantasy looming slowly into focus.

I met your mother in December of 1962. She was studying

French civilization on a year abroad program through her American university. I was in Paris on a holiday trip from Copenhagen where my law school class had just completed the fall term. I was in France for less than two weeks as I recall, nineteen years old, and when I met Julie I thought I had died and gone to heaven. She was young and beautiful, I was hopelessly besotted, and we were inseparable for those few days. One night we ended up at the Hôtel Oxford & Cambridge, 11 13 rue d'Alger near the Tuileries. We were given room number 22 and split the cost: 37 nouveaux francs. You might be wondering how I know these details. It is because I am looking at the hotel receipt in an old scrapbook I made and saved.

We were lovers one night only, but if Julie is to be believed, that one night was the beginning of your life.

I know, what are the odds, what are the chances—it sounds impossible, delirious, insane. Yet Julie read me the information off your birth certificate, it fits, and she filled in the rest of the story: her shock at discovering she was pregnant, hiding it from everyone, deciding not to contact me, her consequent flight back to California intending to have an abortion, her last minute change of heart and your eventual birth. She told me other details, but you are probably aware of most of them, and perhaps they are not important anyway.

For some incomprehensible reason, after nearly twenty years of complete silence, your mother recently decided to trace me, which wasn't that difficult as I have lived all my life in the same district of Copenhagen. My law practice takes me to Paris from time to time, and to get to the point, I would like to meet you, Melissa, not to interfere in your life—I realize, after all, that we are absolute total strangers—but I think I would like to look into your eyes and see if any of this Hans Christian Andersen fairy tale might be true. I refuse to believe that Julie would totally fabricate this bizarre story and track me down to spring it on me: what would be the purpose, what would she gain? Yet it is more than odd that she waited so long. It would be sad if it turned out to be only a pathetic, demented lie: something rotten in the state of Denmark. Excuse my attempt at Shakespearean humor.

Nevertheless, I am a believer, an optimist. If you are also, perhaps you will contact me. I can be in Paris during this Easter holiday, or any time really.

It is not often one has a chance to become a long-lost father.

Sincerely yours,
Anders Bak

I looked at Melissa, she looked at me, and we both started talking at once. I let her go on.

"This is Julie's final attack. It must all be a preposterous fiction. It has to be."

"Perhaps, Melissa, but I'm not sure. Why do we always assume every word out of Julie's mouth is a lie? I know, I know, because it always is. But so what, as Miles would say. This story is almost too monstrous for even Julie to conceive. And this Dane at least is beginning to believe her, and, don't forget, lawyers believe nobody. They're trained to destroy lying witnesses.

That's how they make their living. Without liars there would be no attorneys, no lawsuits, no courts."

"So you think I should respond to this?"

"Why not? Just tell him to keep Julie out of it, that you are unequivocally, irreparably estranged. It was Julie who deceived everyone. If Anders didn't even know you existed, how can you blame him for anything? He is your father, after all . . . I guess."

"Maybe we should sleep on it."

"Very funny. His phone number is on his letterhead. Call him right now."

"Fine, I will. So I have a new father—is Julie still my mother?"

She did call him, and Anders seemed pleased to hear from her, though he was very polite, even a little shy on the phone. Yet he did not want to let the moment slip away: he would fly to Paris tomorrow and a meeting was set up at the Café de la Paix of the Grand Hôtel—no shabby Latin Quarter hostel for Anders.

DIARY OF MELISSA ARTEMIS

April 25, 1984

My heart was thundering against my chest at some insane ragtime tempo as Darneau and I made our way up the steps of the Opéra métro station. We dodged traffic across la Place and le Boulevard des Capucines toward the café, already crowded at three o'clock with tourists and Easter week visitors. Anders had told me, "I'll be the guy with the blond hair, sunglasses, wearing a navy blue blazer. You'll recognize me immediately provided there are no other Scandinavians in the area. I'm a walking stereotype."

Darneau and I hesitated as we entered the café's bright ornate interior. I assumed Anders would be alone, I don't know why. The most likely possibility we saw was a blond man sitting with his back to us; at the same table were two towheaded kids, a girl about ten and a younger boy. As I stood just a few steps from them, the children suddenly pointed at me and blurted out something to their father—incomprehensible to me—they were speaking Danish. Then the girl smiled directly at me, her cerulean blue eyes locked onto mine, almost hypnotically, and I felt that I was looking into a trick mirror at my ten-year-old self.

Darneau later claimed that she didn't look like me until she smiled, but I knew right away who she was. My father's . . . other daughter.

CHAPTER 28

MELISSA AND I HAD WALKED INTO THE INTERIOR OF the café. No one we saw sitting outside appeared to be a good-looking forty-year-old Dane, to reprise Julie's brief description of him, which was about all we had to go on. So we wandered inside and I actually noticed the children before seeing Anders. Melissa saw them too, and stood there almost transfixed, gazing intently at a young girl who was looking fearlessly back at her with her deep blue eyes . . . almost identical to Melissa's, but more peaceful, like a gently rolling, tranquil Aegean sea. Then her face broke into a dreamy grin that bore such a striking resemblance to Melissa's wistful smile, that I had absolutely no doubt that this was her little sister.

It seemed as if all the clocks had stopped while Melissa stood there staring at the child, who never took her eyes off Melissa. Finally, Anders turned to face us and laughed. "I seated everyone like this to see if Rebekka could pick out Melissa. I told her how old she is and that she'd be searching, too. It worked out perfectly, I think."

He stood up and extended his hand to Melissa. "I am Anders Bak. And you are Melissa Artemis."

We introduced ourselves and all shook hands, including the two children, Rebekka and Pascal. Anders signaled the server to bring over a couple more chairs, one of which Rebekka pulled close to hers and beckoned to Melissa. The conversation then began, slowly at first, curiously with Rebekka doing much of the talking in her schoolgirl English. Questions like: "How old are you, Melissa? Are you now my big sister? Do you speak any Danish words?"

Melissa smiled. "Not yet, but I will. You can be my teacher, Rebekka."

"Yes," she said seriously. "Your first word will be søster. Say it."

The boy Pascal was shy and talked very little, but he too did not take his eyes off Melissa. Anders let Rebekka go on for a while, then suggested we park the kids with their mother, who was out shopping but had arranged to be back at the hotel to take Rebekka and Pascal to the Tuileries for ice cream. The idea was to give Melissa and Anders time to get to know each other. My place in all this was not well defined, to say the least, but Anders was more than welcoming and Melissa had made me promise we would stick together. So Anders took the kids up to their mother, whom he said we would meet later, perhaps for dinner. Rebekka was reluctant to leave Melissa, her new søster, but was satisfied that we could all be rejoined for dinner, which I mentioned might be pizza in the Latin Quarter. Pascal's face brightened at the sound of the Italian word pizza, the same in all languages, and he whispered, "Ja!"

Anders, Melissa, and I decided to head down the Avenue de l'Opéra and then wandered over to le Jardin du Palais Royal, where we found a stone bench and settled in to talk. Anders gave us the short version of his whole adult life: including marriage after completing his degree, building his law practice, then the birth of his first child Rebekka, the years passing without the slightest suspicion that he had another daughter growing up without him somewhere in California or Switzerland or France. He smiled at Melissa. "Now you will never be safe from Rebekka."

And Melissa answered him. "Those big round eyes of hers fixed on me, I will remember them forever."

Anders was quiet for a moment, then said, "I suppose I should hate Julie for concealing Melissa from me, but at the same time I'm grateful now that she finally decided to track me down. What in the world could have motivated her to do this after so many years of secrecy? It's beyond belief."

I had my own answers to that question: guilt, fear, atonement, a last-gasp effort to win a measure of forgiveness from Melissa. Good luck with that one.

Melissa posed her own answer: "You can never comprehend Julie's motives—her mind is not like any other. It's beyond the pale, ego-driven, abnormal; compassion and empathy are not words she relates to. Mostly she's probably trying to impress Darneau with her pitiful attempt to be truthful for once. Of course, it's a pose. Who wrote there is no point in looking for a noble motive when you have already found a base one? Gibbon, I think, and that's appropriate for Julie: he was an expert on decline and failure."

I said quietly, "Maybe Julie has many motives, some she isn't even aware of, doesn't recognize, couldn't describe. She was never cast in the role of an honest confidante, true best friend, the girl next door. She must always play the role of the tragic heroine in life's drama, especially in her own eyes. Her motives can't be known and so she can't be trusted until she dies in the last act, and even then . . ."

I didn't touch on my affair with Julie—which of course had begun with my coming in the door as Anders was going out. It would surface later, I knew, but today it was not worth mentioning. Melissa and Anders (I couldn't quite yet bring myself to write "her father") had a lifetime of catching up to do, and it would not be accomplished in one short afternoon—the story of two decades cannot be told in two hours. But they did the best they could, and when we said our goodbyes till we would meet later for dinner, Melissa hugged Anders, as if the feeling of being his daughter had already started to inch its way toward her heart.

⚜

Melissa and I chose a family-friendly pizzeria in the Latin Quarter, just a block over from the Place Saint-Michel. We met the Baks by the fountain with Rebekka running toward Melissa and holding her hand. Pascal was less excited, no doubt his mind already mulling over the toppings he would order on his pizza. Anders's wife Karina was a little reserved, but friendly and smiling, exchanging two cheek kisses with Melissa. All the time that I had been concentrating on Melissa's reaction to the sudden discovery of her father and new siblings, I hadn't given much thought to Anders's wife. Finding this lost daughter out of nowhere—it must have also been shocking news to her. But as far as we could tell, she was handling it with the cool aplomb the Scandinavians are deservedly known for.

The restaurant was decorated with posters of Italian movie stars from the fifties and sixties. Melissa carefully chose her place at the table with her back to a striking black and white publicity shot of Gina Lollobrigida. Melissa explained to Rebekka, "I can't eat pizza and look at her—her hair is so dark and curly, it reminds me of someone else."

Rebekka asked, "Is the someone else beautiful like this picture?"

"Yes, she is too beautiful, and too clever. Let's talk about how handsome Marcello is, instead. His picture is there, right in front of you."

The pizza was also beautiful: perfect thin crust, just enough pungent tomato sauce to balance the mozzarella cheese and bits of bacon, onion, and black olives that Pascal had requested. He asked his father something in Danish, then told me that the pizza cheese came from bøffel mælk. I said I didn't know that, and he smiled proudly as if he had just given me the password to enter Ali Baba's treasure cave.

Our server was hustling around the few tables in the busy little restaurant, his call of "J'arrive!" answering the frequent requests for more food or wine or desserts. Karina seemed to enjoy herself, watching Melissa intently, asking her questions in the typically good English spoken by educated Danes, which includes almost all of them. The burning topic for Rebekka was when would Melissa come to Copenhagen for a long visit and sleep in their guest room which, she confided, was right next to her bedroom. Melissa promised to come as soon as her classes finished in early June. The children were amazed that she had never been to the Tivoli gardens and told her that Paris has nothing like it, and Denmark has palaces and old churches, too, although, they admitted, nothing like the great stone towers of Notre Dame which looked down on us from across the Seine. We left the restaurant and walked the short block to the river. The cathedral façade softly reflected the early evening sun, now a red disc sinking in the clear western sky. But Pascal pointed out that he didn't care much for old churches—he preferred parks and playgrounds. So we made plans to meet in the Jardin du Luxembourg the next morning and if the weather stayed nice, to take the métro out to the Vincennes Zoo.

It was remarkable how easily Melissa fit into the Bak family picture, despite the fact that this afternoon was the first time she had seen them. I credit Anders primarily for this. He knew just how to reach out to Melissa without overdoing it. Not once was there any mention of paternity testing or of any doubts in his mind. She walked into his life, he looked at her, he accepted her. There was no hesitance. Melissa was his . . . and Rebekka's.

DIARY OF MELISSA ARTEMIS

April 27, 1984

I telephoned Nico with the news. He already knew it—Julie had told him what she was doing. She had used her same French detective to trace Anders Bak. But Nico, too, had no idea why she had tracked him down after so many years—it made no sense—not that any part of Julie's whole life made any sense. He guessed that she had originally decided to conceal the pregnancy from Anders and tell no one of the planned abortion for the same reasons: confusion, shame, self-punishment, regret, remorse, take your pick. When the abortion didn't happen, she must have decided to keep Anders out of the picture and out of her life, as she sloughed off the care of her child to her parents and later to Nico, who confessed he never felt the urge to cross-examine Julie about my biological father. He said he didn't need another mad, irresponsible, irrational figure in his life—one was enough. Now two, he added, though politely not mentioning Darneau by name.

I asked Nico if he wanted to meet my new family and he said, "Sure, if you want me to."

I told him, "You have been like a father to me all my life—that's not going to change now."

Darneau is flying back to Italy on Friday. I think he was almost as overwhelmed by the Baks' sudden emergence as I was. Pascal hung close to him at the zoo: two like-minded animal lovers. It looks like Darneau will return to teach at ACP next year, and maybe pick up the part-time gig at the *Herald Tribune*.

That would be nice. And maybe the Arno will flood again this spring like it did a few years ago. That would also be nice, if they had to close the school and he came back early.

I think I'll ride out to Orly with him. I'm going to give him another song to keep on his desk, and a little cassette tape player so he can listen to it this time. I'm going to talk him into coming to Copenhagen with me for two or three days, then I'll stay on longer to play big søster to Rebekka. She is only ten—how could she learn to steal my heart so young?

CHAPTER 29

It's late. The wind has diminished or moved on, and I sit here at my old, scuffed desk in this quiet pensione feeling utter peace and harmony after the pounding din of Haussmann's great boulevards. I realize how lucky I was to have surfaced here last August, under these wide Florentine skies, after nearly drowning in the troubled Parisian waters of my own making. I talked to Melissa on the way to the airport—she rode the bus with me—asking her if Julie's recent efforts toward reconciliation earned her a sliver of forgiveness. But Melissa was having none of it.

"She cares nothing about forgiveness. She wants to steal you back from me, enticing you with her phony rebirth of love and honesty, resurrecting old dreams by purging years of guilt. When will you finally begin to see through her?"

"Well, Melissa, I'm getting older, but not wiser, I guess. I thought her spontaneous, candid confession to Anders was something, at least."

"It was less than nothing, Darneau. She deprived me of Anders for all my life. What is the mortal sin called when you rob someone of her father? What is the hottest circle of the Inferno? She will burn there."

When Melissa kissed me and said au revoir through a few blinking tears at the gate, she handed me a wrapped package.

"A little gift for your soul," she said, smiling softly. "Play it just before you leave to walk with your Italian teacher."

⚜

Gina picked me up at the airport, her endearing grin the same, but her deep-set brooding eyes adding a wary look to her cheerful "Saluto!" She asked me about my ACP prospects, and I filled her in on that and the *Herald Tribune* interview. Then I plunged into the Anders Bak story, and Gina was dumbfounded.

"You mean for all those years"—and she paused to search for the most damning epithet she could find—"that stronza kept Melissa and her father completely in the dark—with neither of them aware of the other's existence? I can't believe it. Jesus got it wrong when he taught that there are no unforgivable sins. Julie should be stretched out on a bloody rack, left there in chains overnight, and thrown to starving lions at dawn—a rusty guillotine would be too merciful for her."

I thought to myself: Melissa and Gina may be completely dissimilar, but they're of one mind in this case. Julie would not want either of them sitting on her jury.

Gina also had some news. The language department at our school was sponsoring a class trip to Paris and a couple nearby châteaux: Versailles and Fontainebleau, and the Chartres cathedral, she thought.

"Maybe you'd like to join me as a chaperone?"

"Sure," I said, "Why not? I could show the senior boys the Place Pigalle and its quartier rouge."

This was followed by the obligatory roll of her dark laughing eyes. Nevertheless, I thought, it wouldn't hurt to stay on good terms with Gina's father, in case I ever have to evacuate Paris again.

I was aware that Easter came late in the calendar this year, but it still seemed impossible that the end of the term was only a few weeks off. There was a lot to do, even more to think about, and I never claimed to be good at either making decisions or getting things done. I am good at putting them off, though. Procrastination is my forte.

Gina dropped me off at the pensione, but not until we had grabbed a quick plate of pasta Bolognese with a glass of vino rosso at our regular caffè. She left me with a full kiss on the lips and finished with, "Thanks for coming back to us from Paris, Darneau. I was afraid when I saw you that you would be shaking like a blushing sinner entering the confessional booth. But, grazie a Dio, you've been acting like your usual indifferent, flippant self." She drove away into the Tuscan darkness, but she was smiling.

I had opened my present on the plane, and I'm looking at it now: a small cassette player and a tape of Ella singing Cole Porter songs. Melissa had Scotch-taped the lyrics of one of them to the back of the player. I have to give her credit: she has no equal when it comes to stabbing my heart with the blade of her emotions. She had chosen, of course:

Every time we say goodbye, I die a little.
Every time we say goodbye, I wonder why a little.
Why the Gods above me, who must be in the know,
Think so little of me, they allow you to go.

I listened to Ella's sad, perfect voice, twice, then turned out my light. In the morning I would write Melissa a thank you letter—in French, I thought . . . yes, sa voix . . . triste, parfaite.

⚜

The last weeks of the academic year always seem to drag a little, as students go through the motions, like tired race horses faltering down the home stretch. The warm sultry air of late May was intoxicating, further slowing the pace as my own classes yawned their way toward the finish line. I was helping to coach the boys' tennis team. Unfortunately, they were learning old-school form, slice serves and one-handed backhands, as I hadn't played competitive tennis since my freshman year at Cornell . . . a generation ago. Some of the kids were dead beginners; one or two showed promise. All in all, my coaching was clearly not a huge positive factor, as we finished a solid last in the league. But the kids had fun, I think, and they gave me a nice plaque at season's end inscribed with my name, the date, and YOU TRIED.

Some of my literature and language students asked me if it's true that I'm not coming back in September. I answered them, "Non lo so," because I never actually know for sure what I'm going to do—that's the way it's all unplanned. You can't achieve chaos with careful planning, I explain to them. (I'm not a good role model—a science or math teacher would suit them better.)

Returning from our last tennis meet the first week of June, I found an airmail letter in my box with an ominous postmark: Santa Monica, California. I told Gina at least a letter is better than walking into the lobby of the pensione to find Julie waiting for me, perhaps dressed this time in the colors of the Danish flag—though she would no doubt look good in red and white stripes. Her letter was not long.

Darneau,

I hope this finds you well and happy in your Florentine paradise, but enough of insincere formalities. Are you going back to Paris this summer? I can't see you staying in Florence. Wasn't it just a stopover on the edge of your existence, a glitch before you move on? Not to worry, I don't foresee dropping in on your strange life again. Nonetheless, I'm sure you were stunned by the Anders Bak reentry into Melissa's—no, reentry is the wrong word. Because there was never an initial entry, no prior rapprochement, nothing but long years of blank obscure oblivion. I can hear you musing: and whose fault was that?

Don't ask me why I looked for Anders. Maybe I just wanted to reach out and touch the past. He was a sweet guy, but I forgot him twenty minutes after I met you. Every choice I made from that moment on I was convinced was the right one. The sad part is they probably were right . . . for me. And wrong for everyone else. The worst part? Even though I can now admit the truth, I'll still go on making the wrong decision, every time. That's who I am. And when the choice is made, that rules out all the other possibilities. It's too late then. Forever.

Darneau, don't blame me too harshly for this last year's débâcle. I simply wanted to recapture part of a dream from another lifetime, fragments of an imperfect love. That was my plan—it hasn't worked out too well, has it? And how could it? Every relationship I had—with Anders, you, Nico, Melissa—was a failure, a defeat. The funny thing is you yourself have no serious ambitions, isn't that true? But you are lucky. I have ambitions, but I have no luck.

Ciao,
Julie

⚜

The last week of school had arrived, closing in on us with long June days and short cool nights, endless blue sky weather and the bittersweet celebrations of high school graduation. Gina had a personal diploma printed up for me: Certificate of Fluency in Italian, Cum Laude. The master of ceremonies (Gina's father Pietro) called me up on stage to receive it and asked if I had anything to say. I told him, "Grazie. Mi capisci?" Then I went on in my best, most ardent Italian to thank Gina for her priceless tutoring, because I didn't pay her anything, hectoring, badgering, and impatient though she was—so I ended up thoroughly intimidated and learning how to stutter in her language, which I had never done any time in my life in any other language. The Italian kids laughed and I slipped back into my seat.

After the refreshments and congratulatory goodbyes, Gina and I wandered back down the country road behind the school where we had walked and practiced my Italian moltissime volte, on just such ordinary afternoons as this. We passed olive groves and vineyards showing their healthy green shoots, everywhere wild flowers and bushes in full bloom, and climbing purple wisteria vines. Tuscan poppies grew right up to the edge of the gravel road, glittering in the late afternoon light like red stars. The burnished sun was beginning to fall in the west, mort de beauté, its slanting light throwing our long shadows behind us. It was a sublime, flawless setting, and I felt that no matter what happened in the rest of my life, I would remember this beautiful moment forever.

Finally, Gina's voice broke the perfect silence. "Darneau, will this be the last time we take this walk together? I think it is the saddest and happiest I have ever been"—the Italian contento and triste rolling melodically off her tongue. "But I have to be honest with you, I have some personal news, although this will not quite rival one of Julie's great admissions—it is just a scrap of truth. The American College of Paris contacted my father as well as the international schools in Rome and Milan to recommend an Italian teacher for a new course offering next fall, someone who could also handle a French or freshman English composition class, as needed. I'm surprised your department head didn't mention it to you; he knows you're teaching here this year. I discussed it with my father, did nothing for a while, then last week I submitted an application."

She shrugged her shoulders in an expressive mea culpa gesture. "I have an interview scheduled with Jack Roth, your boss, I believe, because he mentioned your name, knows you're teaching here and wondered, in fact, why I hadn't listed you as a reference." There was a short rest in Gina's story, just a beat.

"Really . . . and why didn't you?"

"I told him by phone that you had been here so briefly and

hadn't really observed me teach in the classroom. I didn't point out that you are far too emotional and undependable to rely on for a professional reference."

She smiled up at me, her expressive eyes and passionate face glowing like a full harvest moon on a cloudless night . . . blinding me.

What could I say? "Gina, once he interviews you, the job will be yours; I know Jack—he will be defenseless. The next question is: will you want it? The college can be frustrating; it is not intimate like the Florence international school. There are no twelve-year-old kids looking up to you, hanging on every word you say, young believers. At ACP you'll have a mix of university-age students—dolts and utter simpletons, Melissa would say—diverse, some apathetic expats, a few serious and talented, it will be different. But I am preaching again. Ignore all of this. The chance to live for a time in Paris is really all you need consider: you would be crazy not to take it. You would look back someday and never forgive yourself."

After a while we turned around and made our way back towards the school, now silent and empty. What I had feared would be my last nostalgic night in Florence, la mia ultima notte, I understood had now completely changed with Gina's application to ACP.

"You are quiet tonight, Darneau. Talk! Or you will forget your new language."

"You will never let me forget it, Gina. You are in my dreams every night, taunting me, terrifying me, correcting every errore that comes out of my barbarian mouth."

"You have your diploma now, Darneau. You earned it. And

I want you to know that I have been happier this year than any year of my life, even with the disruptive, sfortunati visits of Julie and Melissa. Those I will not soon forget."

Looking back as I write these words many months later, in a different city, in a different country, I realize now that it did turn out to be our last walk there, speaking her beautiful language, inhaling the warm scented Italian air. The gentleness of it all seemed to reprove my sadness over the prospect of leaving, and I felt grateful for the quiet harmony of the fading afternoon. It had ended in the rich emerald Tuscan dusk, our passions and feelings left behind in the indifference of time, like all memories.

We wrapped up the evening early. Naturally, I hadn't packed yet for my trip back to Paris, by train this time so I could bring my cassette player, my tennis plaque, my Italian diploma, and all my other worldly possessions—they would fit nicely into two boxes. Gina would drive me to the station . . . and I could sort out my life on the tracks of the long ride home. You might think that my feelings for Gina and Melissa were uncertain then, shifting wildly as I left Gina's side for Melissa's, or the reverse. It was not so. My love does not flutter in the wind like a false flag. I felt an unconditional constancy in my emotions. I loved them both every day, all the time.

Yet there was a profound distinction between those two loves. It's one of my regrettable character failings that I tend to picture real life through the fictitious lens of the books I teach and love. Melissa, the young Phoebe Caulfield, her naïveté redeemed by her unsurpassable honesty—her persona is wistful

Salinger. Gina comes from another literary world—she is amore incarnate, Hemingway's Catherine Barkley, the wounded soldier's beloved nurse—her optimism always protecting them from loss or defeat, like the adamantine shield of some invincible knight.

And these books do not end happily.

PART THREE

Le monde est comme un concombre: aujourd'hui dans la main, demain dans le cul.

—Justine

CHAPTER 30

Even though I had visited Paris twice during school holidays, returning now felt more like a true homecoming. Still, it wasn't quite that simple. Melissa was comfortably ensconced in my old apartment, which really wasn't big enough for two people, and that's assuming both of us wanted to stay there together for more than a day or two, which I wasn't sure either of us did. Coming in from Florence by train and taxi, I did find my way to the rue de Sèvres address almost by default, taking turns hauling my two boxes and duffel bags of clothes up the steps—I'd forgotten how many there were. Inside, I collapsed on Nico's red couch, as Melissa laughed at me and said that she would have helped me schlepp my stuff up except she was on the phone long-distance talking to Rebekka.

She did give me an iced drink from her new Frigidaire—mine had barely kept bottles of vin blanc at serving temperatures, which was as cold as you need a fridge to be, according to my French landlord. Melissa announced that Rebekka had politely invited me to accompany her to Copenhagen, but had added that I would have to stay in a hotel, as their guest room only had one bed. She was not sharing her new sister with some strange teacher from Italy who, she pointed out, needed a klipning, as she taught Melissa the word for haircut. Her brother

Pascal, on the other hand, said I could share his big room which did have two beds, and he was already planning our trip to the Copenhagen Zoo where he would take me up the tall wooden observation tower. I would have to hide my fear of heights from him . . . remember, never look down.

I was going over a lot of things in my mind, one of them how to broach the subject of Gina's interview at ACP. As it turned out, Melissa fortuitously opened that door herself.

"Darneau, I picked up my registration catalogue for this fall and I noticed they are offering a new Italian elective. I may sign up for it so I can finally communicate with you."

I smiled warily. "You won't believe this, Melissa, but my friend Gina has applied to teach it. I just discovered this myself. That's not to say she will get the position, or even want to leave Florence if it's offered to her."

Silence . . . then, "You have always been good at making up nonsense, Darneau, but if this is a joke, you have crossed a red line."

"C'est pas une blague, chérie." And I reached out to her. "My boss is interviewing her later this week. I suppose you can blame me for everything, as I think he got the idea when I met with him over Pâques and offered to teach conversational Italian. He laughed at me then, but now, I guess . . ." and my words trailed away like the sound of a train whistle somewhere in the night, fading sadly in the distance.

"Bien! Just when I think I'm getting you back to myself in Paris, you drag along your dreadful bella Italian tutor to ravage my happiness. This is not good news, Darneau. And where will the unlucky members of your ménage à trois rest their demented bones? This place is too tight for the two of us, and I'm tired of lugging groceries up uncountable steps to this primitive little kitchen."

"Melissa, you bring up a good point for once. I don't think we can live together here, or anywhere at this time. You have a life to live—where would Liam bring his poems for you to read?"

"You're not in good form today, Darneau, resorting to a vicious low blow like that. You no longer love me."

"You know that's not true."

Then, out of nowhere, as only Melissa can strike: "Perhaps we should get married now and find a real place to live, not this little wreck of a hovel. And there you would learn how to make love to me. Once we're engaged, even your tender conscience might let you sleep in the same room with me."

"Yes, of course, marriage would solve everything. Shall I get down on my knees here in the hovel? Or should I first go to Copenhagen and ask Anders for his blessing?"

That finally drew something close to a smile from her petulant features.

"I guess I won't take Italian after all. Maybe Danish is offered at the Sorbonne—then I can speak Lego to my little bro."

CHAPTER 31

THE RESTLESS MUSIC OF HUMANITY IS PLAYED AT A faster tempo in Paris than in Florence—it didn't take long for me to notice this. And the rhythm here is uneven, staccato, the tones more dissonant. Some days I found myself missing the graceful legato of the Tuscan countryside, her mellow harmonies soft in the sunlit mornings. And they grow even softer in the late afternoon, then fade away faintly into the encroaching dusk—when time can stop completely—and shadows walk you gently to night's obscure edge. This peaceful flow never happens in Paris. There's always something forté going on here: discordant events continuously taking place, nonstop, crashing together like cymbals; problems arise, big or small, new or old—decisions have to be made—all at the same time, yesterday, today, now! Words are tossed out and voices lost in the wind: where should I live, could I squeeze in a trip with Melissa to Copenhagen, what would Gina decide to do? Did I dare put her up in the apartment while Melissa was in Denmark? No, even I realized I couldn't go that far.

Plus I had my first assignment from the *Herald Tribune*, a piece I had pitched on the terrorist group Action directe. That should take at least a week of interviews and background research. Melissa understood that and was thoroughly excited about the trip to her new Danish family. She only advised me four or five times not to bring Gina anywhere near our apartment, or her embassy would be shipping a body back to Florence for a big Italian funeral, closed casket.

The student field trip from Florence was scheduled for late June, and I had promised to help guide and chaperone on the Paris end, which did not, happily, obligate me to stay with them at the youth hostel. But it would delay any visit to Denmark until early July. Meanwhile, I started looking for another place to live. I didn't have the heart to move my stuff out of Melissa's apartment, to leave her again while she was gone. We'd have to work something out, I'm sure we could. Or could we? I pictured Melissa's probing blue death ray eyes on me, opposing, disapproving, vetoing any plan that did not include her front and center. We'd have time to straighten everything out when she got back from Copenhagen . . . wouldn't we?

Then Gina blew into Paris for her interview—Melissa needn't have worried as she had booked a room at the Hôtel Lutetia near le Bon Marché. I walked down la rue de Sèvres and met her there, after she had toured the ACP campus and talked at length with my boss. As I had anticipated, she bulldozed Jack and was quickly offered a contract to set up an Italian language and civilization course of study, and he had persuaded her to show up for registration and orientation to help drum up interest in her classes. There could be no one better for that job. I could see the waiting list filling up with freshmen boys once they caught a glimpse of her in one of her Italian summer outfits. She did ask my boss for a day or two to make a final decision, but I could sense she was ready to sign. Was I happy for her? Of course. Yet I couldn't help thinking of Melissa's quivering, fragile love: I knew I should never have kissed Gina in Sienna, if I was to honor Melissa's love, but . . . I had.

Gina and I made plans to have dinner at a brasserie on la rue des Lombards, and maybe listen to some jazz at one of the local clubs. We took the bus to the Boulevard Saint-Michel, strolled north past the Conciergerie and over the Pont au Change, crossing the two rippling arms of the Seine. The great summer city was at her transcendent best, giving us a soft warm evening, the quartier overflowing with Parisian joie de vivre. Yet we spoke only Italian to each other, reminiscing about the past anno a Firenze, our scuola, her father, my win-less tennis team, our long walks, her teaching me funny Italian idioms and slang expressions, so many momenti belli. Gina was more tactful than she usually was—careful not to come near the topic of my now half-Danish petite amie. I wondered to myself if she would change her last name to Bak? Apply for citizenship there? With Melissa you could rule out nothing, because she lived her life without rules, erratically, unpredictably. The only guiding force hanging over all of us was the city of Paris, manipulating her players, her students, professeurs, artists, writers, and lovers, all of us who lived here. Gina was just the latest, the newest victim to be tempted and inspired and pushed around by this unreadable city . . . her heart would be tested, but tonight her face showed nothing.

The next day I called Annelise, who was teaching some summer German classes at the Berlitz language school. I wanted Gina to talk to her before she reached any final decisions on her move to Paris. Gina knew of her from me, of course, and knew her reputation for infuriatingly sound advice. We met in the Lutetia hotel bar, dead quiet on a weekday midafternoon. The two hit it off immediately, not surprising me given Gina's positive outlook on everything everywhere in the world and Annelise's enviable, all-consuming sensibility. She knew how to find a solution to anything. At the end of our meeting she handed Gina a list of six rules by which to safely navigate the waters of the American College of Paris.

1. Don't go for a petit apéritif after class with Darneau's boss, Jack—you will never get home before dark and you will be paf.

2. Don't expect more than a quarter of your students to be paying attention to what you say at any given time. Remember the old college joke: I think I'll go to class today—I need the sleep.

3. Do expect more than a quarter of your students to be late every day; make that higher for the first class in the morning.

4. Homework assignments in your eyes are mandatory, obligatory; in your students' eyes they are optional, discretionary.

5. Never sit in on Darneau's poetry classes. After his lecture and class discussion, you will be confounded, bewildered, mystified, though you will love the poem.

6. Never go out for coffee with one of your more perverse, sensitive, smart, nice-looking students. You might end up stranded in the middle of a shoreless ocean on a ship without a sail . . . like Darneau.

Gina laughed and smiled her Danke to Annelise, we paid the tab and went our separate ways: Annelise to correct papers written in fractured German; Gina to trail around with her apartment rental agent; and I to look for Action directe communists to interview—all three challenging, unpleasant, discomforting tasks.

⚜

The field trip from our Florence school went pretty well. One kid got separated from the tour and was lost for two hours in the four hundred salles of the Louvre, said it wasn't his fault—that none of the guards spoke Italian, which they should because all the worthwhile art he saw was from Italy.

Gina formally accepted the ACP position and leased a furnished apartment near the ghost métro station, Croix-Rouge, which remains closed by the RATP authorities. Its old platform is still faintly visible in the dim underground light, if you look sharply as your train rumbles through without ever stopping or slowing. Millions of people ride the Ten Line, but nobody has gotten on or off at Croix-Rouge since before the war.

Melissa returned to Paris after her nearly three-week sojourn in Denmark, already making plans to have Rebekka come here for a visit in August. She immediately recommended a semi-furnished one-bedroom apartment for me in the same rue de Sèvres building she was living in, ideal for her to keep an eye on me, she explained, or to drop in when she felt lonely every day. My first instinct, which I have learned is invariably worthless, was to keep looking for a place, but Melissa knew I was too lazy to do that, and in the event the move down the deux étages was successfully accomplished in less than two hours. She kept me entertained with stories of her trip to Copenhagen and sightseeing under the supervision and guidance of Rebekka and especially Pascal. It occurred to me that the sudden entry of the Baks into Melissa's life might create a gap in our relationship. Neither of us could know for sure yet, but I thought it probably already had. Melissa had a new family in another country, maybe a new surname; what I had was another little apartment in my old familiar septième arrondissement, same street number, same rue, same colorless stone walls.

Gina headed back to Florence to pack up and ship what she would need for the coming year, having decided to leave her Fiat at her father's villa. As the philosopher Charles S. Harris put it: a Parisian without a car is like a fish without a bicycle. Gina mentioned to me that she had run into Melissa at an ACP open house, a chance meeting that both told me was amicable enough. With Gina's unflappable temperament, what else could it have been?

Melissa later told me that in their brief conversation she half-seriously mentioned she had proposed we get married.

Gina asked her, "Did he say oui?"

And Melissa answered, "He didn't say non."

Then Gina: "Where's the engagement ring?"

Melissa: "You must be confusing Paris with Brooklyn. We never wear the ring here before les fiançailles."

Gina: "D'accord. I'll take the ACP job then. Help Darneau make up his broken-down mind."

Melissa: "You were clueless about the ring. But spot-on about his mind."

DIARY OF MELISSA ARTEMIS

le 14 juillet 1984

La Fête Nationale: storming the Bastille. One thing I hate is a parade. It makes me think of wars and students my age drafted to fight and die in them for les vieux maréchaux sitting safely back at headquarters, plotting where to send their young crusaders to attack. I'm much more likely to show up on the Champs Élysées for the last Sunday of the Tour de France. Bicycle racers are never shooting at anybody.

Darneau has been pretty busy with his journalism gig. Now that's how to get shot: interviewing terrorists. But he seems to like it. His new apartment is working out, I guess—I found him a trap. One of my life's small but satisfying victories. And with Gina in Italy most of July, it's working out even better. With her away, each day goes by without the threat of some ruinous loss or some piece of bad news, some sad change in the flow of summertime. I know, I know . . . les bons temps won't rouler forever.

Last night it poured, the wind sweeping the rain over the tops of buildings, heavy drops spattering and dying on the sidewalks, like dark voices warning of unlucky endings, the mist concealing the love and fear I knew were there. It's been a while since I've written in this diary. Choppy similes and stray metaphors: I've got to get back in shape.

Jesus, what did I do to deserve Gina descending on ACP like a bird of prey? What were the odds of her landing a job there? I wonder how people ever came up with the notion that things are supposed to be fair, that it will all work out for the best. Where in the Bible do they talk about fairness? They don't. They talk about perfect, pitiless revenge. That's all you need to know. C'est dingue!

I am living in such a mad world here—this year will be a test. In so many tragedies, comedies even—often with Shakespeare's heroines—the woman has power over the man who loves her, who follows her desperately, who fights or dies for her. Where is the power here? Darneau wouldn't understand power if he had it. Would I? Would Gina? Probably Gina, yes; let's hope she has the least power of the three of us. Why am I holding my fainthearted breath? I wonder if a person in love and a person who feels she's in love is the same thing? This is not one of life's great mysteries, and I'm stopping here because I'm making no sense.

CHAPTER 32

I FINISHED THE ACTION DIRECTE PIECE WHICH RAN IN three installments in the *International Herald Tribune* and was picked up by the Sunday New York magazine. Melissa advised me to start wearing a bullet-proof vest and to buy her one, too, seeing that I now would have time to take her to dinner or a show. Coincidentally, I received a short, rather pessimistic letter from her mother.

Darneau—

A line or two from beautiful California with its gridlocked smogged freeways and overcrowded summer beaches where you can't find an empty spot to put your towel down. I've been thinking less of Paris and all of you lately, probably because I never hear a word from anyone . . . other than Nico who deserves a lifetime award for human kindness. Myself, I will never again ask for forgiveness from you or Anders, my two long ago Paris lovers, or from Melissa, who even sends back my birthday wishes unopened. It's not enough for her to rip them up; she has to be certain I know she rejects them. Why would anyone forgive me when I can't forgive myself? Am I repeating myself? Too bad it's not as easy as going to confession. I could use some sacred priestly absolution.

Perhaps my sins were as simple as not being able to distinguish right from wrong. Blame it on my youth.

This is the last letter you will ever receive from me . . . I think. I am running out of moments of madness. The lies I tell myself! This is the final one.

I love you,
Julie

P.S. Contact me if Melissa talks you into getting married. A sacrilege to think if you have a son or daughter, it would be my grandchild. Somehow you have been left with the gift of eternal youth, like Dorian Gray, while you are making me feel old. That is not a gift I am looking for. How did this happen? My masquerade is over. I am damaged beyond redemption. Salut.

⚜

C'est déjà août. Strangely, when I first learned how to say all the months in high school French, the final *t* of août was silent. But almost every local Parisian I know pronounces the *t*. Such are the consequential matters that occupy my mind as I sit here writing down these thoughts in my new apartment, wasting my time, when I should be planning ahead, setting out great pretentious designs for the future.

Melissa Artemis (although she is signing her name Bak these days) and Gina Lorentino: it's rare to come across a novel or drama with two equally strong compelling heroines. While profoundly and beautifully different, both of them are always ready, willing, and capable of putting me down into my deserved place in the real world (in accordance with their mood that day). They can do this easily enough with a look or a word. It seems that it would be impossible for me to narrate their stories, to see and feel and write about them . . . let alone live with them. I can't imagine trying to hold onto Melissa and Gina with any carefully thought-out plan. I have no plan at all. I am crap at making plans. Perhaps I will go on loving them both until my soul dies completely. I could never choose between them. It would be like forcing Anders to choose between Rebekka and Pascal.

Yet someday, perhaps, I will be able to write about these years, including my time in Florence, to distill it into a coherent histoire with a modicum of honesty mixed with a defensible amount of self-delusion. Unfortunately, my own Florentine version of events would have the glaring weakness of lacking the private reflections of Julie, Gina, Pietro, Annelise, and even Melissa's insights, save for the parts of her diary that she has shown me. I suppose this lack is the inevitable misfortune of all story tellers: you're limited to one set of eyes, one voice, one version of what happened. The rest of it is the reality that you have to fabricate as you go along.

In any case, my own retelling of these events would not be meant to reshape how other participants understand them, nor would it necessarily assist any of us to wade safely into the future without getting in over our heads. When I write about these last years, it will simply be to draw the truth out of my deepest memories, for my own benefit, my own awareness. If anyone else wants to read it, someone who seeks out sad stories, that is not my concern. No one will claim that my scribblings are a work of deathless genius.

When I finished expounding on this to Melissa, I could hear her polite laughter—for a moment I thought she was taking me seriously—but then . . . (there is always a "but then"). "Darneau, you don't know anything. You have finally utterly lost your mind. Oui, c'est comme ça, alors"—as she cast her steel blue eyes at me like Athena's deadly spears.

CHAPTER 33

I MET ANNELISE EARLY ONE AFTERNOON SITTING OUTSIDE in our favorite Place Dauphine café, set down in the true historic heart of Paris, but despite the location, usually calm and uncrowded. We ordered a demi of chilled rosé and began talking of the coming school year, her new German civilization class, Gina's Italian ventures, and my literature classes.

Annelise smiled. She never moved her eyes around looking for something to focus on but kept them fixed on the person she was talking to. "Darneau, I hardly know Gina but she has swept into ACP, dominating Jack Roth and enticing students into her classes like the pied piper Tuscan diva she is. She flashes her willing smile and the boys at orientation sign up for Italian 101 in droves. You are her only flaw: she adores you. How do you do it? You aren't that good-looking, barely presentable, some would say, with your hair falling around your neck and shoulders."

"Thank you for noticing. Pity, it must be, or compassion, because Gina recognizes what I am . . . how can I put it? Meshuga, unbalanced, daft, there is not un mot juste. Of all people you should know what I have sought for years and failed to find in this city. I used to blame all my disappointments on Julie for destroying my first love. I was a young student searching for molten, eternal truths, and she was living with me while carrying another student's child. Then she left me in that freezing winter with snow falling on my dreams. And there were no stars in my frigid dark sky, not that you could have seen them anyway through the neon signs and bright street lights of Paris."

"Listen to me, Darneau. Your only fault was not allowing yourself to forget Julie, and later comparing everyone to her: what chance, my friend, did anyone have against that beautiful ghost-memory? You fixated on a shattered dream and let it crush all the chances that followed. You carried your crève-cœur with you wherever you went, never trying to piece it back together . . . until, it seems, you met a nineteen-year-old enchantress who understood what you were going through, though she would never admit it to you. She reached out and slowly reassembled those broken heart pieces. Then she took them all back, stole your new heart before you could stop her, and she made it her own. She ripped down your psychic scaffolding and forced you to flee from the city you love. But then the Italian gods of love played a trick on you. They would not leave the fugitive in peace, would they? They threw a fascinating, alluring Tuscan charmer at you and you succumbed like the shameless romantic fool you are."

"Yes," I managed to get out. "And it all started after long walks and the innocence of learning Italian vocabulary."

"No, it didn't, Darneau. Gina told me she loved you from the first day she saw you, when she walked by your open classroom door and heard you teaching a Petrarchan sonnet to your students, mispronouncing every Italian word that you were errantly yet fearlessly translating."

"She said that? It was a brutal beginning, to be sure. What a pair of cold-blooded critics I have collected: Gina laughing and shaking her wild dark curly hair, abusing me for the slightest Italian colpa; Melissa looking fiercely straight through me every day, her eyes and her words frozen daggers of truth."

"Do you believe, Darneau, that time will mediate between your two loves? Or will it only deepen both of them?"

"I don't believe anything, Annelise. Melissa talks about marriage like it's two people walking in a park holding hands. Gina understands everything about me—the good, the bad, and the barely presentable, as you say. So we'll all stumble ahead through different shades of love and loyalty and conscience, some beyond reason."

"Darneau, you have lived in Paris too long. You are becoming like all the French romantics: floundering, falling, crashing in confusion, born of centuries of doing nothing but sorting out love affairs. And you, holding on to your grief like a pit bull terrier instead of letting it go. Why do you make people fall in love with you?"

"I don't know—remind me."

"They love you not because they think you will make them happy forever, but because they believe you will never betray them. Later they will learn that you can do both without even trying, without even thinking about it, without even knowing."

A pause followed, then I shrugged. "Melissa and Gina are both incredible women. Maybe they'll meet someone, find their true loves this year."

"Is that what you are hoping will happen?"

"I am hoping for the best."

"The best for you is never to have to choose between them.

And this fits right in with your implacable indecisiveness, for once. Maybe Melissa thinks you will move in with Gina. Maybe Gina thinks you will marry Melissa. But neither of these outcomes is possible. Neither of these possibilities is true. You are lost, Darneau. You want to hurt neither of them so terribly that you will hurt them both, terribly."

A rueful smile touched Annelise's face. I felt a rush of feeling for her as she got up to leave for her next class. And I poured the last of the vin rosé into my glass where it settled like faint red tears.

A few days later a postcard arrived from Florence: the picture side was an Italian Renaissance painting of the martyr Saint Sebastian tied to a tree and pierced by multiple Roman arrows. I tried not to read too much into it. Gina wrote:

I am gathering my stuff for the year in Paris. I seem to be the antithesis of women who complain they have nothing to wear—I have way too much. My father sends his best. Told me to warn you of Goethe's "night phantom of disbelief." I have no idea what this means—I'll have to ask Annelise. He said you would understand.

Con amore, Gina

But I didn't understand. I would have to be there too when Annelise broke the code.

DIARY OF MELISSA ARTEMIS

August 2, 1984

I will keep this short, as I'm meeting Rebekka out at Orly this afternoon. The rest of her family will be here next week to join her. They are staying at the Lutetia this time, just a short walk from my apartment. Darneau surprised me by asking if Pascal was coming—I wonder if he ever thinks about being a father—he would be a natural. And I can't see him living alone forever. He is ready to be loved, I think. It will be by me, if I can somehow dispose of Gina. Not that I blame her for anything. It is absolutely altogether Julie's fault: her insane lies caused Darneau to run from me last summer like a spooked deer, and the frightened cerf ended up in the clutches of a Tuscan huntress. I will have to think this through myself. I can't depend on the Croix-Rouge ghost to frighten her away. I wish I could. La misère ou le bonheur: which is waiting for me at summer's end?

CHAPTER 34

I SPENT THE AFTERNOON AT THE COLLEGE, TALKING TO Jack, sorting through reading selections for my fall courses. It brought to mind the famous one-line literary review attributed to Ambrose Bierce: "The covers of this book are too far apart." The challenge is always to choose great novels that are not too long for my students to get through in a reasonable amount of time. That rules out whole swaths of nineteenth century works, especially the Russian masters, not that they didn't write some immortal short fiction, too. Naturally, Jack and I ended up at a nearby bar for un verre ou deux, and there he pointedly asked me if I was in a serious relationship with his new Italian teacher.

"Serious is a meaningless word, Jack, it's indefinable, really. It's not in my vocabulary."

And I quickly changed the subject, like a rhythm guitarist deftly modulating into a lower key to fit the singer's range, as Jack turned and caught the serveur's attention. We lingered in the bar for a while, enjoying a last round, un petit dernier pour la route. We left just as the orange sun was beginning its slide down the western sky, and I walked alone up to le Pont Neuf, crossed over to the Île and descended the steps to the little Square du Vert Gallant where Hemingway liked to go. There I found a place to sit and watch the summer river, its wine dark blood surging through the heart of the city, capturing a mélange of my confused thoughts to carry toward la pleine mer. I could feel the centuries of beauty, tradition and history which are Paris, in the truest sense, as the lights along the river banks came on, wobbling in the watery mirror which was quietly slipping by.

Annelise was right, of course, as she always is. I had no right to choose between them: Melissa, who would never lose her tender wistfulness; and Gina, the nonpareil avatar of love . . . the three of us besieged in the hazardous throes of this city, consigned by some fate to work or study closely side by side in the same college, walking around and living in the same vibrant quartier just a few blocks apart from each other. Melissa, hopeful and fearful at the same time: she has absorbed some grim lessons of ambivalence from me, I'm afraid, though she is a soaring ardent romantic at heart. Gina will settle in perfectly here and be her own sensible, easygoing, honest self. And what will I do? Play my usual blind supporting role in this outré triangle, apprehensive, hesitant, inept, undoubtedly the least content of the three.

The school year will be starting, and our hopes, plans, and dreams will soon be scattered all around us, swirling on the sidewalks of Paris like wind-blown candy wrappers or stray pieces of torn affiches or canceled métro tickets tossed away by heedless wanderers like the three of us, climbing up the station steps into the precarious city.

Annelise told me that both Melissa and Gina had a better grasp of what is happening and what might happen than I ever could. The reason, she said, was that I couldn't bear to see

Melissa defeated or Gina saddened, and that I would surely be the one most disappointed. . . because they were both braver than I. In the end, Annelise had summed it up in her precise analytical way. (She should have been a psychologist, though my problems are plainly untreatable.)

She said, "Even if Melissa realizes you may never marry her, she does not want to let you go; and Gina will soldier on through the Maginot line of your suffering irresolution—excuse my military trope. She knows your personal mot de passe, she knows your unchanging answer to every one of life's unsettling questions: which is that time will tell, the motif honnêtte of failing lives. And there you have it."

I took a long last look at a couple of bateaux-mouches pushing upstream between the banks of gray stone, their happy passengers blissfully ignorant of my pathetic, convoluted, ego-centric deliberations. Throwing them a wave and my best self-effacing smile, I began the slow trek home, yet thinking rapidly, desperately—vowing that at the end of my route I would have worked out at least the potential beginning of a plan to confront reasonably, once and for all, the discord of my life, as it drove me recklessly through the shadows cast by Melissa and Gina. A stray breeze from the north followed me across the bridge onto the left bank, as if to cool and soothe my jangled thoughts, setting to rights my dissident reflections. So I began the thought process, a bit disorganized yet strangely, cheerfully hopeful for once, determined, almost confident, as I meandered through the early soft summer evening. First, I reminded myself, Melissa with all her Sarah Bernhardt theatrics is too young for me—or am I too old for her—explain to me again, Annelise, what the difference is? Melissa is unjaded: full of hope, curiosity, passion, youth . . . I was like her once, but those days are gone and they will never come back for me. It would be unforgivably selfish if I hung on to her simply because she reminds me of what I have left behind.

And Gina? She is far too stronghearted for me—she lives her life with effortless, nonchalant insouciance—her laughter is both her favorite defense and preferred strategy of attack. But I can deal with her formidable good humor.

Already I felt better, the cacophony of my delusions fading away as I turned up the two flights of stairs to my new apartment. Yes, once I've carefully thought everything through, once I've reached the top of my mountain of misgivings, the rest will be easy, downhill. I will adapt. I will be flexible. I have a plan. And the essence of a plan is to understand what not to do, how not to act. I will write it out: a consilium vitae.

So I let myself in, turned on the radio, and sank into my one comfortable chair. My mind was at ease—my conscience for once was quiet. Then without warning the haunting words of an old French chanson came flowing out of the radio, cascading into my peaceful mind . . . which was not ready for them.

Je suis seule ce soir, avec mes rêves.

Je suis seule ce soir, sans ton amour. . .

It was a song I had heard many times with Melissa, that I knew she loved. A minute later I heard her footsteps descending the deux étages, the door was flung open, and she stood there, smiling at me despite tears welling in those angel eyes, ominous tears that your heart and soul could drown in.

"Darneau, you are listening to the same station. You heard

my song. When you were in Italy, every time I heard it I could have died of sadness. It hammered my soul."

And she began to sing, first in English, then her soft contralto voice switching into French.

I'm alone tonight, with all my dreams.

I'm alone tonight, without your love.

Je suis seule ce soir avec ma peine.

J'ai perdu l'espoir de ton retour.

I heard it, and I felt my ten-minute-old life plan plummeting helplessly, as Melissa would write later in her diary, into the unfathomable chasm of her love.

"Oui, c'est vrai, Melissa, I was listening. It was Juliette Gréco—her version is the best, I think, even better than Django's. By the way, where is Rebekka?"

"She's staying at the Lutetia with her family. I have time for you. Maybe I will unlock your heart tonight."

I stared at Melissa, who still hesitated on the doorstep as if she were waiting for someone to call to her. Her deepest feelings were unspoken—like her love—they needed no poet's words. She wore no trace of makeup, no jewelry, no clips or ribbons to hold her hair which tumbled loose around her shoulders. She had on the simplest little summer dress—dark blue cotton powdered softly with stars.

Où sont-ils allés, mes rêves?

Ne me laisse pas seule, sans ton amour.

Her song ended, and she came into my arms. C'était le moment juste.

My plan could wait. It would begin tomorrow.

CHAPTER 35

THE ACP SCHOOL YEAR KICKED OFF WITH AN AFTERnoon cocktail party to welcome new faculty members. Gina was the undeniable star attraction, friendly, affable, but unforced and sincere, a good listener like all authentic people. And impressively conversant in all her three languages, not that she utilized her Italian much except for occasional asides to me. We stayed till the end and resisted Jack's entreaty to carry on with him and a few of his copains at one of the local watering holes. Instead, Gina suggested we have dinner at the Italian ristorante I had told her about on rue du Cherche Midi—where I had first ventured speaking Italian over the Toussaint holiday. Gina had not forgotten my promise to take her there—and I hope I hadn't been putting it off because Melissa loved this little restaurant, but maybe I had.

In any event we slipped into a small table (they are all small really), and were greeted by Tomaso in his effusive Italian—with a strong Milanese accent, Gina told me later. She ordered a Porcini Mushroom Risotto and soon complimented Tomaso with a heartfelt eccellente, and I had Vitello Tonnato served with fresh asparagi. We shared both dishes and Gina said it was the best food she'd tasted since leaving Firenze. Tomaso told her he would never let her down.

We talked about a lot of little things, but it was a conversation where nothing, really, was said. Mostly I was asking about her impressions of ACP and the Croix Rouge quartier where she was now living. She seemed happy, relaxed, naturally missing her family and our old school, but getting acclimated to the pace of Parisian life. She'd been settled in her apartment for a couple of weeks and, with Jack's help, had pretty much successfully cut through the maddening red tape of French bureaucracy, arranging for her carte de séjour, work permit, phone and mail service, utilities, etc. I had stopped over there twice, helping her unpack, move boxes and furniture—the place was freshly painted, nicely furnished, conveniently just down the street from a good boulangerie. And Gina needed no clocks as she slept in the shadow of l'Église Saint-Sulpice with the hourly tolling of her great bells. You could set your watch by them; on one visit I did. Mine was five minutes behind . . . l'histoire de ma vie.

I felt lucky to be able to keep up my Italian which, I feared, would have rusted away if Gina had not come to Paris. As for our future, or anyone's, we instinctively avoided talking about it—we were running in place, marking time. It was enough to enjoy the beautiful September weather without worrying about what sinister storms future months would bring.

I took Gina through the Hôtel de Ville, the Hôtel Matignon, and the Medici palace during the Journées du Patrimoine, a new annual tradition opening Parisian monuments and government buildings for free tours one weekend only, in late September. Our classes were also off to a good start, with cries of ciao and a few other Italian words echoing through the school halls. I had some students return who had been in my classes two years back. Life and times were good, too good to last as it turned out. Hazards were lurking just around the corner, though I suspected nothing. I suppose perfection in any logical sense of the word is unreachable; or if we somehow reach it, it doesn't last, because—as Melissa would say—in the end there is no perfection, just brief moments of escape from sadness.

⚜

October in Paris: they don't write songs about it . . . for good reasons. One damp, gloomy day Gina invited me for a drink, and we met at a little brasserie near the Croix Rouge Carrefour. After we had settled in, she began a conversation that was even more threatening than the cool misty weather.

"Darneau, I have been thinking about a lot of things, not just about us, but about my year here in Paris."

I was about to say something back to her, but I saw then how serious she was, so I stayed silent. But so did she.

Finally I said, "Come va?"

She looked away and said, "I need to talk, that's all." Another pause, and then, "I think that we should take a break from each other, call it a trial separation, if you want, or the war to end all wars. I cannot spend my time here always thinking of you and Melissa. I want to get to know Paris, to look forward to every day, to live freely without a guillotine of suspicion and jealousy hanging over my head wherever I go. Capisci?"

What could I say? I understood perfectly and could not disagree with a word she said. I knew she was doing the right thing, for herself and maybe for everyone, seeing the true picture, diamond-sharp, looking presciently into the future. But nonetheless it still hurt. It hurt deeply.

I wanted to let Gina's words slip by me as if they were a momentary abstraction, insignificant, illogical, although I knew they weren't. Yet my thoughts made no sense to me or anyone—they were meaningless, useless. What could I say . . . or do?

"Gina, I'm searching for words and they are not coming. Nothing I can say to you would express what I feel, so I won't say anything except that I will always love you."

"Don't lie to me, Darneau. It only makes it worse."

"It's not a lie. I think you know that."

"What I know is that your love comes at a cost I will not pay. I've given up trying to reach your heart, trying to convey my feelings to you. You never really listen anyway." Her lips were tightly pursed. "That's all I have to say."

And I thought of Hamlet's last words: the rest is silence.

I knew in all honesty that I deserved this, to be shunted aside, like an empty railroad car, shuffled out of the way of Gina's blooming future at ACP and her path to felicità in Paris. Yet this break was something I would never have arrived at myself. Telling someone you love, perhaps someone who loves you, that it is over takes more courage than I will ever have.

When we got up to leave, Gina looked at me and smiled, "Don't be so morose, Darneau, I will see you at school tomorrow."

I said, "D'accord . . . à demain." But I knew it would not be the same. I will watch her shining and charming her way around the college: it will be totally different, and the first sharp splinters of jealousy began to prick into my soul . . . but there was nothing I could do.

⚜

The next day I took a long slow walk alone by the Seine, past the tall, ancient lime trees, along the banks of that river road that ran from Paris to the sea, right through the center of the city. The day was suitably overcast: the sky was a color that has no name. It seemed that this was where I always did my most serious thinking, where I gazed at life's metaphysical mysteries and never failed to arrive at perfectly calamitous solutions. And so it happened again. I decided to break with Melissa, not just because of what Gina had done to me, though doubtless she had planted the seed. There were other, more important factors.

I considered them all: Melissa was a twenty-one-year-old university student with unlimited potential. She needed to live her life fully without my intrusive, perplexing presence. What good could I do her now, in love with two women, reluctant, no, unable to choose between them? I didn't want to hurt either of them—I didn't want to ruin this year in Paris, even if I was going to be unhappy myself. I would get through it. I've done it twenty times.

Back in my apartment, I considered whether I should move out of our building, out from under Melissa's thumb. But that was ludicrous—it's not sharing an address on rue de Sèvres that is the problem. Then, as if on cue, Melissa dropped in on me, complaining about this or that professeur, but I wasn't listening to her rant. She soon noticed my lack of interest and said, "What's the matter, Darneau? You are pretending not to pay attention to me today." And she rolled her eyes heavenwards.

My answer was not a lie, but it was not an honest one, either.

"Melissa, listen to what I'm going to say, and don't go charging out of here like a stricken bull until I'm done."

I paused, gathering my thoughts, marshaling my words, summoning my courage. "I think we need a break, some space between us, a chance for you to cut loose a forty-year-old English teacher who is holding you back, dragging you down. Let's be honest, Melissa. I am a generation removed from you, and I'll never be what you want me to be. In fact, I fall far short of the mark."

She answered, "You don't know what I want you to be."

"I know you deserve more than I can give you."

"Okay, fine. But it's you, Darneau, who don't know what you want, don't know how to get it; and maybe you're right, maybe I deserve more than a bloody, bungling coward who is too lost in his addled dreams to make sense half the time."

When I said nothing, she stormed on. "Tu es lâche, and the saddest part is you know it and are able to live with it. Alors, je te quitte! Don't call me unless you completely change, and you never will."

She slammed the door as she walked out of the apartment and my life. I thought back to my saddest days after Julie first left me, now a vast, incredible age ago. That was not a separation, it was a permanent estrangement, a cold-hearted execution. So how long will these two breakups last this time? Gina is punishing me, probably without meaning to, and Melissa . . . there I'm punishing myself, without wanting to.

DIARY OF MELISSA ARTEMIS

October 15, 1984

I should have walked up to D. and slapped him in his puzzling, absurd face, but I wouldn't want to insult his indignity. And he might have laughed at me. Yet he's probably right—maybe we should separate for a while. At least he's made a decision for a change without having to ride the train to another country. Or I could have wept and hugged him, but instead I walked away. As I climbed back up my stairs, I was thinking of that mystical farewell scene when Alan Ladd rides off into the valley, ignoring little Joey's desperate cries of "Shane, come back." That was a good movie, but Joey's sad role is not going to be mine. I am too proud to give in, and I'll keep my cries to myself. Unlike my uninspiring life, in American movies and their romantic novels everyone eventually gets what they deserve. But that is a different world. What are my chances of a happy ending here in the cruel realpolitik of day-to-day Parisian street theatre?

DIARY OF MELISSA ARTEMIS

October 30, 1984

Enceinte, pregnant, schwanger: it sounds threatening in any language. And there must be several Italian words for it. I used a home test kit but didn't trust the result, so hoping against hope I went to my doctor—the news was not good. She told me I was due May 14, not just around the middle of May, pas au printemps prochain, but precisely May 14, 1985. Just what I need: a doctor who can also foretell the future, a prophetess. I will not tell Darneau. Well, at least not for a while—I have to think this through. He will not be able to handle it. And I do not want to win him back that way. It would not be a victory.

I'll call Nico tonight. He will want to talk to me about an abortion, but that is unthinkable, impossible—or he might suggest I go back to Geneva, take some classes there, have the baby secretly, and . . . and then what? I know Nico would want to put the baby up for adoption, but in a way that's even more impossible. Could I look into my baby's unsuspecting, trusting blue eyes and whisper goodbye, little one? I think I know what Darneau will say: he will ask me what I want. That's what he will do. And the first random thought in his time-locked mind will be about Julie's abandonment of her child, when Julie was just my age. Darneau never forgave her for that, even though I told him to forget it, as I had. But after that he despised her, or he despised himself for still loving her.

And then there is Gina, the one solid leg of our strange triangle of pain and love . . . which is collapsing. I don't even see them together at school anymore, speaking Italian like conspirators. But I've changed my mind. I won't call Nico, not now at least. I'm going down to talk to Darneau, even though he cut me loose. I've always trusted him, and he will not lie to me about his feelings or anything. That for one thing is unequivocally true.

CHAPTER 36

With my windows open I could always hear Melissa scuffling down the steps, usually looking in even if she were just going over to the Monoprix, though she has stayed away since our recent talk. No communication at all, just the hurt of my self-imposed solitary confinement, the pain increasing by the hour. Today, however, she knocked on the door and looked in. This time she didn't appear to be on her way anywhere, standing there in a pair of wrinkled khaki shorts and a mismatched, faded PSG T-shirt. I realized something was different the minute she stepped through the doorway. She looked at me with a skeptical, questioning expression fixed on her face, then added to it her singular wistful smile and complained, "I don't know why I love you, but I do."

"Ah yes, the Frogman's song."

Then, "Darneau, I have some news." And she gave me a cheerful look of defiance, as if she had just glanced up from her crystal ball with a blush of understanding. Her eyes were almost serene.

I said, "Good or bad news?"

"That depends . . . on you."

"Then try me."

She shuddered and said, "Anders is going to be a grandfather . . . on May 14th."

She burst into tears as I went to her and we hugged like two lovers united for the first time after years apart. Our actual separation could have been counted in days, not weeks or months, let alone years. This had nothing to do with time.

Sobbing quietly, not letting up at all, like a little girl waking up from a violent nightmare, terrified, unable to find her way in a pitch-black forest, she finally said, "Don't be mad, Darneau, I told you I couldn't get pregnant, but . . ." and she said uncertainly, "You love me so much my pills couldn't stop you. I can get an abortion if you want."

Then, speaking with her wet, silent eyes, she stared at me brazenly as if I were the author of some catastrophe, which, of course, I was. Her lips were betraying the end of a grimace or the beginning of a smile, I couldn't tell which.

"Melissa, if you love me, I would never agree to an abortion. Don't mention it again. It is not an option. I will marry you tomorrow or the next day or any day you want, or never; we can just live together, the choice is yours. I may not deserve you, but I love you. And I want to see Rebekka's face when you tell her she will be an aunt. We'll look up the Danish word."

"Darneau, you won't believe this, but I was not afraid to tell you the truth because you always know how to answer me. But I think we should just be together—maybe think about marriage later—we do not need it now. The baby to come will be our wedding vows. You've never had a wife, Darneau. You might not be ready for one yet. You might never be ready."

"The word wife is just a label, Melissa. It's got nothing to do with love, does it?"

I poured us each a glass of ice water and sat back down.

"Melissa, I need a minute, this is . . . this is mind-shattering news. But I think it calls for a celebration, n'est-ce pas? Shall we go out to dinner?"

"Dressed like this, Darneau?"

"I am going to be a father, but I am not yet a fashion plate?"

"You never will be. C'est un pont trop loin."

So we decided to clean up, change, and head out to dine and face the future together, a little unsettled, but for me at least with a uniquely fresh outlook, a new bold feeling of belonging after so many long years on my own. How could all those years add up to zero? Ça doit changer.

We ended up at La Petite Chaise just around the corner on rue de Grenelle, one of several restaurants claiming to be the oldest in Paris. (I wasn't quite ready to speak Italian with Tomaso so soon again, for obvious shameful reasons.) We were guided upstairs to a table in their intimate (some would say tight) salle à dîner, but the cuisine was faultless classic French, a promising start to our changed life. I knew it would take time for everything to sink in, but it was a good beginning. On a commencé à partager, a consummate French expression. Melissa did not seem too concerned about telling Nico—he had already been through so many other unfortunate disasters with his stepdaughter. She was also anxious to call Copenhagen and spread the news to her new family. There was no mention by either of us of telling the baby's maternal grandmother, no need to interfere with Julie's solitary expiations.

Pour ma part, il va sans dire, I was not in any way anxious to convey the news to my Italian teacher and former confidante, to have to confront Gina with this climactic implausible twist in my life. Yet I could not keep it secret, that would be far worse. I said nothing to Melissa about this—though I'm sure it was also in the back of her mind—she knew only too well what was ahead for me. She also knew what a breathless coward I was, but there was no running away this time.

⚜

We made the call to Denmark after our dinner at La Petite Chaise, during which Melissa had only a sip of champagne, explaining to me that our baby would not want even good French sparkling wine running through her little self. The god Dionysus would have to wait.

Anders and the Bak family, especially Rebekka, were excited beyond words. Pascal asked his father if the baby would be a Dane, saying to him, "You're a lawyer, you'll take care of it." Anders laughed and told Melissa he would be the youngest grandfather in Copenhagen. Rebekka finished the conversation by telling Melissa she would start today making a list of her favorite Danish names, one column for girls and a smaller one in case it was a boy.

The evening ended with our first practical accomplishment, making a decision together: choosing which apartment to settle in, at least temporarily. Melissa nominated hers, explaining to me, "Since it's higher in the building, it's closer to heaven. And so we'll paint the bedroom walls sky blue."

I told her, "I like when you reason things out like that. It's a good sign."

"Of what?" she asked.

"I'm not sure."

"You are never sure. But I think you would have come to the same conclusion, though you might have no idea why."

"You know, Melissa, I've kind of missed arguing with you."

"So have I, Darneau, so have I."

I didn't mention that she also had a newer, more comfortable bed. In any event I wasn't sure how much sleep we would get, as we talked quietly late into the night. So much was said during those tender hours, mostly passing dreams back and forth, but I remember above all else what Melissa told me just before falling asleep.

"Darneau, when you made love to me, I felt you were happy making me happy, even if it was only a beginning. Everything was together and not separate at all anymore and it didn't matter then who I was or who you were because we had reached that point and passed it already and now, for a second, we could be us."

CHAPTER 37

THE FOLLOWING DAY I WENT LOOKING FOR GINA AFTER her last class, shaking off a vague nostalgic mood as I recalled the countless times we had met at the end of the Tuscan school day and then walked down our tranquil country roads, sharing a new language, forging a new friendship. She was always skilled at drawing out information from me; my evasions never did me much good, my lies were worth nothing. We left the ACP building and headed down to the river. She was reading my mood even before I started talking.

"You have reached a decision, Darneau, and it has nothing to do with my breaking things off with you. Something has tipped the scales in Melissa's favor—I don't want the details, I think I can imagine them. You have been different these last few days, guarded, cautious, apprehensive, I should say. Some warning shots have missed me, some have not. But today is even worse. Your eyes are dark with pity."

I denied this, but told her the truth anyway, as I knew I must, never mentioning the word amore. But she did.

"Do you love her, Darneau, truly love her? Because if it's just the pregnancy . . ." and her voice faded away until the only words I could make out were "del tutto impossibile."

She looked away and went on. "But I shouldn't have to ask. For over a year now I have known that you love her. Time has not changed that, neither could I. That's why I finally told you goodbye and wished you buona fortuna. I could not wait for you to change because you never would. You once mentioned that you had never seen me weep. You won't now. If tears come later, you will never know about them. As you said to my father: sunt lacrimae rerum."

"You studied Virgil in school, Gina, so you know the meaning."

"Yes, it means that Melissa is with child, and I don't suppose this is a virgin birth. That hasn't happened in quite a while."

I struggled to find words to answer her. I felt like some diabolical sinner stabbing a beautiful, flawless saint in the back.

Gina, as always, was ready to help me out. "Say something, Darneau. Talk to me. Just leave out your words of sympathy. I'm not in the mood for your facile irony, and I don't have any faith in self-pity. There will be no suicide in the last scene of this play."

Never, I thought, had I seen her so pensive, so melancholy, but still smiling, resolute behind her curtain of hidden tears. At the same time that I was filled with my new sense of hope, I never felt more unnerved, more weakened by tristezza.

The fall day was sunny with pockets of cool air filling in the shadows. I gazed upriver toward the ancient buildings on the Île de la Cité, past the great Linden trees, their branches hanging over the quais like a lovers' embrace. Then I looked back into her glistening, wide open eyes. "Are you sorry you came to Paris, Gina? Will you stay? What are you thinking?"

"Of course I will stay. What am I thinking? I think you and Melissa have a fifty-fifty chance of felicità—but that is likely better than most people have. And if you lose, I may be there to hold your hand, or I may not be—don't count on it. If somehow you win, and I am still in Paris, perhaps I will teach your dark-haired child to speak Italian like a Tuscan, senza il tuo accento."

By now we were walking down the Quai d'Orsay near le Palais Bourbon, the diffused late afternoon light reaching down toward the unwavering current of the Seine, marking the end of another histoire d'amour. Gina had not run out of questions, but I had run out of answers. I wanted to be the one to comfort her; yet at the same time I was the one holding the knife.

Then she looked away. "Darneau, you have always been very good at expressing final thoughts, even in Italian."

"No, I don't think I would agree. Truthfully, I should say, it's one of my worst failings, in any language."

Finally, she again broke a long silence. "Did you know I have been seeing Jack Roth's younger brother, Mark? He is a bravo ragazzo."

"Gina, he is a flamboyant gambler and celebrated Don Juan. You must be careful with Mark."

"Grazie per la tua sollecitudine, but when he gambles, maybe I will bring him luck. More than I brought you."

I tried to smile at her, but I could not hold off the stray pang of jealousy jabbing at my heart. Then she said softly, "Darneau, when you write your book, your tear-stained romanzo about your life and loves, will it be a novel or a memoir?"

"There is no difference . . . or is there? I suppose you can call it a novel, if you like. Or a memoir. Although most memoirs are books full of lies written by retired generals, politicians, and celebrities. In novels the stories are truer, but the names have been changed to protect the guilty. Wasn't it Hemingway who said all first novels are autobiographical?"

"Then yours will be une mémoire de Paris, perhaps. Does your book have a title?"

"Not yet. What do you suggest?"

"How about Un Cri de Cœur?"

"Maybe that's too bleak, Gina. Too desperate."

"No, actually, I think not for you, although it doesn't translate well into Italian. But you're the English teacher, you'll come up with something. And what about your year with me in Firenze? Will you include that?"

I looked at her. "Of course . . . shouldn't I?"

"Yes. Just remember that felicità is more important than amore, and they are not the same thing. And don't worry about how you describe my deepest feelings. Just be sure you get the Italian dialogo right and spelled correttamente."

A couple of days later I was walking through the Jardin du Luxembourg breathing in the warmth of a mild afternoon, nodding contentedly to strangers who somehow looked familiar. The whole Latin Quarter was like a small college campus: it was amazing how you were always running into people you did know, purely by chance. I found a bench to sit on and watch the little French kids poking and sailing their model boats in the Grand Bassin—watching them as I had a thousand times before. Yet this was the first time I observed them with the beginning of a paternal gaze, wondering whether Melissa and I would be raising a family here in the midst of the old weathered statues of French queens and the leafy trees of this great romantic park, the very setting where Marius and Cosette first met. Yes, I will be a father . . . in some sense I already am. It's inexplicable how your vision changes—the image is the same—but the meaning is altered beyond belief.

Life with Melissa has been sweet, though we're talking again about days not years. She doesn't seem concerned at all about a marriage date. Oddly, I probably think about it more than she does—I'd at least like to give my surname to our gosse. Maybe next spring would be nice, before the due date perhaps? I suppose if it doesn't matter to her, why should I worry about it? If Gina were pregnant, on the other hand, she'd be spending all her spare time planning a big Italian wedding, roping me along for the ride. No, that's probably not being fair to her. To tell the truth, Gina is never far from my thoughts, though I haven't seen her since our last talk. My chief consolation is that I'm convinced she can do better than me, though maybe not with Mark Roth. Paris is full of worthier prospects—one of them will find her. She is hard to miss.

The prospect of becoming a father is somehow prompting my mind to wander back in time, to think about what I have missed, to reflect on all those wasted years. Or am I simply suffering from a recurrence of a hopeless, mystical nostalgia, as I revisit the history of my three Paris loves: Julie, the beautiful, enigmatic Californian from long ago that I have tried so hard to forget; Melissa, her haunting, enticing daughter, impulsive, unpredictable, whom I can hardly believe I've known for two years already; and Gina, a soft twilit sinfonia of amore whom

I've known for only this one tumultuous year, but it seems as if I were with her every day of it. How can you put them in order in this brave iconography of love? You can't. I suppose you can have a favorite color, even a favorite movie. But loves are too ambiguous, too mystifying, too complex. You can't rank them. It would be like comparing angels.

Melissa recently told me, "You don't understand women, Darneau. You are even more delusional than I first thought."

I think I said, "That's true, and I don't want to understand them. I try not to worry about it too much."

And just as I was getting up from the park bench to leave, my new roommate came walking towards me, flashing unconsciously the wide-eyed smile that could melt even my icy soul. I pulled her down beside me and said, "Melissa, how did you know where I'd be? Did you follow me here?"

"No, I just knew. It helps that you are a creature of habit."

"You mean routine, I guess. Unremarkable."

"Darneau, you have on your serious look today. I think you have been sitting here writing your Paris novel in your meandering mind. But I do have a couple of editorial suggestions. Can you make Julie completely disappear well before the end, at some point when Satan needs a new archfiend in Hell. And, mon chéri, if Liam sometimes uses too many words, you sometimes use too many quotes."

"I am an English teacher, Melissa. Quotes are the flowers in my novel's field of mud and weeds. But actually I was just now thinking only about the very first sentence."

"You mean: once upon a time?"

"That's a possibility."

"Darneau, make sure you put some lies in your book. People never believe what rings true. But I have a better opening line for you. What about: This is not a love story."

"But perhaps it is."

"Of course it is! Have you forgotten that you are the maestro of irony? Irony is your only weapon. You have stabbed me with it a thousand times."

"Fine. I will consider your first sentence. And do you have an ending for me, too? Irony again?"

"No, no, it will be truthful, beautiful, happy—I will make it so . . . peut-être. Ça reste à voir, comme tu dis."

I smiled at her. "I am not adept at happy endings, Melissa. I know they exist everywhere: in movies, songs, literary romances, just not in my life story."

"I can see, Darneau, that I will have to edit your roman triste. And when I do, I will not let you forget that in Paris love is the greatest virtue; it is even more important than happiness. If you are good to me, I will let you quote from my diary to spice up your mordant musings . . . I will give your sad life a happy ending."

ACKNOWLEDGMENTS

My thanks to John Knight, editor sans pareil. No glitch, no faute, no slip was faint enough to escape his hawk eye.

And to my daughter, M.K. King, a romance author of twenty novels, written under a nom de plume I have promised (to protect and preserve her readers) not to reveal. Her professionalism provided the structure on which this amateur book stands, and her judgment and sensitivity softened the edges of Darneau's story of love and remembrance.

ABOUT THE AUTHOR

Michael Brady lives in Port Sanilac, Michigan. He can be reached at authormbrady@gmail.com.